PRAISE FOR TAHC

PRAISE FOR TAHOE ICE GRAVE

"BAFFLING CLUES...CONSISTENTLY ENTERTAINS"
- *Kirkus Reviews*

"A CLEVER PLOT... RECOMMEND THIS MYSTERY"
- *John Rowen, Booklist*

"A BIG THUMBS UP... MR. BORG'S PLOTS ARE SUPER-TWIST-ERS"
- *Shelley Glodowski, Midwest Book Review*

"GREAT CHARACTERS, LOTS OF ACTION, AND SOME CLEVER PLOT TWISTS...Readers have to figure they are in for a good ride, and Todd Borg does not disappoint."
- *John Orr, San Jose Mercury News*

PRAISE FOR TAHOE BLOWUP

"A COMPELLING TALE OF ARSON ON THE MOUNTAIN"
- *Barbara Peters, The Poisoned Pen Bookstore*

"RIVETING... A MUST READ FOR MYSTERY FANS!"
- *Karen Dini, Addison Public Library, Addison, Illinois*

WINNER! BEST MYSTERY OF THE YEAR
- *Bay Area Independent Publishers Association*

PRAISE FOR TAHOE DEATHFALL

"THRILLING, EXTENDED RESCUE/CHASE"
- *Kirkus Reviews*

"A TREMENDOUS READ FROM A GREAT WRITER"
- *Shelley Glodowski, Midwest Book Review*

"A TAUT MYSTERY... A SCREECHING CLIMAX"
- *Karen Dini, Addison Public Library, Addison, Illinois*

TAHOE DEATHFALL

by

Todd Borg

Todd Borg

THRILLER PRESS

Thriller Press Revised First Edition

TAHOE DEATHFALL
Copyright © 2001 by Todd Borg

Library of Congress Card Number: 00-111552

ISBN 10: 1-931296-11-1
ISBN 13: 978-1-931296-11-3

Cover design and map by Keith Carlson.

Manufactured in the United States of America.

For Kit

ACKNOWLEDGMENTS

I'd like to thank my agent Barbara Braun. Her efforts on my behalf are as helpful to my confidence as her perceptive comments are to my manuscripts. She helped me make this a much better novel.

Many thanks are owed to Kate and Tim Nolan whose thoughtful examinations of my characters and suggestions for making them work better contributed much to this series.

More thanks to Sandy Bryson and her book Police Dog Tactics. What Owen and Spot know of K9 techniques come from Sandy's expertise.

Thanks as well to Elise and Richard Erickson and the staff at Neighbor's Bookstore in Caesars Tahoe for their ideas and support.

Much credit is due to forensic entomologist M. Lee Goff, author of A Fly For The Prosecution. His groundbreaking work in forensic entomology is the foundation on which I based Street's career. I owe him a great deal and only hope I haven't made too many entomological mistakes in my story.

And, because people *do* judge a book by its cover, special thanks to Keith Carlson for his fantastic cover design.

Most of all, I would like to thank my wife Kit who provided me with tremendous writing support, gave Owen his fix on great art, and was my editor and story coach throughout. She is in possession of one of those rare detectors that Hemingway spoke of, and her ability to separate good writing from bad is a gift beyond words.

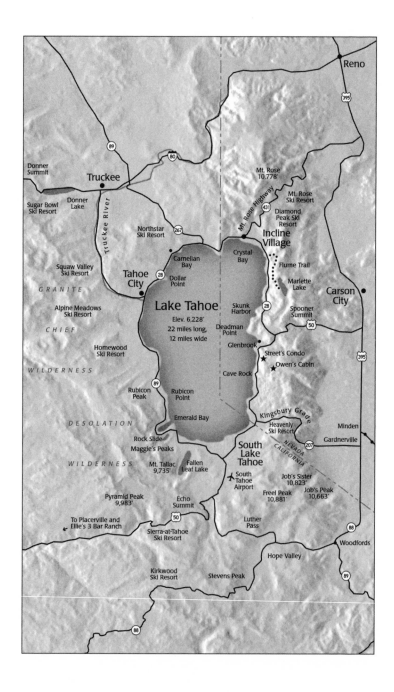

PROLOGUE

The fall from the cliff was so sudden it was as if God had yanked Melissa off her feet and hurled her into the air.

She plunged through space, accelerating like a rock until the wind roared past her ears and sucked the air out of her lungs. One of her tiny red sneakers fluttered behind.

Like a cat Melissa twisted as she fell, her small six-year-old body moving with natural athletic grace, and, trying to see what happened, trying to understand, she looked back up at the top of the cliff.

But there was only rock to see.

Melissa fell one hundred forty feet, struck and broke a small gnarled pine that clung to the vertical rocks, bounced off a protruding boulder and smashed onto a ledge of granite.

The landing knocked Melissa out. Yet her brain, like a bulb that dims to orange before it goes dark, shut down with reluctance, aware in the fading consciousness of a loud crack in her right leg and another in her right arm, sharp snapping sounds like breaking pieces of sun-dried fir.

When Melissa came to it was dark. She clenched her teeth against the terrible pain from her splintered bones. She concentrated on the pain because it helped her to shut out the fear, fear so intense that it overwhelmed her shame at falling.

Melissa's shivering became violent. The muscle spasms jerked on the shattered bones, intensifying the pain. She looked away from the indigo water down below and saw through the darkness a depression in the rock where she might be warmer.

Melissa used her unbroken limbs to push at the frost-covered granite. It was a slow, painful, crab-like motion, dragging her broken body back in from the edge of the ledge, away from the wind. And there, Melissa thought of hungry coyotes and closed her eyes one last time.

ONE

I was trying out my new second-floor office up on Kingsbury Grade, Monday morning, May 4th, when I got a client.

I normally didn't hustle into work so early. Especially when I didn't have any work. But my office had a view of Lake Tahoe and a framed print of my newest favorite painting, Edward Hopper's New York Movie. The print hung opposite the window wall so that no matter which way I faced I had something wonderful to look at. Now my pretensions to gainful employment were at least visually stimulating.

Spot, my Harlequin Great Dane with more polka dots than any six Dalmatians, finished his olfactory inspection of the carpet and showed his approval by sprawling over by the door. He lowered his massive head onto outstretched paws and sighed. His jowls flapped with the outgoing rush of breath.

The woman in the Hopper painting was incandescent. She stood alone inside a movie theater on a side aisle away from the screen and the patrons. Her beauty was as radiant as her sorrow was dark. I was about to speak to her when there was a soft knock on the door. Spot's chest rumbled for half a second. He lifted his head and craned it sideways so that he could watch the door. His pointed ears were held high, but he decided that he needed a better reason than two diffident little taps to raise up his 170 pounds.

"Door's open," I said, impressed that my new digs might bring a customer so fast. Clothes make the man. Office makes the business.

The knob turned, the door eased open a few inches and then stopped. Spot watched to see who might appear. He was in the path of the swinging door, but out of sight from the hall. A face leaned in through the opening. My visitor was a young, teenaged female with large dark eyes and a gawkish nose. Her brown hair was tucked up under a purple baseball cap that sported a snowboard logo. The girl saw Spot and gasped. She jerked her head out of sight.

"It's okay," I assured her.

Her head reappeared in the door opening. She inched the door open farther but stopped it before it hit Spot in the chest. "Can't you make him move," she said, a tremolo of fear in her voice.

"Just jump past him," I said. "He won't hurt you."

"He's awfully large," the girl said. She reached a tentative blue-jeaned leg and a mustard-colored high-top basketball shoe up and out and, after a pause to gather her courage, made a little leap past Spot's body. Spot followed her with his eyes. The door stayed open near his side. The girl stood in front of my desk. She tucked some loose hair behind her ear, which then stuck out. I saw her make a surreptitious glance back to make certain that Spot wasn't about to include her in his lunch plans. Her eyes alighted on the New York Movie print and stayed there a moment.

"Is this McKenna Investigations?" she asked. "It doesn't say on the door. It only says Suite Six."

"One can't be too careful with one's name." I stood up and reached out my hand. "Owen McKenna."

She shook. Her chewed-off fingernails didn't go with her grip which was firm and dry and not nervous at all. "Jennifer Salazar," she said. She turned. "And your dog?"

"Spot. He knows how to shake, but he doesn't look very motivated at the moment. You can pet him if you like." I was thinking about the name Salazar. It sounded familiar.

Jennifer bent over and, moving in slow-motion, pet Spot. Her hand looked tiny between his upright ears. "Hello, Spot. My, what big eyes and ears you have. No doubt big teeth, too." She turned and looked at me. "Does he help with your investigations?"

"Yes, if what I'm looking for is buried under a ton of dog food. What can I help you with, Jennifer?"

Jennifer spied one of my visitor's chairs and sat down. She perched on the edge of the seat with her back straight, knees together, her hands holding a small, red purse in her lap. "I'd like to know your qualifications, Mr. McKenna."

I sat down in my old desk chair. "Please. Call me Owen."

"Owen."

"I'm ruthless with bad guys."

"You don't take mercy on them, turn them over to the justice system that slaps their hands and lets them back out on the street?"

I looked at her for a moment. "Isn't the quality of mercy supposed to drop like a gentle rain from heaven?" I asked.

"No. Portia had it wrong."

The kid was impressing me. "I don't take mercy on them. But I live by the law, more or less. If the cops want the bad guys, I hand them over."

She looked disappointed.

"Though sometimes I thrash them around a bit first."

"What kind of gun do you use?" she asked.

"I don't," I said.

"But you used to be a cop in San Francisco."

I raised my eyebrows.

"You don't think I'd approach you without doing basic research, do you? Anyway, I thought ex-cops always carry guns."

"I'm a private investigator, now"

"Oh, I get it," she said. "Something happened, didn't it?"

I didn't respond. We sat and studied each other.

"Okay," she said. "I'd like to hire you."

"Jennifer, at the risk of sounding indelicate, you're a kid. I don't think the rules let a kid hire a private cop."

"Rules?"

"Yeah," I said.

"I'm sure there aren't any laws or precepts that say you can't do some investigating for me."

"Just rules," I said.

"I have my own money."

"I'm sure you do."

"Please don't patronize me, Mr. McKenna. Owen. I mean it. I'm rich. I can pay whatever you charge."

I leaned back in my chair and it squeaked. Should've bought one of those, too. "Jennifer, how old are you?"

"Fourteen. I'll be fifteen in August."

"More than three years until you are of age to enter into contracts. To be a legal adult. Until then I'd have to deal with your parents if I wanted to help you."

"I thought you might say that, but I intend to convince you of how responsible I am." She pulled an envelope out of her purse, opened it and removed a piece of paper. "I wrote this myself, so if you find the wording somewhat irregular I hope you'll understand. 'I, Jennifer Salazar, being of sound mind although only fourteen years of age, do hereby release and hold harmless McKenna Investigations from any liability for actions taken while in my employ. If any party attempts to interfere with McKenna Investigations' work on my behalf, I will use my full resources, when I turn eighteen and get control of my money, to seek redress against them. I know my mind and I am not to be trifled with. Signed, Jennifer Salazar.'" She handed me the paper. "You'll see that I had it notarized. This document should give you some protection."

I glanced over the writing and noticed its perfect spelling and clean formatting. "Do your parents know you're doing this?"

"I have no parents to speak of. My father is dead and my mother is confined to a hospital outside of Las Vegas. She's schizophrenic."

"Your guardian, then?"

"Gramma Salazar. No, she doesn't know. She would have tried to talk me out of coming here if she did."

"Why?"

"Because she doesn't believe I'm right."

"About?"

"About why I'm hiring you."

"We haven't decided you are hiring me," I said.

Jennifer rolled her eyes, the first kid gesture she'd made since she walked into my office.

"Nevertheless, what is it you want?" I asked.

"I want you to find out who murdered my sister."

"What would be your grandmother's problem with finding out that?"

"She doesn't believe she was killed. She thinks it was an accident like everyone else does."

I paused. "Why don't you tell me the circumstances."

Jennifer shifted back into her chair. "My sister Melissa was my identical twin. We were hiking with Gramma Salazar when we were six years old. I should probably back up and say that Gramma is one of those sturdy German types. Hikes the mountains all the time. Used to hike in

Bavaria when she was a little girl. So when her son Joseph - my father - married mama, who never used to go outside, Gramma was very disdainful. My father and Grandpa Abe died in a plane crash on a business trip in Indiana. Melissa and I were three. So we were too young to remember either of them very well. After that, mama's sickness got worse. Her name is Alicia. I see her once a year. She's a benign zombie. Sweet, but her brain is somewhere else. Probably the drugs they've got her on. I don't think I've ever seen her smile. Anyway, Gramma was convinced that mama was sickly because she stayed indoors. When they committed mama, Gramma became our guardian. Gramma believed we had bad blood in us from mama. So Gramma took us hiking all the time because she thought that exercise and fresh air would keep us mentally healthy.

"The summer we turned six Gramma decided we should celebrate our birthday by climbing a mountain. Do you know Maggie's Peaks over on the California side of the lake?"

"Yes. Up above Emerald Bay."

"Do you know the rock slide?"

I nodded. "Nineteen fifty-five, I think. A big chunk of mountain slid down toward the bay."

"Gramma took us up South Maggie's the morning of our birthday. She brought a little cake and surprised us with it when we got to the top of the mountain. She lit twelve candles, six for each of us." Jennifer was looking past me out my window. I realized she could probably see Maggie's Peaks over my shoulder.

"On the way back down the mountain, Melissa and I started playing hide and seek among the giant fir trees. Somehow we got separated and when Gramma and I got back together, Melissa was lost. We searched all day but couldn't find her. So we ran down the mountain. Gramma drove into town and we got the police.

"By the next day they had search parties all over the mountain. One of the rescue dogs found Melissa's body about half way down the rock slide." Jennifer appeared pensive.

"The authorities decided it was an accidental death?"

"Correct," she said.

"And you don't believe them."

"I don't now and I didn't then."

"Why?" I asked.

"It was a visceral sense. By the time we were six we had hiked all over the Tahoe Basin. We were agile and co-ordinated. We'd run through boulder fields jumping from rock to rock. We'd stood on the edge of cliffs. Speaking for myself, I was too sure-footed and sensible, even at the age of six, to accidentally fall off a cliff. It's like a geometry proof. Genetically, we were two copies of the same person. If I couldn't fall accidentally, then neither could Melissa. Therefore she was pushed."

"What about a sudden gust of wind? I've stood on that spot above Emerald Bay and felt the fear that the wind could blow me over."

"It was a calm day. They checked the weather reporting stations around the Tahoe Basin. There was no wind. They decided Melissa must have stepped on a loose rock and tumbled off." Jennifer's large eyes were direct and unyielding. "They all thought she was just another unfocused six-year-old kid. But I know that she wouldn't have done that. That would be like a cat falling off a couch or a mountain goat tripping over its own feet. She had to have been pushed."

"Who would push a six-year-old off a cliff?"

"That's what I'm hiring you to find out."

"I don't mean to be tedious," I said. "But I haven't

agreed to take on the job."

"Why not?"

"Look, Jennifer, it's been almost nine years, a long time to carry the torch. You're fourteen. You've got your whole life ahead of you. Why concentrate on something terrible that happened so long ago?"

"Because," she said, "if Melissa was pushed, and I'm sure she was, then that means there is a killer who's gone unpunished. I waited nine years to do something because I was a little kid and no one believed me. Now I'm old enough and mature enough to have some control over my life. I have the financial wherewithal, and I intend to use it to bring the killer to justice."

I gestured with the paper she'd handed me earlier. "This money you get when you turn eighteen, is it a lot?"

"As of my last monthly statement from my broker, three hundred and ninety-four million dollars."

I wasn't sure, but I thought I saw Spot perk up his ears.

"Grandpa Abe started a textile firm when he was twenty-one. It is now the fourth largest clothing company in the world. He left me some stock. The dividends alone amounted to seven million last year. Naturally, I only get an allowance until I turn eighteen. But it is a large allowance. I have my own checking account and I've written you a retainer check to get you started." She handed me a check. It was for twenty thousand dollars.

I looked at the clock on my desk. 11:00 a.m. "I don't mean to pry, but wouldn't a kid like you normally be in school on a Monday morning?"

"Yes. But tracking down my sister's murderer is more important than school."

"Public or private school?"

"Private. The Tahoe Academy in Zephyr Cove. Grandpa Abe started it just so we would have a place to go that he approved of."

"Do your teachers get upset when you play hooky?"

"Look, Mr. McKenna. Owen. You can stop worrying. I already took my S-A-Ts, three years early because I'm graduating this spring. I got seven twenty-five on the verbal and seven ten on the math. I've already been accepted at Stanford, Caltech, Harvard and M.I.T. I think my teachers will understand."

TWO

I reached across my desk and handed the check back.
"I'm sorry, Jennifer, but even if I put the same
stock in your convictions as you do, I could not work for
you. Your grandmother, maybe, but not you."

Jennifer looked profoundly disappointed.

"But," I said, "you and I are friends almost. Lot's of
times I've done some detecting on the side for friends."

Jennifer gave me a huge gap-toothed grin that showed
the hardware of extensive orthodontia. "If you won't work
for me, I should at least pay you for such favors."

"Kids who are fourteen don't pay for favors. They rely
on wise, mature and altruistic adults to guide them and
protect them from harm."

"Wisdom and maturity and altruism your specialties,
no doubt," she said.

"No doubt," I said.

"When I turn eighteen and gain access to my money,
maybe then I could make your activity on my behalf remunerative."

"Remunerative. Sounds exciting."

"Four hundred million is very exciting," she said.

After Jennifer left I stood up and looked out the window to see what kind of transportation she was using to

skip school and visit her friendly local detective. Stretch limo? Helicopter? Harrier jet?

Jennifer appeared down below. She looped her purse around her neck and climbed onto a dirty green mountain bike. She pedaled fast across Kingsbury Grade, dodging between a U-Haul truck and a red Lexus. At the opposite shoulder, she bounced up the bank and disappeared into the pine trees carrying the biggest check I'd seen in a long time.

Another cyclist appeared, went up the bank and into the trees in the same direction as Jennifer. Maybe there was a trail I'd never seen before. Maybe I should look.

In my peripheral vision I saw a silver BMW with smoked windows pull out from a tree shadow up the hill and drive to where Jennifer and the other cyclist had gone into the forest. The driver's door opened and a man in white pants and white T-shirt got out. His T-shirt was stretched tight by muscles. The man ran around his car, up the bank and into the woods.

Popular spot, these woods suddenly were.

"Hey, Spot?" I said. "Wanna see what the body-builder is doing in the woods?"

He jumped to his feet. His friend Treasure, the toy poodle who lives down the street, tried to teach him to do a handstand and stick his butt and hind legs in the air when he's excited, but Spot would have none of it. When he's excited he just rises to his feet and starts sweeping tables clean with his tail.

I glanced at the woman in the Hopper painting and left the office.

Spot ran down the stairs, put a paw against the glass door and pushed outside. I clicked my fingers and walked to the road. He trotted over to my side and waited with me for a break in traffic. When it came, we ran across the road and up the bank where everyone else had gone.

The tire tracks from the mountain bikes meandered into the pines. They were marred here and there by widely-spaced footprints. Spot was at my side waiting for permission to run around when the bodybuilder reappeared in the trees.

His heavy panting was audible as he walked toward us. He was in his late thirties with thick black hair set in such a perfect wave that he must have used a spray-on plastic coating. He was a half foot shorter than my six, six, but he had 240 pounds of hard beef on his frame. Even his jaw muscles bulged.

I touched Spot's neck, a gesture that meant stay at heel. The hair on his back was up and stiff.

"Interesting place, these woods," I said. Friendly. Just walking the dog.

The man glared at me as he approached. He had feral eyes, dark little obsidian beads that were close set and made his nose look pinched.

"You looking for one of those bicyclers?" I asked.

He gave Spot a careful appraising once-over, one animal to another. "What bicyclers?" he said at last.

"Two guys," I lied, watching for a reaction.

He shook his head. "Never saw them." He was wired tight as a piano and his eyes flicked from me to Spot. The man knew I was messing with him and he looked ready to spring. Neither my size nor my dog seemed to intimidate him as common sense would suggest. But then men don't build muscles like that because it makes sense.

I casually shifted toward what we used to call our "ready" stance on the San Francisco Police Department. "You ran into the woods right after the bicyclers and you didn't see them?"

The man ignored me. His eyes were on Spot, no doubt

wondering what the dog would do if the man were to teach me a lesson for being flip. "That dog's the size of a donkey," he mumbled. "A polka dot donkey." He laughed with gusto, a reaction I thought strange.

Spot must have agreed with me. He growled, deep and loud, his lips lifting.

The man moved to our side and hustled away in the direction of his car.

"Enough, Spot," I said.

Spot stopped growling. He held his tail high.

"You study that at the Actor's Studio?" I said.

He wagged.

I turned and saw the man running for his car. I ran after, intent on getting his license number. We came out of the woods and slid down the bank. The silver BMW was a flash of light down the road.

When the traffic eased we walked back across Kingsbury Grade.

I let Spot in the rear door of my Jeep. He sat his butt on the passenger seat and his feet on the floor. I rolled down the glass and he stuck his head out and became Tahoe's number one traffic distraction.

We drove down Kingsbury and across Stateline to the California side of Tahoe. It was another typical spring day with hot sun and cerulean skies. The mountains were white with snow that would last through July. Three or four cotton-puff clouds competed for the best reflection in the deep blue mirror of the lake. If I could take the woman in Hopper's painting out of the movie theater and bring her to Tahoe on a day like this, it would go a long way toward mitigating her anguish. For a moment I wondered about myself that I was playing make-believe knight to a fictional maiden, but I let the thought go as I pulled into the lot at the Tahoe Herald building and parked.

"Don't howl with loneliness if I leave you for a moment, okay?" I said to Spot. I grabbed his muzzle and shook it, but he was ignoring me, turning his head to watch a cop on horseback over by the beach.

I went inside the Herald building. "I'd like to review a story you printed some years ago," I said to a woman at the front counter.

"Do you know the date?"

"I'm sorry, no. But it would have been in the month of August. Nine years ago this coming August"

She picked up the phone and pressed three buttons. "Glenda? I'm sending a man back to look at the microfiche. Could you please pull August of nine years ago? What? Years. Thanks." She looked up at me. "Just go down that aisle, sir, to the second door past the drinking fountain."

I entered the darkened room. It had two microfiche machines on modular tables. "Just a minute," a woman's voice called out. She appeared from between rows of floor-to-ceiling shelving.

"Owen!"

"Hi, Glennie."

She gave me a fierce hug. She was wearing navy blue stretch pants, a white turtle neck and over it a light blue Norwegian cardigan with metal buttons. In the dim light I could see under her blonde curls the tan that comes from spring skiing. She was all curves and all of them still firm. She looked up at me, bending her neck back. "Owen, honey, you ready to try a new woman, yet?"

"Thanks, but I'm reserved until further notice."

"Street still hasn't given you a commitment."

"No." It was a sore spot.

Her arms were still around my waist. "I cook the best stir fry at the lake, you know. And my house is off limits to all bugs."

"An entomologist needs bugs around the way an astronomer needs stars."

"Sure, but maggots?" Glennie stepped away from me. "Come on, Owen. One time in her kitchen I saw jars with white things in them. I thought they were little noodles. But Street said they were maggots. How can you eat food made in a kitchen with maggots on the counter?"

"She does forensic consulting. The maggots they find on the body can tell when a person died."

"That is disgusting." Glennie screwed up her nose, then gave me a sad little smile. "Anyway, if you ever want dinner, I'm available."

I nodded. I was thinking that most men would think Glennie was a prize, not a compromise. Most men would take her in a second rather than wait for Street, a too thin, too edgy, too fragile woman with eyes that could see my soul and a voice that could melt it.

"I get it. All business. What is it this time? Casino espionage? Jealous spouse? Oh, that's right. Privileged information."

I smiled.

"Okay, you're not talking. But remember me if that girl ever skis off with someone else."

"Promise."

"Here's your August from nine years ago." Glennie handed me a roll of film. She left me alone while I perused the tape. I zoomed around on fast forward and fast rewind until I found the story on August 17th. The headline was bold.

SOUTH TAHOE GIRL KILLED IN
CLIMBING FALL

Melissa Salazar, one of twin granddaughters of Abraham Salazar, the late chairman of the giant clothing company Salazar West, was killed yesterday in a tragic fall on the rock slide above Emerald Bay. She was hiking with her grandmother, Abraham's widow, and her sister Jennifer.

I paged ahead to the obituaries.

Melissa Salazar, aged 6, survived by sister Jennifer, mother Alicia and grandmother Roberta Salazar. The family requests that memorials be sent to the Sierra Club and the League To Save Lake Tahoe.

I made a few notes, thanked Glennie and left.

I decided to drive out to Emerald Bay. As the road zig-zagged its way five hundred feet up the moraine ridge between Cascade Lake and Emerald Bay, I thought of the two glaciers that had gouged them out ten thousand years ago. The Cascade glacier stopped short of Lake Tahoe and left a postcard lake nestled in a small valley below a waterfall that plunges down from the mountains above. The Emerald Bay glacier won the race and pushed all the way to Lake Tahoe forming a picture-perfect bay of water surrounded by granite walls three thousand feet high. Both lay below the Wonderbra peaks that were named for a well-shaped maiden named Maggie.

I turned into the parking area at the Bayview Trailhead. The lot was still covered with a foot of snow. I ground forward in four-wheel-drive and parked.

My snowshoes were in back. I strapped them on,

slipped on my anorak and headed up the trail that leads to Maggie's Peaks and the place where the mountain had fallen away half a century before.

I set off at a good pace, my snowshoes sinking just a few inches into the firm spring snowpack. When I entered the dark fir forest on the east side of Maggie's the snow was soft and much more work to hike in. Spot ran ahead, oblivious to the deep snow. He powered up the mountain without regard to the terrain or the low oxygen of high altitude. He followed scents that were as plain to his nose as Dayglo orange trail ribbons are to my eyes. Fifty yards ahead he jerked to a stop and pushed his head completely under the soft powder that lay below the shade of the dense firs. I hiked on past him while he investigated the criminal transgressions of squirrels and other creatures of spring. After a minute Spot raced past me, then veered off the trail and disappeared into the woods.

It is customary in Tahoe to worry about your dog in the back country. The concern isn't about the bear or mountain lion, but the ubiquitous coyote. A single coyote will serve as bait and lure an unsuspecting dog out to a waiting pack, there to be devoured. But I didn't think coyotes would make an attempt on Spot any more than they would try to bring down a bear.

The trail steepened. The fir forest thinned and in the bigger spaces were occasional large pines. I stuck my nose in the bark of one and inhaled. It had a strong and delicious butterscotch aroma which meant Jeffrey Pine.

The trail broadened. The trees opened up before me and I crested the top of the rock slide. Emerald Bay lay twelve hundred feet below me, as dazzling and richly colored as any water on earth.

Near the sandy beach where the wealthy widow Lora Knight built the Vikingsholm Mansion in 1928 in the style of a medieval Norwegian castle, the water was pure emerald. Heading out toward Fannett island where the heiress had her butler row her daily to take afternoon tea in the teahouse, the emerald color blended into turquoise. Past the island, the color turned to deep marine blue. And beyond, out in the main body of Lake Tahoe, the color was indigo, so deep in tone it was as if the blue light had traveled all the way up from the bottom, one thousand six hundred feet below the surface.

I stood at the top of the rock slide and thought of little Melissa plunging toward that saturated color. It was dizzying. I wavered for a moment, my legs seeming to sway. Could I lose my balance as I contemplated the height? And what of Melissa? Could a six-year-old child be carried away by such a view? Did she step on a loose rock and tumble? Was it possible for a sure-footed youngster to slip?

Or was she pushed to her sudden death?

Something cold and wet slapped my hand. I jerked with adrenaline, then realized it was Spot's nose. I rubbed his head as he stood at the edge of the precipice. One of the large tourist stern wheelers was entering the mouth of the bay so far below.

Thinking it some strange white bug, Spot did his rumbling imitation of a Panzer tank.

I recalled the day a few years ago when my neighbor's toddler had escaped the baby sitter and discovered how much more fun his toy car was in the middle of the road. Spot ran out and stood in our street as a truck roared up the mountain and around the corner. The angry driver screeched to a stop, honked and eventually got out carrying his tire iron before he saw that beyond the giant dog was a tiny child.

If only Melissa had been so lucky.

THREE

It seemed that Melissa's death was likely an accident. But to do Jennifer any service required me to consider that Melissa might have been murdered.

What could be a motive for killing a six-year-old kid? Because she saw something she wasn't supposed to see? Such a scenario presumed that someone was doing something abhorrent up on the mountain and didn't want a six-year-old to be able to finger him. Which was a far-fetched notion.

I took another look down the rock slide and imagined the path a falling body would take. The slide got steeper as it went down until it was near vertical. Being early May, it was still covered with a heavy layer of snow. I stared for another minute down the wide white swath trying to intuit something more about Melissa's death, but realized I would learn nothing further until I knew where they had found the body. I hiked back down Maggie's and drove south around the lake. It was too late to stop at the police station and ask my friend Mallory about Melissa's death, so I headed back up the east shore.

North of Cave Rock, I turned right onto a private road that winds its way two miles up to a small group of homes. My four-room log cabin was the original building. The previous owner had subdivided the land. Now there were five other houses, all grand assemblages of glass and rough-cut beams with prow fronts and cedar shake roofs. My humble structure was the black sheep of the bunch, but my stock broker, software engineer neighbors didn't seem to mind. I think they felt it was good to occasionally rub elbows with common folk who didn't even have a garage, never mind a Range Rover to put in it.

But I did have a ten million dollar view.

My cabin sits at 7,200 feet above sea level, 1,000 feet above the lake. The best place to see the view is from the deck which projects out from the mountain.

Street Casey's VW bug was in my drive and Spot got excited when he saw it. I told him to be quiet as we went inside. Street was not in my small cabin. I went out to the deck.

Street stood at the railing facing the lake, her body silhouetted against the sunset. She was skinny, but she looked great in her black blouse and black jeans. I touched Spot, held my finger out for silence and lingered at the view, then said, "Get you a beer?"

Street turned and grinned and patted her thighs.

"Spot, honey, c'mere!"

He bounded to her and, lifting his snout a few inches, licked her chin. Street hugged him, then swung a leg over his back and, giggling like a little girl, rode him around in a circle. "I'll take a light," she managed through her giggles.

"A whole one?" I said.

"Just half."

I went inside, poured half a beer into a tall narrow glass and brought it and another bottle for me back outside.

Street was back at the railing, facing across the water toward Emerald Bay, Maggie's Peaks and the white snow-covered gash of the rock slide. I set the beers on the railing and put my arm around Street's shoulders. I ran my fingers over her prominent jaw bone, across the tiny acne scars, down to the full, red lips. She'd put on a hint of shadow under her cheekbones, making them look even more dramatic than normal. She was gorgeous in spite of her flaws and I wondered for the thousandth time why she used cosmetics to make herself look more severe. I kissed her. The warmth of her high metabolism radiated like a heat lamp.

"Catch any bad guys lately?" she asked.

"Nope. But I've got a new client. Thinks her sister was murdered. If so, there's a bad guy in there somewhere."

The sun was disappearing behind the mountains making God rays flash through the clouds. The last of the sun made the amber liquid in Street's glass glow like a danger beacon.

As if on cue, a large spider came strutting down the railing toward us. I cocked my finger to shoot it into space and then remembered Street's presence. The woman had spent a sizable part of her life studying creepy crawlers. I let the bug pass by unscathed.

"What's this?" Street said. "A sudden case of arachniphilia?" She took a tiny sip of her beer.

"Did you expect anything less around you?"

"Yes, actually." She pointed a delicate finger at the spider. "That guy is a Turret spider. Makes his living eating insects, mostly ants. You want to be nice to insects, you should squish the spiders."

"Figures I'd get it wrong," I said. "I guess I don't find bugs interesting enough to keep the different types straight."

"Some night I'll sneak a couple of Cow Killers under your sheets. You'll become interested pretty quick."

"What's a Cow Killer?"

"A type of wasp, red and black. Got a sting so severe people claim it could kill a cow."

Street looked at her watch. "I better go," she said. "I

have to give a paper at an entomology conference in Oakland at eight in the morning. If I leave now I can get to my hotel by eleven p.m. I just wanted to see you before I left."

I walked her to her car, kissed her goodbye and watched as she drove away. A sadness, out of proportion to the moment, washed over me. I gave myself a shake and went inside.

My art books sit in a disheveled row on a long shelf that is open above so that the tallest hardcovers can sit side by side with small paperbacks. Although I never seem to get them organized, I knew right where to find the big Hopper monograph. My little cabin doesn't have a table so I sat down in my leather chair and opened it in my lap.

I wasn't looking for a specific image so much as a feeling that many of Hopper's paintings give me. My eyes lingered on certain reproductions. The lighthouses all alone on a hill. A group of people in a cafe, together physically but disaffected and emotionally alone. An old building in a forgotten part of town, past its prime and facing abandonment at best, demolition at worst.

The New York Movie painting flashed by and I turned back to it. I realized I wasn't drawn to the young woman so much as I was drawn to her pensiveness. Like Street, her loneliness was hidden from the world, revealed only to herself and only when she was alone. For her, self-reliance was more than just a worthy goal, it was a survival code as necessary as food or shelter.

I lingered on the image, fighting back my own loneliness at Street's departure. She had a conference to go to, no doubt important to her career. That I would give up my entire career if it meant I could spend every evening with her didn't mean I should judge her for not doing the same. Our driving forces were as different as our backgrounds and I should expect nothing else.

I'd come from a long line of Scots and Irishmen, scattered in big cities from Boston to Philadelphia to San Francisco. My father and uncles and grandfathers were gruff, loud-talking, beer-guzzling street cops, tough but fair-minded if a suspect was white, tough and not-so-fair-minded if the suspect was brown. The women in my family tree were plump, cheerful mothers, equally prejudiced but devoted to their kids like mother bears. If we didn't grow up with a broad and liberal view of the world, we at least grew up loved and cared for. And our families were intensely focused on protecting their own.

Street, in contrast, came from a union of two broken people who thought of her not as a child needing their love and attention, but as a problem interfering with their lives. When Street's only brother died after a beating by her recently paroled father, she ran away at 15 and never went back.

It seemed the rest of her life was going to be an exercise in self-reliance. When a young child is burned by the very people she is dependent on, that child learns never to get too close or dependent again.

I knew Street cared for me, maybe even loved me, and I knew I was as large a part of her day-to-day life as anyone had ever been. But she always kept me at an emotional distance. Oftentimes, I thought I could break through and get her to finally share some essential aspect of her inner self with me, but it never happened.

The cliché says that in the end one is always alone. But I thought maybe it is not just in the end. I looked at the Hopper book some more, then went into my kitchen nook to find something for dinner.

The next morning I was up early. Mallory would not be in the station until 8:00 or 8:30. I pulled on my sweats.

Spot and I walked down our road until we came to the highway at the base of the mountain. There we turned and started back up. Spot was excited, knowing that it was time to run. His slowest loping gait matches my fastest uphill run so it was hard for him to stay with me. Then we both settled back, me to a fast jog, Spot to a slow trot, as I forced myself up 1,000 vertical feet. It is a ten percent grade for two miles and takes me twenty minutes. At the top we turned around and did it again.

When we reached the cabin, Spot lapped heartily from his water bowl while I drank two glasses of water. Then Spot fetched a piece of rawhide that looked like old road kill. I put on coffee and got in the shower.

When I came out Spot was still working on the rawhide, his paws holding it in place. He rolled his big eyes up at me. It's hard to imagine a beast with claw and fang looking tender and feminine, but he could have been Rita Hayworth caught nibbling beef jerky in her dressing room.

After a late breakfast, Spot and I drove to the South Lake Tahoe police station.

Spot stayed in the car while I went inside.

"Mallory in?" I asked the burly young man behind the desk.

"Who's asking?" he said, his voice thick like a big city cop on a TV show.

"Tell him McKenna wants to take him to Mulligan's. Buy him a Guinness."

The young cop frowned at me. He picked up the phone and relayed my message.

Mallory came out sashaying and twisting. "Hey, hey, hey, McKenna, where you been!" He grabbed my hand, shook it like he was snapping a towel. Then he turned to the young cop on the desk and was all serious. "I'm going out for an important conference," he said in a deep voice.

"Hold my calls. No paging, no radio. I don't care if the Huns take the town. Got it?"

The cop at the desk smiled. "Sure, captain. An important conference."

Mallory poked a big finger at the young cop's chest. "You'll go far, kid."

We walked toward my Jeep. Mallory saw Spot with his head out the rear window. "Sure you don't want to take my Blazer? Those cherries'll get us there in a hurry."

"Spot likes you," I said.

"He likes beach balls, too," Mallory said. "That doesn't keep him from putting them in his mouth."

"Your head looks nothing like a beach ball," I said as I opened the door. "Size and shape and lack of hair, maybe, but no blue and yellow triangles."

Mallory got in and sat stiffly. "There ought to be a law," he said, looking over his shoulder. "Used to be a guy up in Montgomery Estates who kept tigers. He needed a permit. So should you."

I started the Jeep and pulled out of the lot. "Permit for a puppy dog?"

Mallory grunted.

Spot, realizing he wasn't going to get pet, hung his head and put on his sad eyes as we drove down Lake Tahoe Blvd. to Mulligan's Irish Pub.

We found a place to sit and ordered a round of Guinness Stout.

"Got a memory test," I said. I sipped my brew and licked the head off my upper lip. "Nine years ago a girl named Melissa Salazar fell off the rock slide above Emerald Bay. She was six years old. Remember?"

Mallory put down his beer. "Let me guess. The grandmother hired you to find out about the sister."

"Jennifer?"

"I don't know the name," Mallory said. "The twin."

I nodded.

"The old lady put that girl through half a dozen psychology examinations. She was convinced the sister pushed her off. Said those girls fought like rabid kittens."

"Anything come of it?"

"The tests?" Mallory said. "Naw. 'cept that girl proved to be a genius. I.Q. as high as the Transamerica Pyramid. The word on the force was that if she did it, she'd never get caught. Too smart. Played those shrinks like a deck of cards."

"Personal opinion?"

"Don't know," Mallory said. "But even if she did it, she was six years old. Can't prosecute a six-year-old. They say some are just born bad. Maybe so."

"Know who found the body?"

Mallory finished off his glass and signaled for two more. "It was one of Ellie Ibsen's search and rescue dogs that found the kid."

"She still around?"

"Down in the foothills near Placerville."

I brought Mallory back to the station, told him thanks and took Spot for a walk. We wandered down the bike paths toward the community college. I ruminated. Spot sniffed.

I remembered what Blakey Yardman, the SFPD-criminologist told me when I was on the force. "Any homicide ain't an obvious drug burn, look at the family first."

Could Mallory's speculations be right? Could a child actually murder her sister? Jennifer was the one who wanted me to find the supposed killer, so I hadn't considered her as a suspect. But maybe I'd fallen for an old trick. There'd been dissertations written on the psychology of guilty people who want their crimes to be discovered. And it was possible that the only two people who knew that Melissa was on the mountain that day were her grandmother and sister.

Which left me with a question of physical strength. Could a six-year-old push her sister off a cliff? The steepest part of the slide was out and down from the top. It would take a tremendous effort for a kid to push another kid that far. Then again, they might have climbed down to one of the boulders that protruded above the vertical drop-off. From that point a little push would do the job.

I found myself going over my conversation with Jennifer, searching for clues I'd missed. Nothing presented itself.

As for the grandmother, any woman in good enough shape to climb a mountain could easily toss a child off a cliff. Although I had not yet met Gramma Salazar, it was hard to imagine a woman murdering her own granddaughter. But if she had done it and worried about being found out, maybe she used the psychological tests to try to throw suspicion Jennifer's way.

Be good to find out.

FOUR

It was a little after 1:00 p.m., plenty of time to drive down to the foothills. Spot and I got in the Jeep and headed west. I got information on my cell phone. The only Ibsen in Placerville was a Mattson Ibsen. Quite a name. I dialed the number.

"Mattson Ibsen," an old man said. He sounded like he was gargling.

"May I speak to Ellie, please?"

"No Sally here," he said.

I thanked him and hung up.

Highway 50 crawls out of town out toward Meyers and Tahoe Paradise and then abruptly climbs up the granite ridge of the Sierra Crest. The pass called Echo Summit is one of the snowiest places on the continent and is often caked in snow eight months of the year. This May was no exception. As I rose up from the Tahoe Basin the snow banks grew by the guardrails that keep wayward vehicles from plunging down to Christmas Valley. The forest air rushing in Spot's open window was humid and cold.

I crested the pass and began the long descent toward California's Central Valley, 80 miles and 80 minutes and 7400 vertical feet from snow to palm trees.

I wound down the American River canyon. To my left was the gush of rapids that delights rafters and hydrologists alike. Above me a Mooney airplane did aerobatic turns as it flew through the canyon. It reminded me of my days off in the Bay Area when I used to take my old girlfriend Hannah out to Lindberg Field, rent a Cessna and fly up through the mountains of Napa. But that was another era, before I met Street.

As I lost altitude, the forest of fir and pines gradually gave way to oaks. The temperature rose steadily. When I arrived in Placerville, I was sweating in the hot sun. I gave in, rolled up the windows and turned on the air conditioning. Spot seemed grateful for the return of cool air. He stretched out across the back seat and went to sleep.

In front of one of the town shopping strips was a pay phone with a book hanging on the cable. I got out and checked in the Yellow Pages.

Under 'Dogs' were Food, Grooming, Kennels, Pet Sitting, and Training. There was no mention of Search and Rescue or the name Ellie Ibsen. I dialed one of the listings under Training.

"Foothills Obedience." A male drawl that could have come from Texas.

"A quick question, please. I'm looking for a dog trainer named Ellie Ibsen. Trains search and rescue dogs. Supposed to live around Placerville. I need to talk to her."

"She does live here. But she's a private trainer. Got an unlisted number. Now, if you want a rescue pup, I'd recommend you come out and talk to us. We're west of..."

"Excuse me. I'm just looking for Ellie Ibsen. If you could tell me where she lives?"

"What is it, an avalanche dog you want? You calling from one of the ski areas? We can help you with that, too. Ellie isn't the only master trainer in the Sierra."

"Sir, I'm investigating a potential homicide. One of Ellie's dogs found the body. I need to talk to her."

"Well why didn't you say so. You head north on forty-nine, you know, out where they discovered gold? Go five or six minutes until you come to a right turn called Winding Way which'll take you down toward the American River. Look for the Three Bar Ranch. It's got a big timber arch over the drive. That'll be Ellie's."

I thanked him and got back in the Jeep. Spot opened his eyes a crack, then went back to sleep.

The Three Bar Ranch didn't look like it would have any ranch animals on it. There were no fences and no barns and no crushed rock on the driveway. Instead, an immaculate blacktop drive with fresh seal-coating led to a large white rambler with light gray trim and a red enamel front door. I parked in front under the shade of a large oak and rolled the windows down.

"Stay put," I said to Spot. The big red door had a button to the side. Chimes sounded from within. A tall, gangly woman in her fifties answered the door.

"Good afternoon," I said. "Ellie Ibsen?"

"She's out back. Who shall I say is calling?"

"Owen McKenna. I have a question about one of her dogs."

The woman picked up a portable phone, dialed. "A Mr. Owen McKenna is here to see you. Says it's a question about one of the dogs. Okay, I'll send him back." She put the phone down. "Just go around that way." She pointed out the door to the right. Her eyes saw my Jeep. "Oh my." She said, looking at Spot. His head was out the window and he returned her gaze. "Oh my," she said again. "Anyway, you'll see the kennels. Mrs. Ibsen is out there."

I walked around the house on a bright green lawn that looked more even than Astroturf. There were no weeds. It was freshly mowed and perfectly trimmed where it met the drive and walkways and the house.

The kennel was a low building, as neat and clean as an outpatient surgical facility. I heard no barking. As I approached, the door opened and a tiny woman eighty-some years old emerged talking excitedly on a cell phone. She stood less than five feet tall and the white smock she was wearing hung down to her knees. Her pants were teal and her white running shoes had teal swooshes. Her hair was up in a lavender scarf and even at a distance she smelled of lilacs.

"You're kidding!" she said in a high, clear voice. "A Harl? This man? Here he is." She folded the phone and slipped it into the pocket of her smock. She squinted her eyes against the sun and looked up at me. "Mr. McKenna? My assistant says you have a large Harlequin Dane in your car. I can't wait to see."

She hurried past me. Upstaged by my dog, I about-faced and walked fast to keep up with her. She rounded the corner of the house and abruptly stopped. "Lordy be, look at the head on that boy! It is a male, correct? It must be. He's huge." She started forward again, almost running. "What's his name?" she called back to me.

"Spot," I said. "Don't worry. He won't hurt you." It was a line I found myself saying to everyone. But it wouldn't have made any difference with Ellie for she'd already yanked open the door of the Jeep.

"Spot, you lovely creature!" she said, holding her arms out to him. "Come out of that car and let me hug you."

I thought Spot would sit still. I thought he'd be suspicious of an old woman who didn't weigh much more than a large bag of dog food. Shows what I know. He jumped out of the car and sat at attention in front of Ellie, his head even with hers. She bent forward and hugged him around his neck. His head went over her shoulder and reached down her back to her waist. He was twice her size.

She wrenched herself away and looked at him as if he were her long lost son. "Okay, boy! Let me see you run!" Ellie smacked him on his chest. Then she took off in a lop-sided run across the yard. Spot loped after her. "Come on, big guy!" Spot galloped past her. Ellie made a tight turn. He followed, circling her while she shouted encouragement. "Lord, look at the conformation on him!" She stopped and turned to me, breathing hard. "You have a beautiful dog, Mr. McKenna."

"Thank you," I said.

She reached her hand up and we shook. "My name's Ellie Ibsen. Pleased to meet you."

Spot charged up and did one of his quick stops. Bits of turf flew. He stood next to Ellie, wagging hard. I worried that he might hit her with his tail, an assault which feels akin to being whipped with a garden hose. Again, Ellie showed her mastery of dogs. She sidled up next to him, and lifted her arm so that his neck nestled under her armpit. When he shifted position, so did she, always staying away from the swinging tail. I'd never seen Spot accept someone the way he did this affectionate woman.

"Mr. McKenna, your dog is well-behaved. You obviously know something about dog training."

"For a brief moment I was a canine handler on the S.F.P.D. years ago. But I haven't put Spot through much rigorous work."

Ellie nodded. "I thought so. Now that Spot has entertained me, what can I do for you?"

"I'm visiting to ask you about a search you were involved in nine years ago."

Ellie looked at me intently.

"I'm a private investigator now. I've been hired to look into an accidental death up at Lake Tahoe. A child named Melissa Salazar fell off the rock slide above Emerald Bay. A friend of mine on the police department said it was one of your dogs that found the body."

Ellie's face darkened. "That was so sad. So sad. Come with me." She started off toward the kennel. Spot heeled perfectly at her side. "We'll get Spot a friend to play with while you and I talk." We walked to the kennel. She turned and spoke directly to Spot. "You stay here."

She disappeared inside the building. A moment later she emerged with a black German Shepherd heeling at her side. "This is Natasha. Natasha, meet Spot. Now you two go play."

Natasha walked forward. Spot stood still. He lowered his head as she approached, she lifted her head and they touched noses.

"Don't worry," I said. "He's a little stiff at first but..."

"I know," Ellie interrupted. "He won't hurt her." Ellie took my arm, turned me around and walked with me into the yard. "Now, about the girl. I remember it like yesterday. It was Miss Lizzy that found her. She's gone now. But she was my best at the time. A lab shepherd mix. So when the police called and said they had a missing child I brought Miss Lizzy and Brandy, my yellow lab. When we got to the top of the rock slide, Brandy wanted to go on up the mountain. I remember how he barked and pulled. Of course he had the child's scent. The child had been all the way to the summit. But Miss Lizzy would have none of it. She turned off at the rock slide and started climbing down those boulders."

Across the lawn raced Ellie's German Shepherd followed closely by Spot, a sports car being pursued by a Mack truck.

"I was worried that we'd lose Miss Lizzy. My goodness, it was a drop off. But she picked her way down, jumping from boulder to ledge and so on. She was way down out of sight when she gave the bark that meant she'd found the little girl." Ellie went silent for a moment. We kept walking, her hand in my arm.

"Do you recall where Melissa's body was found?"

"You mean could I go and show you? No. One of the climbers brought the body up. But I gather it was on a ledge somewhere quite far down the slide."

"Do you know who the climber was?"

She shook her head. "A young man in his early twenties. Blond hair."

"Did the climber use the word 'ledge?'"

"Yes. Seems the poor thing crawled back under an overhang after she hit." Ellie's eyes teared up. "I can't stand to think of that little girl lying there slowly dying of her injuries." Ellie turned her eyes up to me. "What if the coyotes had gotten to her? What if she laid there half the night freezing to death?" Ellie's head shook with a tremor. "Why would she do that, crawl under a ledge? It would only make her harder to find."

I took her hands in mine and held them. "Maybe it was cold. Maybe she wanted to get out of the wind."

Or, I thought, maybe she was hiding from a killer.

FIVE

We spoke another fifteen minutes, and when I felt I would learn no more I excused myself, telling Ellie to come over for a barbecue the next time she was up in Tahoe.

It was early evening when I got home. The phone was ringing as I let myself inside. Street would be done with her conference by now and was possibly calling as she headed back home from Oakland. I hurried to the phone, but when I picked it up there was only a dial tone. I dialed Street's cell phone but got routed to her voice mail. I left a message, then headed for the kitchen, wishing once again that she were with me so I could cook her dinner.

I couldn't articulate well the nature of how I was attracted to her. But it wasn't anything like other relationships I'd had. Where other women had given me plaid flannel shirts or concert tickets for a present, Street would take me on a hike up a mountain summit and read a Yeats poem or one of Shakespeare's sonnets. Where other women spent time shopping and socializing, Street spent her time alone, reading books and studying bugs. While I didn't love bugs myself, I found her devotion to such tiny creatures very alluring.

The phone started again. I was bent over, head in the fridge, hands full of green and red and yellow peppers. I got to the phone after the second ring, but again there was only a dial tone when I picked it up. I thought of trying Street again, but realized she would be on the highway and driving through a dead spot between cell towers. I went out on the deck and lit a fresh pile of charcoal. A hundred stories below, Lake Tahoe lay gray and flat like a plate of fresh forged iron. The sunset reflected on it like the fires from a dying blast furnace.

I scrubbed a potato and put it in the microwave to jump-start the slow cooking of high altitude, then took a New York Strip steak out of the fridge. The microwave beeped. I wrapped the potato in foil and transferred it to the charcoal. To mix up a marinade I squeezed a clove of garlic into a pan, diced some green onions, poured in some soy sauce and a touch of Napa Valley Cabernet.

Twenty minutes later I put the steak on the grill. Spot lifted his nose in the air and flexed his nostrils.

"Don't drool," I said. "It's not polite."

He went back to chewing his rawhide, dejection on his face.

When I sat down and tasted my steak, it was all I could do not to call Jackson Bullman, my venture capitalist friend, and offer to start a restaurant chain with his money. But I couldn't have called because the phone started ringing again. I jumped up and answered it.

"Mr. McKenna?" It was Jennifer Salazar. She'd said only my name, yet I could hear the terror in her voice.

"Yes, Jennifer. What is wrong?"

"I think someone is trying to kill me! Someone is in our house! He broke in! I grabbed my cell phone and hid in the closet of the study! Then I heard someone go into the room next door. I ran out."

"Where are you now?"

"I'm in the library. Hurry!"

"Did you call nine-one-one?"

"I tried, but my phone keeps cutting out. He broke in last night, too! I got through to the police last night. I explained about it on the machine at your office. But you didn't call. Can you come to my house? Can you come right now?" Her voice was sobs and mumbled words. She sounded like she was choking.

"I'm on my way. Where am I going?"

"South of Zephyr Cove. Around the curve. On the lake side is a drive with two stone columns and yellow Tiffany lights on them. It's a wrought iron gate. I'll push the button to open it. Hurry, Mr. McKenna! Please hurry!"

SIX

My untouched steak and potato went into the fridge. I pulled on my leather jacket and ran outside with Spot next to me.

I drove down the dark mountain as fast as I dared. Guilt over not checking my messages at the office crowded my thoughts.

Highway 50 had lots of traffic for a Tuesday night. I stomped on the accelerator and jumped out after a Cadillac limousine and in front of an eighteen-wheeler.

Jennifer's driveway was as she described. The wrought iron gate was open. I turned in and raced down a paved road lit at intervals with yellow lights on two-foot-tall stone columns with elaborately-carved caps. Neither the house nor lake was visible through the pines. The drive curved left and went around a hill of granite. I went by a good-sized home on the right. Probably the caretaker's.

The Salazar mansion appeared through the trees. It was made of stone, with turrets and towers and giant bay windows, each with a hundred small windowpanes or more. A steep slate roof swept down beside third-floor gabled windows. I hadn't come to a complete stop in the circular drive when the front door opened and Jennifer ran out.

She came for my Jeep and ran around the far side as if to use it as a barrier between her and the house. Her eyes were wide with fright. I grabbed the flashlight out of the glove box and got out. Jennifer held her hands in front of her mouth. Her eyes darted from me to the house.

Her voice was high and tense and insistent. "I keep hearing noises! Last night they were in the north wing. So I hid in the closet off the parlor when I called nine-one-one. The police came but they couldn't find anything. Now tonight I heard more noises. They were upstairs where the bedrooms are. My cell phone kept cutting out. I tried calling you over and over until you came home." Jennifer's voice choked up. She put an ice-cold hand on my arm. "I watched through the window from the library. When I saw your headlights I ran outside." Jennifer was shaking.

"Are you staying here all alone?"

"Gramma is visiting friends in Salt Lake City. I convinced her I was okay alone. Samuel Sommers, the caretaker, was supposed to be back from vacation yesterday, but he never showed." She started to cry. "Why did he have to pull his disappearing act when Gramma is gone?"

"You're okay, now," I said. "Let's have a look." We walked toward the house. Jennifer took hold of my hand. I could feel resistance as I moved forward. "Spot will help us check the house," I said.

When we reached the open front door Jennifer stopped. "I'm afraid," she said.

"Spot will go in first." I gave him the hand signal to stay with me. "You are certain no one else is supposed to be with you?" I asked Jennifer. "Are there any servants around?"

"No." She said, her voice quaking. "I'm all alone."

Spot and I stepped in through the front door. I called out in my loudest voice. "THIS IS THE POLICE! YOU HAVE THIRTY SECONDS TO COME OUT!

AFTER THAT I'M SENDING IN THE DOG. THE DOG WILL FIND YOU AND ATTACK YOU. I

REPEAT. YOU HAVE THIRTY SECONDS TO COME OUT OR YOU WILL BE BITTEN."

Jennifer shook at my side. Her frightened eyes went from me to Spot. Thinking of the size of the mansion and the likely number of servants and helpers, I asked her one more time. "Is there anyone else who has a right to be in the house tonight?"

Jennifer shook her head. "Only Sam the caretaker, and he would come to me if he were around."

Thirty seconds were up. "Okay, Spot. Find the suspect!"

Spot shot into the house.

I grabbed Jennifer by the hand and pulled her at top speed after Spot.

Spot ran into the mansion, claws scraping the carpet. He went to work, his nose to the floor. He ran a zig-zag pattern through the cavernous entry hall, inspecting the walls and floor. He turned right and disappeared into the house.

"What part of the house is he going to?" I asked.

"That way is the main staircase. Beyond is the living room, the library and the parlor."

Jennifer and I ran after Spot. He rushed up the stairs, his nose alternating from the steps and handrails to the air above him. I tugged Jennifer's hand.

"Wait," she said. She pulled back. "What if he finds someone? What if the intruder has a gun?"

"If Spot finds someone, he will let us know before we get there."

We went up the stairs two at a time. It curved around in a half circle. When we got to the top, Spot was disappearing down a hall.

"That's toward our bedrooms!" Jennifer said in a hushed voice.

We went down the hallway. Spot was thirty feet in

front of us, his nose to the floor. He alerted at a doorway, whining, pawing and biting the doorjamb.

"That's Gramma's room," Jennifer whispered.

I ran up and turned the knob.

Spot sprinted into the dark room. He growled. I reached around the door jamb, feeling for the light switch. Spot growled louder. I flicked on the light.

The room was empty. Spot was over at the far wall. His head was out an open window. The rumble in his chest grew.

I flipped off the light, ran over to the side of the window and peeked out above Spot's head. It was dark outside, but I could see a long, wide roof about four feet below the window. The dark lake was beyond. Nothing moved. "Jennifer?"

She came slowly into the darkened room.

"The roof below this window. Can you get from it down to the yard?"

"Yes. That's the roof over the swimming pool. It's not a long drop."

I shut the window. "Let's go downstairs," I said. "Hurry!"

Jennifer and I rushed down the hall. Spot passed us at a gallop and ran down the stairs. "Is there a door on the lake side near the pool?" I called out as we ran.

"Yes! Behind the staircase!"

Spot was pawing and biting the door frame when we got there. I opened it and he charged out into the night.

I grabbed Jennifer's hand and we ran into the cold breeze off the lake. The lawn was uneven and scattered with large pines. Spot raced down toward the dark lake. We stumbled after him. He headed toward a building on the shore. Jennifer stayed by my side as we ran. "Is the boathouse kept locked?" I asked.

"Yes," Jennifer said. "You have to enter the code on the alarm panel in the house in order to unlock it."

As Spot approached the boathouse, he veered off down the beach toward the wrought iron fence. We turned to follow. The fence projected several feet into the water where it ended. Spot dashed into the waves, went around the fence and headed back into the woods. He disappeared in the direction of the highway.

I realized that the intruder would reach the highway before Spot caught him, putting Spot at great risk among the vehicles on the road, so I called him off. "That's enough, Spot! Come on back."

Jennifer and I stopped running. "Let's check the boathouse." She stayed back of me while I walked toward the building. In the twilight stood a modern structure with a blue metal roof and exterior walls of cedar varnished to a high sheen. The boathouse projected out over the water with a pier on each side. There were French doors on the side that faced us. A pile of concrete blocks sat next to one door. I walked down the pier to the door and tried the knobs. Locked. The doors had multiple window panes. I cupped my hands and peeked inside. I could see nothing in the darkness except the windows in matching doors on the opposite side. Spot reappeared and came running down the pier.

"Other side, boy," I said. He followed me back onto land, around the building, and we ran down the other pier. I tried the other doors and they too were locked.

Spot was out at the end of the boathouse, lowering his head down toward the water. I ran out to him. The water was four feet below the dock and was black as ink. Spot sniffed the air. Nothing seemed to move below. He trotted down to the end of the pier, his nose to the boards. He didn't seem to have a scent so I wasn't alarmed.

I hung onto the edge of the boathouse and leaned out over the water. I reached out and felt the door where the boats would go in and out of the boathouse. It appeared to be a ribbed fiberglass garage door that rose vertically like that on an ordinary garage. I tugged up on the ribs, but it would not move.

"C'mon Spot. Let's go."

Jennifer stood on the pier not far away.

"All locked," I said. We walked back up the dark lawn to the house.

We went inside and Jennifer showed me to all of the outer doors which, counting the six car garage, numbered fifteen. All were locked. Next, we toured the ground floor windows. I lost count of the number when I passed one hundred. They all were secure. "Any other higher windows, like in your grandmother's bedroom, that you can get to from a roof?" I asked.

"There are two or three rooms down past Gramma's that are also the same height above the pool roof, so I suppose someone could climb up to any of them. And there are the third floor windows which all are gables in the roof. If you could get up on the main roof, you might be able to get in any of them. But the roof is very steep."

We went through the house and verified that it was closed up well.

"Does your grandmother ever leave her bedroom window open?"

"She often sleeps with it open. But she never leaves it open when she's gone."

"Does she keep it locked?"

"I don't know."

Jennifer stopped walking. "You think Spot is smelling Gramma?"

"Could be that the only other strong human scent in

this house is her."

We were coming down the stairs from the third floor. There was a noise from somewhere below us. Spot growled and ran down. We took the steps two at a time. We stopped at the corner where the stairs met the second floor. I peeked into the hallway. Spot was again entering the door to the grandmother's room. Jennifer stayed back as I approached the dark doorway for the second time. I followed Spot into an empty room. He was sniffing the sill of the window. I looked out at the darkness. It was the same as before.

Jennifer came in behind me. "Was that window open?"

I nodded.

"You shut it before." Jennifer said.

I tried to remember. It seemed that I had, but I had checked more than one hundred window latches since then. I wasn't sure.

"You shut it the last time we were in this room. And now it's open." Jennifer voice broke. "Oh, my God!" Her eyes darted around the room. "Owen! Someone was in the house. While we were outside. Or maybe they just came in while we were up on the third floor! Maybe they're hiding in here at this moment!" She seemed to implode. Her knees bent. She hugged herself.

I took her by the elbow and steered her out of the room. Spot led the way down the stairs and out the front door. He did not alert again.

We got into my Jeep and I drove out the drive.

"When does your grandmother come home?"

"Not until tomorrow. I'm supposed to spend one more night alone. If Samuel were doing his job as caretaker he'd be just down the driveway. But he's gone and I won't stay alone in this house again."

"Can you sleep at one of your friends? I can drop you

off."

"I don't have any friends. None close enough that I could sleep over on short notice."

"There must be somebody."

Jennifer looked down. "You don't understand. I'm a fourteen-year-old in a class of kids who are all seventeen. Two are eighteen. They think I'm weird. I make them insecure. And the kids my own age treat me like I'm an alien." Jennifer turned her head toward me. "I'm embarrassed to admit to such social dysfunction. But the truth is I don't have any friends. Haven't for years."

"Okay. We'll go to my house."

SEVEN

We sat in my living room in front of the wood stove. I built a fire and got us drinks. Tea for Jennifer, a beer for myself. Jennifer tentatively pet Spot who sat next to her. "What about the alarm panel you mentioned?" I asked. "Aren't the windows tied into the system?"

"The entire house is wired. But the only thing we use the system for is unlocking the boathouse and operating the front gate. We never turn on the alarm because it always goes off. The sensors are too sensitive. Every time the house creaks, the system fires. Because it's connected to the police, they were always coming out on false alarms."

"But tonight and last night weren't like any of the times you had false alarms?"

Jennifer looked startled. "The last two nights weren't like any night in my whole life."

"The noises you heard couldn't have been the groans of an old house?"

"Not a chance. I've lived there all my life. I know that house."

I sipped my beer and looked at the fire through the glass door of the stove. I wondered if she could be lying.

Jennifer shifted to the edge of her chair. Spot leaned his body toward her, the better for her to hug him. She ran her hands over his head and chest, then laid her head on his neck. His eyes were half-closed and his ears were relaxed. Dog heaven wasn't any better.

"Ever since I ran the ad in the paper," Jennifer said, "things have happened. The phone rings, but there's no one there. I feel like someone is following me on my bike. Now someone's been in the house."

"What ad?"

"A few weeks ago I put an ad in the personals. In the Herald. I offered a reward for any information about the accident on the rock slide that took the life of a girl nine years ago. I thought that might loosen something."

"Jennifer, why didn't you tell me about this when you came to my office?"

"I didn't think it germane to your investigation. I'd run the ad and gotten no response. I don't even know if I remembered it yesterday when I went to see you." She gazed into the fire. "The murder happened nine years ago so I didn't really expect a response. And I suppose I didn't want the lack of response to discourage you."

"Anything connected to Melissa's death is germane to my investigation. Including your previous efforts to gain information about it. Especially when your efforts have been followed by strange events." I was thinking about the bicyclist who took the same path into the woods that Jennifer did, followed by the belligerent bodybuilder.

Jennifer took a drink of her tea. "Those events seem important now. They didn't then. It's easy to give credence to small things after their possible significance has been established. Prior to that, well, I just didn't think of it. Maybe part of me worried that you'd think I was wacko. As if I don't have enough of that in my family what with mom."

"You said Alicia was schizophrenic?"

"Yes. We see her once, maybe twice a year in that prison they call a hospital. She's so out of it, I can't even imagine she's my mother."

"When does your grandmother get home?"

"Tomorrow afternoon. The people she's visiting in Salt Lake are family friends. Stockholders in Salazar West, too. They have a private jet. They'll fly her into the airport in South Lake Tahoe."

"She'll take a cab from there?"

Jennifer closed her eyes a moment and sighed. "That's right. Sam is supposed to pick her up. But who knows where he is." Jennifer's eyes opened wide. "My God, I just thought of something. A couple weeks ago Sam said something unusual. I was leaving on my mountain bike and he asked me which way I ride to school. I told him about my path through the woods. Then he asked if I met friends or if I rode the whole way alone. At the time it seemed like benign curiosity. Now I wonder."

"Does he do this often? Disappear without advance notice?"

"Often enough that behind his back we don't call him Samuel Sommers, we call him Samuel Sometimes."

"Why keep him on?"

"Because even though he has these lapses, according to Gramma he's the best we've ever had. He's kind, polite, puts in extra hours, doesn't drink, doesn't crack up the cars. He just disappears here and there."

"Any idea where he goes?"

Jennifer shrugged her shoulders. "This time it was his vacation. He went down to Cabo for a week on the beach. But other times we don't know where he goes. He has his own car. Probably goes to the Showgirls Ranch and spends his money on hookers."

"How long is he usually gone?"

"A day or two. Never longer. So I suppose he'll be back tomorrow. If he's not back in time, I'll have to send a cab to pick up Gramma and Helga. Although she despises cabs. Maybe I can pull some strings and get one of the hotels to send a limo."

"Helga is..."

"Helga is our housekeeper. At least that's her title. But she's actually more like Gramma's personal attendant. Helga practically raised us. Gramma never did like kids much, not even my father Joseph, if I can believe Helga's off-hand comments. You remember the room just down the hall from Gramma's? Helga has lived in that room for forty years. Gramma brought her over from the old country, as they call Germany. Helga was only twenty. She was studying to be a nun. Gramma knew her parents. They introduced Gramma to their daughter hoping Gramma could take her to America and talk her out of serving her religion so monastically. So Gramma met Helga and convinced her that she could serve God in America just as well as in Bavaria. Gramma was thirty-six when she brought Helga to Lake Tahoe. Ever since my father and Grandpa Abe died, Gramma never goes anywhere without Helga."

"They leave you without a sitter? Just Sam?"

"This was the first time. I had to talk Gramma into it. When I was young they'd leave me with some friends of Gramma who live in Glenbrook."

"Tell you what," I said. "If Sam doesn't get back in time I'll pick you up and you and I will go get them at the airport together."

"Pick me up? Where? I'm not going back home. No way. I'll sleep on your couch." She glanced around my tiny cabin and saw that I didn't have one. "I'll sleep right here in this chair. With Spot."

"My friend Street lives just down the mountain, nine hundred feet below us. She has a pull-out couch. It's more comfortable. You'll be better off there."

"Street?" She sounded suspicious. "I won't sleep at a stranger's. What kind of a name is Street, anyway?"

"Street Casey is my girlfriend. Her parents named her Street because they didn't make it to the hospital in time. She was born in the street."

Jennifer started to grin, then abruptly stopped. "I'd rather sleep here. I know you. You're safe."

"Jennifer, you just met me yesterday. I'm a grown man, as they say, and you are a kid of the female variety. People would be uncomfortable. Grandmothers especially." I looked at the clock. One in the morning. Street would be home from her conference. I went into the bedroom and brought the phone out so that Jennifer wouldn't think I was talking behind her back. I dialed. "Street? Hi, sweetheart. Sorry if I woke you."

"Not to worry," Street said. "I was up revising some notes." Her voice had a husky fatigue in it. "Trying to get it all out of my system." While I listened to Street I saw Jennifer mouthing the word sweetheart to herself.

"Was it a bad conference?"

"No. But after I gave my paper, two bug guys from D.C. tried to put the make on me. Real cockroaches. They kept asking me to come to their condo in the Oakland Hills when the conference was over," Street said. "Said their hot tub had a great view of the Bay. Then, get this, one of them said that there was an inverse relationship between cup size and leg quality. He looked at me and said I must have great legs."

"Well, at least they're right on that account. What'd you do?"

"I told them that I was a great judge of character, hence I'd rather spend my time with maggots. Too bad, being that these guys have done a lot of consulting for the FBI. I might have gotten forensic referrals."

"Street, what am I gonna do with you?" I said. Jennifer was watching me carefully.

"Come and check my cup size."

"I already have. There's enough to keep me busy. But I have something else to ask." I explained about Jennifer and her situation.

Street was predictably gracious. "Of course she should stay here! Hey, I rented a great classic. Hitchcock's Dial M for Murder with Grace Kelly. Bet she hasn't seen it. I'll start making popcorn. It'll be done by the time you two get down the mountain. And tell her I have pizza in the freeze. We'll cut up some extra cheese and some bell peppers and pineapple and make like it came from the Lake Tahoe Pizza Company."

I thanked her and hung up. Jennifer looked at me like I was turning her out into the cold. "Trust me," I said. "You'll like Street."

EIGHT

I dropped Jennifer at Street's. I winked at Street while I explained that I couldn't stay. The two of them would get comfortable with each other much faster with me gone. Jennifer gave me a look of betrayal, but seemed resigned to her lack of alternatives.

Back in my log cabin I placed a call to the pager of Diamond Martinez, a friend and Douglas County deputy on the Nevada side of Lake Tahoe. I didn't know if his schedule put him in bed or on the highway at two in the morning. I hoped that he had the pager turned off if he was asleep. The phone rang two minutes later.

"Diamond, I hope I didn't wake you."

"Late for a gringo like you to be working," he said. "Maybe you're getting smart and taking a siesta during the heat of the day."

"Not much heat at this altitude," I said.

"Altitude alone won't do it. Gotta have latitude."

"What?" I asked.

"My home town Mexico City is even higher elevation than Lake Tahoe. It's how far north makes the difference."

"Ah," I said. "Just a quick question. Couple of your boys responded to a nine-one-one at the Salazar place last night. Find anything?"

"Found a very excitable girl. That's all. If you're working

for the family you should be watching more closely. They've got enough bank to hire every baby-sitter in California and Nevada. Yet they leave that girl alone."

"Your boys left her alone when they were done checking the house."

"She refused to come. What would you have them do, kidnap her and lock her in the station house? The Salazar lawyers would sue us off the map."

"Anyway," I said, "there's supposed to be a caretaker. Some disappearing act named Samuel Sommers."

"The kid mentioned him."

"You run his name?" I asked.

"Yeah, there's a funny one. He's got no sheet. He doesn't even officially exist. DMV in both Nevada and California have no record of a Samuel Sommers. We're checking Social Security. You believe what the kid is saying? About her sister being murdered?"

"I don't know, Diamond. She seems sincerely afraid. She called me tonight, very upset. She was convinced someone was in the house just like last night. Spot and I checked the house."

"You find more than we did?"

"I don't think so," I said. "There was a window that was open that the girl said was previously shut. But I'm not certain of that. Nevertheless, she seems fixated on murder."

"Speaking of which, we've had some of our own excitement in Douglas County tonight. I need to call your lady friend and ask her to do a time-of-death estimate on a decomposed body we found down below Spooner Summit."

"When was this?" I asked, immediately thinking about the missing caretaker.

"A hiker found the body this evening at seven o'clock. He reported it when he got back from his hike. That was about ten-thirty. Two of my deputies followed the hiker's directions. It was slow, going by flashlight. They found the corpse around midnight. It's down in a ravine about a half mile from Highway 50."

"Murder?" I asked.

"There were two bullet holes in the skull, side by side. From the look of the bone chips, they were both entrance wounds and there were no exit wounds. Small caliber, no doubt."

"Close range, execution style?"

"Maybe," Diamond said. "I've heard of Mob hits using twenty-twos. They don't have the punch to pass completely through the skull. Instead, they ricochet around inside the brain causing more damage than a bigger round would going all the way through. But I don't know that we've ever had Mob activity in Tahoe."

"How long dead, do you think?"

"Hard to say. That's why we need Street to do her thing. The body is mostly skin and bones. I'd guess death was a few weeks ago."

"Which would rule out the missing caretaker," I said, "because he only left on vacation a week ago or so."

"The guy with no sheet? Right. Plus, these bones look to be female."

"Unusual for a female to be killed execution-style," I said.

"I agree with you there. But the bones are small and a bracelet on the wrist said, 'to Maria, I'll love you forever.' Hey, what time does Street usually wake up?"

"I just spoke to her a few minutes ago," I said. "I'm sure you could still call."

"It won't ruin her night, calling about a corpse?"

"No," I said, thinking of the demons that Street wrestled with on a regular basis. "Unless she knows them, bodies aren't the kind of thing that bother Street."

I hung up, went into my kitchen nook and put my cold steak and potato in the microwave. It smelled good when it got warm, but the steak chewed like a rubber eraser. I gave part of it to Spot. The way he inhaled it, you'd think it came from Morton's of Chicago. After I ate I sat in front of the fire and communed with Sierra Nevada Pale Ale. Only one was for enjoyment. The other three were purely medicinal.

I'd seen my share of psycho-pathology over the years, but I still couldn't accept that some creep might be stalking Jennifer in her mansion at night. Harder still to think that the same creep might have murdered her six-year-old sister nine years ago. But one would explain the other now that Jennifer was running ads in the paper and inspiring a private cop to stir up trouble.

I got out the Hopper book and paged through it. The color plates of famous paintings flashed by. Sunlight In A Cafeteria. Office At Night. Sea Watchers. They each had two people in them, yet the people seemed alone, lost in private thoughts. They looked as if they wanted a bond but were unable to connect. I felt like there was something in the paintings that would illuminate my case, but nothing came to me. I finally went to bed with many questions and no answers.

I didn't sleep so much as occasionally nod off only to awake at 3:00 a.m. with pounding heart and heavy breath. A dream about the way people prey on others was fresh in my mind. I opened the Hopper book again. I didn't think I'd find any comfort. Maybe I was looking for a small measure of understanding of the human psyche. But if Hopper revealed these secrets, they were lost on me.

In the morning I took my coffee out to the deck where it steamed vigorously in the brisk air. The sun was dazzling on the snow-covered mountains across the lake.

From my deck railing I could almost see Street's condo

in the trees down the mountain. If the night had gone well for them they would still be asleep for hours. I showered and dressed in jeans and red plaid flannel shirt. Spot was particularly lethargic having only had a few hours of sleep, so I left him on the big braided rug and drove into town. I had an omelet and more coffee at the Red Hut Waffle Shop and then drove down the street to the Herald.

Glenda Gorman said she had nothing else to do so she helped me look for the ad. I told her what the ad would say and roughly when it ran, but I did not say who placed it. We sat in front of one of the microfiche machines, side by side on padded metal chairs. Glennie scooted hers sideways until it touched mine. I looked at her.

"I just need to be close so I can see the screen," she said. She fiddled with the focus knob. "And so you can smell my new perfume."

"Glennie, it's a little naive, without any breeding, but I'm definitely amused by its presumption."

She slugged me hard on my shoulder. "You're using Thurber to mock me. Remember, I'm a trained journalist."

I rubbed my shoulder.

Glennie was running the film on fast forward. "What is it anyway? That she's got and I haven't?" She stopped the film, backed it up, stopped it again.

"You shouldn't ask such questions." The page on the screen was the classifieds from a couple of weeks ago. I took the adjustment knob and slowly scanned the Personals column. "Anyway, you've got it backward," I said. "It's not just what Street has, it's partly what she doesn't have." Jennifer's ad wasn't there. I fast-forwarded to the next day's paper and slowed to find the Personals. "Street doesn't have your solid self-confidence. She doesn't have your stable career. She doesn't have your Cover-Girl face and your body that goes in and out so dramatically."

Glennie turned and looked at me. "What do you mean? She has a great body. Skinny as a model and legs that won't quit."

"That's what I said."

Glennie noticed the way I was working the microfiche machine. "Here, let me do it. I'm practiced at this." She took over the search. "Don't you like confidence and career stability? Don't you like my body?"

"Of course I do. But you're too perfect a package. You're the cheerleader who turned out to have brains and heart. For most guys, having you would be like winning the lottery. Someone hands you what you've always wanted on a platter and the ambition and dream to make it happen by yourself is blown apart."

"You're trying to flatter me."

"No, I'm telling the truth. I'm attracted to you. But I'm more attracted to Street's vulnerability, her incompleteness, her small share of insecurity."

"Is it a challenge or something?"

"No. It's more a connection to my own insecurities. Street and I share something dark."

"I can be dark. I can be insecure. Give me time. Practice makes perfect."

"No, Glennie. You stay exactly the way you are. You're perfect. You're going to meet some guy who makes me look like a geek in a cowboy suit."

"Right. Someone with your brains, your blue eyes, all in this little town."

"You forgot my dog."

"Best part about you. But I didn't think it necessary to state the obvious." Glennie pointed to the screen. "Here it is."

I leaned over to look.

She read the ad out loud. "'Reward paid for any information about an accident that killed a little girl August of nine years ago on the rock slide above Emerald Bay.'"

The ad had Jennifer's phone number but not her name.

"That's it?" she asked. "That's what you're investigating? I get it. Someone thinks the kid's death wasn't an accident. But if it wasn't, then the only person who might have information would be the killer. If someone else had information, the killer would have killed them long ago. So the person who placed this ad is basically sending up a flare saying, 'come kill me, too,' right?"

"Glennie, you are saying some very disturbing things."

Her eyes got a wild look. "Who is it? Who placed the ad?"

I was too disturbed by her premise to respond.

"Owen! I can easily look it up in the computer. Save me the time."

"Melissa Salazar had a twin sister named Jennifer. Jennifer is convinced that Melissa was killed."

"That was what you were looking up the other day. The story on Melissa's death. I'll go get that film. I want to read it."

"There was nothing revealing in the story," I said.

"Not to you maybe. But remember..."

"I know," I said. "You're a trained journalist." I thought about what Glennie had said while she fetched the tape I'd reviewed earlier.

"Here we go," she said, returning from the shelves with the tape. "August of nine years ago." She put the film in the machine and found the story in seconds. She read it and immediately forwarded to the obituary as I had done.

"Did you find anything else besides the story and the obit?" she asked me.

"No. What else would there be?"

Glennie looked at me, disbelieving. "We always, always run a follow-up story on any unusual death." She paged ahead. "Sometimes the next day. Sometimes two or three days later." She worked the control. The screen blurred, stopped, blurred again. "Here it is. What do you think? We could be McKenna and Gorman Investigations."

"I don't think Street would be wild about the idea," I said, studying the screen. The date in the corner was two days after the earlier story on Melissa's death.

FREAK ACCIDENTS CLAIM
TWO LIVES IN TAHOE BASIN

Catastrophe struck in two separate hiking accidents this week. On Wednesday six-year-old Melissa Salazar, one of twin granddaughters of the late clothing magnate Abraham Salazar, was hiking with her sister and grandmother when she slipped and fell off the rock slide below Maggie's Peaks.

Search and rescue teams from Eldorado and Alpine counties were brought in. Thursday morning a rescue dog found the body partway down the rock slide.

Preliminary investigation suggests that the young girl slipped on loose rock near the top of the rock slide.

On Friday afternoon across the lake on Mount Rose, Truckee hikers found the body of Penelope Smithson, wealthy North Shore socialite. Smithson, an avid hiker, was ap-

parently hiking alone on a narrow trail that
leads to the 10,600 foot summit of Mount
Rose when she slipped on loose scree and
plunged 1000 feet to her death.

Glennie looked at me to see if I'd finished reading. I
nodded. She paged ahead to the obituary.

Penelope Smithson, aged 49, Reno arts pa-
tron and benefactor of a Truckee theater
group, survived by husband John.

"Strange coincidence," Glennie said.

"Yes, but every year several people die in Tahoe while
engaging in some kind of outdoor recreation."

"Sure. Usually it is skiers who hit trees, or snowmobilers
who head into the back country and get caught in fierce Sierra storms. Rarely do hikers fall to their deaths."

"Yeah," I said. "To my knowledge, that was the only
time two hikers ever died at nearly the same time." I looked
at my watch. "I better run. Got chauffeur duty. Thanks,
Glennie."

She stood and gave me a goodbye hug.

NINE

I pressed Street's doorbell button early in the afternoon. The condo rattled with the bass of loud rock 'n roll. No one answered. I knocked hard, but again there was no response. Street had given me a key that I had never used. Until now.

The blast of music hit me like a punch in the chest when I opened the door. Off-key vocals competed with the recording.

They were in the living room. Street was in her bathrobe, standing on the couch, twisting like Chubby Checker. Her head was back. Her eyes were closed. She mouthed the lyrics and shook her head. Her hair was a blur. Jennifer was doing an a-go-go dance on the glass cocktail table. She, too, had her eyes closed. Her long brown hair shimmied. She was screaming along with the lyrics, "Ooh, yeah, yeah!"

It must have been a minute before they saw me up on the Jennair cooking island in the kitchen. I was on my back, arms and legs in the air, trying not to smirk. Shaking and shuddering like a Holy Roller. I heard a howl and turned my head just in time to see Street leaping onto my body. She landed in a swan-dive position and we jerked and shook together like bacon in a frying pan. When the song was over Street slid off onto the floor. Jennifer collapsed on the couch in giggles.

When the next song started, Street grabbed Jennifer and they waltzed around the floor. Their timing to the music was horrible. But their camaraderie was exquisite.

The CD ended and they fell back onto the couch, arms around each other.

"Oh, God!" Jennifer yelled, her words choked with giggles. "I've never had this much fun in my life!"

"The drugs are working," I said.

"Yes," Street screamed through her laughter.

Jennifer looked at me, then Street.

"Owen says we all self-medicate," Street shouted.

"Owen uses Sierra Nevada Pale Ale." She turned to Jennifer. "You and I just used Pearl Jam and a pound of Sara Lee chocolate cake!" They both shrieked.

After they calmed I pointed to my watch. "Chauffeur time."

Jennifer turned to Street on the couch and shrugged. She reluctantly got up and rummaged around the living room collecting her shoes and other items she'd brought with her. When it came time to leave she hugged Street for a long moment. "You are so..." Jennifer said, searching for words. "I've never met anyone like you before. I had so much fun."

"Me, too," Street said. "You come anytime. Don't wait for this guy to drop you off, you hear?"

I kissed Street as we were leaving. "Thanks," I said softly.

"Thank you." Street pulled me back inside the door. Jennifer was out putting her things in my Jeep. "Jennifer thinks you might be wondering about her. Like maybe you don't believe everything she's told you? Well, I just want to say that I think she's sincere. She's a good kid, Owen. Trust her."

I nodded.

"And by the way," Street said. "Diamond called me last night about that body. So when I'm through collecting samples I'll be at my lab all day."

I said goodbye and went out to the Jeep. Jennifer was smiling. "What's so funny?" I said as I pulled out of Street's drive.

"I'm amused at how rarely adults are right. But you were right. I like Street. She's great."

"Yeah," I nodded. "I think so, too."

"She likes all the same music I do, the same food, the same movies. She remembers what it's like to be a kid."

I nodded.

"You'd never guess that she has a Ph.D. in Entomology from Berkeley," Jennifer said.

"Not until you look at her books."

"So what exactly is her job?"

"She's a bug consultant. The Forest Service hires her to do bark beetle counts every year to keep track of the infestation level in the basin's forests. And she also consults with law enforcement agencies on suspicious deaths."

"You mean that she can tell something about how people died by looking at insects?"

"Right. Forensic entomology."

"Like what?" Jennifer said. "What can Street learn from bugs?"

"Are you squeamish?"

"I guess that means you're going to tell me something gross," Jennifer said. "Go ahead, I can take it."

"There are certain insects associated with dead bodies. By studying them, she can often establish time of death."

"What kind of insects?"

"I don't know a lot about the specifics," I said. "I know there are a variety of bugs that show up. But the main ones are flies which lay their eggs on the body. When the eggs hatch, the maggots use the body for food. So mostly Street looks for maggots."

"She finds maggots on dead bodies?!" Jennifer sounded aghast.

"In."

"In dead bodies?!" Jennifer smacked her hand down on her thigh. "Oh, my God, that is so gross!"

"I asked if you were squeamish."

"I know, but I didn't think you were going to tell me something like that!" Jennifer was silent for a minute. She stared out the side window as I drove. "Do all dead bodies have maggots in them?"

"I think so. I suppose that if you get a body into a sealed environment right after death, then flies wouldn't be able to lay their eggs on them and the body wouldn't end up with maggots."

"I think I'm growing up too fast."

"It happens," I said.

We drove a mile before Jennifer spoke again. "What does Street do with the maggots?"

"She collects them and takes them to her lab. It's in a warehouse off Kingsbury Grade. Not too far from my office. She kills some of the maggots because their size reveals how long they've been growing which can indicate how long since the person died. But first she needs to know what kind of maggots they are which can be nearly impossible to tell by looking at them. So she takes the rest of the maggots and raises them to adult flies so that she can determine the species."

"Is that where all flies come from? Maggots in dead bodies?"

"From what I gather, that's where most come from. Of course, most dead bodies that flies find are not people, but animals."

"I remember a dead squirrel I found once..." Jennifer's voice trailed off. She shivered. "It kind of gives you a new perspective on those flies that land on your food."

"Kind of does," I agreed.

"Maybe we should change the subject," she said.

"Sure."

We rode in silence. Eventually, Jennifer spoke.

"I've been thinking about what Street said about studying insects."

"What was that?"

"Before we went to bed we talked about the difference between meaning and purpose. She said that in watching insects she's learned that even if you can't find meaning you can still find a purpose."

"The unexamined life is not worth living."

"God," Jennifer said, "how did I get to be almost fifteen years old without anyone ever talking to me about such ideas?"

She stumped me there.

"Do you think you'll marry her?"

I turned toward Jennifer. "You got a question, feel free to ask it right up front."

"I'm sorry. That was intrusive."

I didn't respond.

"I just think," Jennifer said, "that if you ever wanted to marry her, you wouldn't want to wait. She's... I don't know, it seems like lots of men would be interested in her."

"Don't I know it." We were silent again. At the far end of South Lake Tahoe I turned left and headed out toward the airport. "I asked her a couple years ago. She said maybe someday. That's all the further she would go."

"Oh," Jennifer said. "I'm sorry. I shouldn't have said anything. It's none of my business."

"Don't worry about it."

We turned left into the airport and went down into the parking lot. Inside, we walked to the windows. A white Gulfstream with a blue pinstripe was coming in over the runway. Its nose was high as the main wheels touched. Blue smoke puffed as tires met tarmac. The nose lowered. The jet quickly braked and pulled off onto the taxiway. A door opened and steps descended. The first person out was a woman in her forties, trim in a gray business suit. She turned and helped two older women down the stairs. The three of them walked to the terminal.

Jennifer and I met them at the door. I could tell which one was Gramma Salazar. She acted the role of the Matriarch.

"Jennifer, honey, how are you?" she enthused as she hugged her granddaughter. Her voice had a smile in it. But her eyes were stern and focused on me. "And this man here is..."

"Gramma and Helga." Jennifer said to the two older women. Then she turned to the other woman. "Mrs. Heinz. I want you all to meet Owen McKenna. He's helping me."

"I'm honored, Mr. McKenna," the matriarch said.

"My pleasure, Mrs. Salazar," I said. We shook all around.

"Your help, sir, is of what variety?"

"Gramma," Jennifer said, "we've had some problems since you left. I'll tell you all about it in the car."

The women stepped back and conferred in a quick conference. I heard the younger of the three speak in hushed tones, "You're sure everything's okay? You want me to wait around?"

"No, no, we'll be fine," Gramma Salazar said. "You go home, now. You'll just make it in time to catch Jacob coming home from the board meeting."

Mrs. Heinz went back outside, turned and waved once

before she climbed into the jet.

Jennifer and I escorted the two older women out to my Jeep. I carried their bags. I detected distaste in Gramma Salazar when she saw my vehicle. When I opened the rear door for her she wrinkled her nose.

"It smells like dog in this car."

"Oh Gramma! Owen has the greatest dog! He's a Great Dane named Spot. A harlequin with all the spots, get it?"

"Jennifer, haven't I told you to use a formal salutation with men?"

"Yes, Gramma, but..."

"Jennifer, you know I have my reasons."

"Mrs. Salazar," I broke in. "I specifically asked Jennifer to call me Owen. She tried to address me as Mr. McKenna, but I objected."

"Mr. McKenna, you would have me believe that there is a reason for my granddaughter to be on an informal basis with a man your age? I must have made a big mistake leaving her."

I gestured toward the car door. "Why don't we get in the car and I can explain on the ride home."

The two women got in the back seat. Helga had still not said a word. Once we were on the road I spoke up before Gramma Salazar had a chance to start her interrogation.

"Mrs. Salazar, I'm a private investigator."

"Fraulein Jennie!" she exclaimed. "I told you..."

I didn't let her interrupt. "Jennifer wanted to hire me. I declined on the grounds that she is a minor. However, I think she may be in danger and in your caretaker's absence I felt it appropriate to be available until you came home."

"Has Samuel gone off again? Oh, my heavens. I just spoke to him on the phone a couple of days ago. He was calling from the beach to say he'd be home the next day. Anyway, Mr. McKenna, I hope you haven't bought all this nonsense that Jennifer thinks about poor little Melissa, may she rest in peace."

I could see Jennifer squirming in her seat. "Mrs. Salazar," I said, "before you pass judgement, let me explain the events of the last few days."

I told her of my involvement from start to finish. Jennifer interjected where I missed a point or got something out of sequence.

When we were through, Gramma Salazar sat in pregnant silence. "I understand," she said, "that Jennifer is frightened of the dark. And I think it very unfortunate that our caretaker has such bad timing with his absences. I'm assuming he'll be back shortly if not already. As for this other notion..." I saw her arm moving in my rear-view mirror. A wave of dismissal. "You and I will talk later, Mr. McKenna."

When we pulled into the Salazar drive and past the caretaker's house, Gramma Salazar spoke. "Sam's car is still gone. So he's really testing us this time."

"When did Samuel start working for you?" I asked.

"Almost nine years ago. I remember clearly because he came to our house right after dear Melissa's death."

"What does he look like?"

"Oh, he's one of those young outdoor types. He always reminded me, sorry for saying this, of a perfect candidate for Hitler's SS. He's short, but he's blond, and strong as can be. Whenever he's not working he's off doing one of those crazy sports."

I pulled up in front of the Salazar mansion. I jumped out and opened Gramma Salazar's door. "How did you find Sam? Did you get a referral?"

"No. We were in such shock after Melissa's accident. And our previous caretaker had died earlier that spring. We hadn't yet replaced him. So when Samuel came and applied for work and he seemed so self-assured and responsible, I just thought I'd try him without going through all the checking. I've always been glad, too. In spite of his lapses Samuel is the best we've had. He was especially helpful right after we lost Melissa. So attentive to little Jennifer." Gramma Salazar glanced at Jennifer as she said it. Jennifer was helping Helga with the bags.

We walked toward the house. "What are Sam's sports?"

"He does them all, it seems to me. But one favorite is para-gliding or whatever they call it when they fly around on those funny-shaped parachutes. And climbing. Especially climbing."

"Mountains around here?"

"All of them. He really likes rock climbing. You know, where they go up impossibly steep cliffs."

I held open the front door for the woman. Jennifer and Helga were already inside.

"Does he go by any other name?" I asked.

"No, of course not."

"You make the checks out to Samuel Sommers?"

"No, I've always paid him cash. Just like he requested in the beginning. He doesn't like banks." She looked at me sternly. "Don't tell me you're going to fuss about withholding taxes for domestic help. I'll have you run out of town."

"No, no. Not at all."

"Good. Then you and I will get along fine." She turned toward the kitchen. "Helga?" Gramma Salazar called out. "Would you please look after Jennifer while Mr. McKenna and I talk? We'll be in the drawing room. She turned to me. "This way, Mr. McKenna."

I followed Gramma Salazar through the entry and the main hall. I was thinking about Samuel Sommers, their caretaker of nine years, the man who Diamond Martinez said doesn't officially exist. He didn't like banks where he'd need proof of his real name. He appeared right after Melissa died. He was particularly attentive to Jennifer. He had blond hair and was a rock climber. I didn't know if it meant anything. But the description fit what Ellie Ibsen had told me about the climber who found Melissa's body.

TEN

"Mr. McKenna, what would you like to drink?" Gramma Salazar asked me as we walked into the drawing room.

"A beer would be fine, thanks."

"Helga, dear?"

Helga came scurrying into the room. She had donned a white apron. "Yes, ma'am."

"A beer for Mr. McKenna and tea for me." Gramma lowered her voice. "And keep an eye on that girl. I don't trust her."

Helga left.

"You sit here." Gramma Salazar gestured at a chair with bowed legs and golden trim. She sat nearby on the window seat. The afternoon sunlight bounced off the lake and back-lit her hair. I couldn't tell if the blue tint came from the lake water or her hairdresser. I sat down and waited. She didn't speak and I gathered that we were waiting for Helga. As if on cue Helga came in pushing a rolling silver cart with a silver teapot and a delicate porcelain cup trimmed with gold. A bottle of Becks stood next to a glass mug that was covered with frost. Helga poured and handed us our beverages.

Gramma Salazar didn't speak until Helga left the room. "Mr. McKenna," she said, "our family situation involves some issues that you don't understand. You have insinuated yourself into my granddaughter's life in a most inappropriate way." She sipped her tea through pursed lips.

I felt like a schoolboy being reprimanded by the principal. "Jennifer is a bright and mature child," I said, "but perhaps a little young to be left alone overnight."

"A regrettable situation to be sure. How was I to know that Sam would run away at this moment?"

"He's run away before. I would think you'd consider the possibility before you leave Jennifer without someone to stay with her." I took a drink of my beer. It was ice cold.

"As I've said, Mr. McKenna, you don't understand. Jennifer is a very headstrong girl. She will hear nothing of a baby-sitter. Believe me, I've tried. Either I'm to be a prisoner in my own house, or I need to occasionally let Sam play the role of guardian. I admit, it didn't work out in the best way this time. Nevertheless, until now Sam has been there when we needed him."

"I believe Jennifer is in danger," I said. "I think someone was in this house last night."

"Nonsense! Do you have any idea of how many times Jennifer has played this game?" She raised the pitch of her voice in mockery. "'Gramma, someone is after me. Gramma, I think someone is trying to kill me.' I swear, that child has the most ghastly imagination I've ever seen." She paused. "I had her looked at, you know. After little Melissa's accident." Gramma Salazar waited to see if I understood her implication.

I said nothing and drank more beer.

Gramma looked around the room as if to be certain no one was eavesdropping. I was going to hear privileged information. Or at least I was supposed to think as much.

"Melissa was the brighter of the two by a small measure," she said. "Melissa was also the more vivacious of the two by a large measure. Born first, you know. From day one Jennifer showed her jealousy by fighting Melissa, by upstaging her. Jennifer used to sneak up on her sister and scream just to scare her. It's no wonder, really, that Alicia, their mother, took ill. Poor thing. She just didn't have the intelligence to deal with such a situation.

"So I had to intervene. I took the children to a psychologist I knew at the time to have them tested. I knew Jennifer was a bad apple and I wanted to know if Melissa would be able to withstand the constant assaults, physical and psychological, that her sister perpetrated."

"What did you find out?"

Gramma held her teacup daintily in front of her as she leaned toward my chair. "The gentleman politely told me that I should watch Jennifer carefully. He said she had anti-social tendencies and a deep hatred for her sister. He thought harm might come to Melissa."

"You believed him?"

"Of course. The evidence was in front of me daily."

"May I have the psychologist's name? I'd like to talk to him."

"Gerhard Kelder. But you won't find him. He made good money counseling celebrities and retired several years ago. He took up with a showgirl and moved to one of those islands in the South Pacific. Fiji or someplace." Her disapproval was palpable.

"You think," I said, "that Jennifer was responsible for Melissa's death."

"I did at the time. If I may confess, it was my first thought."

"Any reason in particular?" I asked.

"Yes. Perhaps you know about our hike on Maggie's Peaks. The girls had been playing hide and seek. After a time, Jennifer came running to me and said that she couldn't find Melissa. Well, you know how it is with children. I could tell immediately that she was lying. She had that breathlessness that children use to hide their guile. It rang false from point A. I challenged her, which in hindsight was probably the wrong thing to do. She dug in her heels and would not abandon her story that Melissa had simply disappeared.

"After Melissa's death I took Jennifer back to Gerhard. He was unable to enlighten me further. But I could tell he had grave doubts about the veracity of the child's story. He wouldn't come right out and say it. But he too suspected that Jennifer had pushed her sister."

Gramma Salazar set down her teacup. She gripped her hands together and looked out at the lake. Her eyes were wet with tears. "Sometimes in the years since I've wondered if it might have been an accident after all. The child has never wavered from her story. If so, I've done her a terrible injustice by suspecting her. Then again, I know how children can come to believe their own lies. The psychologist said something about mechanisms of self-protection."

"Does Jennifer know you've suspected she pushed her sister off the cliff?"

Gramma swung her head around to face me. "Of course not! What do you take me for?" The tears were suddenly gone.

I decided to change the subject. "You referred earlier to Jennifer being paranoid."

"Yes. It's been a nightmare. There is a boogey man in every closet and under every bed. Gerhard warned me about this. He said Jennifer had paranoid tendencies. He thought she'd grow out of it. God forbid she should end up like her mother who is a paranoid schizophrenic."

"You don't think there is anything to her claims that someone might be after her?"

"No. That is rubbish. Nothing more. We've had enough evidence over the years. Now and then she is convinced that something is finally going to happen to her. But of course nothing comes of it. I suppose I can forgive the child for being afraid what with the bad blood she got from her mother and after what happened to Melissa. But it is a child's fantasy nonetheless. If what I suspect is true, that Jennifer pushed Melissa off the cliff, then what is there for Jennifer to be afraid of? Her own conscience?"

I drank the last of my beer. "Last night when we searched this house my dog appeared to smell an intruder. And we found your window open after I'd previously shut it."

"You let your dog in my house?! I thought I smelled an odor." The woman wrinkled her nose.

"I feared for Jennifer's safety."

"I told you Samuel has been a good caretaker except for his lapses. I guess I lied because I've asked him to fix that window a dozen times if I've asked him once. The latch is faulty. You think it's locked and next thing you know the window is swinging open in the wind."

"May I see it again?"

"My window?" She looked at me. Her eyes were blank. "Of course. Come with me."

I set my glass on the silver cart and we left the room.

Upstairs we passed the door to Jennifer's room. It was closed. There was no sound from inside. Once in Gramma's room I walked over to the window. It was latched tight.

"You'll see," Gramma said, "that if you wiggle the window a little the latch pops open. I suppose it is the movement in this old house that does it. Changing temperatures and such."

I wiggled the window and, sure enough, the latch popped up and out. The window was then free to swing open in the breeze. And last night there had been a strong breeze off the lake. Then again, just because a window can open of its own accord doesn't mean that someone couldn't have come through it. "I see what you mean, Mrs. Salazar," I said. "Even so, I'd like someone to stay with Jennifer at all times. I don't think she should stay alone. Not until I do some more checking."

Gramma Salazar looked up at me, a small forced smile on her face. "Mr. McKenna. I appreciate your attention to this. But I have opened up to you and told you family secrets to allay your concerns. I have told you our story and shown you our house. I believe I've been very generous with my time. Now apparently I must explain to you that you are not working for the Salazars. Therefore you will do no more checking, as you call it, on our behalf. Furthermore, if you do not leave us alone I will be forced to ask the authorities to intervene. I take my responsibilities seriously, Mr. McKenna. As you probably know, Jennifer has a little money coming to her. As such, she must be protected from outsiders who would involve themselves in her affairs. Until now I've assumed your motives to be pure. Don't make me go further with this line of thought. Helga?" she called out loudly.

I got the picture, loud and clear, and allowed myself to be ushered out by Helga.

ELEVEN

Spot came to my office with me the next morning. He looked out the window and I looked at the Hopper painting while I hit the play button on the answering machine.

Jennifer's messages from the previous nights came on. They were bracing to hear. Her frightened voice whispered frantically, her fear very real. I tried to imagine that the late-night intruder was merely the product of a paranoid imagination. Who knows how the mind works? But I couldn't make myself believe it.

I had gotten Salazar's unlisted phone number from Jennifer. I dialed and Helga picked it up after three rings.

"May I speak to Jennifer, please?"

"Who's calling?"

"Owen McKenna."

"I'm sorry, Mr. McKenna. Mrs. Salazar has requested that you do not speak to Jennifer again. I must say goodbye." She hung up.

I thought about driving over there and breaking down the door. Then I remembered that it was Thursday morning and Jennifer would probably be in school. I could catch her later.

In the meantime, I could check up on the other story in the paper from 9 years earlier, the one about Penelope

Smithson, the woman who fell to her death from Mount Rose a day after Melissa's death. The obituary said she was survived by her husband John.

I paged through my phone books looking for John Smithson. No luck.

I picked up the phone and dialed Diamond Martinez.

"Do people ever call you Di?" I asked him when he answered.

"If you ever see this brown boy in spike heels, you address me Senorita Di. Until that happens it's Officer Martinez."

"You guys get so feisty when you get your green card."

"Remember, California used to be ours. We might take it back."

"We're in Nevada," I said.

"Picky, picky. Suburb of California. We'll take Nevada while we're at it."

"Got a question for the conquering army. Shortly after Melissa Salazar died on the rock slide nine years ago, a woman named Penelope Smithson was found on Mt. Rose. She'd also apparently died in a hiking accident. Kind of rare for two hikers to slip and fall at the same time, don't you think? Her husband was John Smithson. Ring any bells?"

"Before my time. You want me to see what I got?"

"Buy you a case of Carta Blanca if it's good," I said.

"You at your office?"

"With my feet on the desk and my eyes on the lovely sad woman in Hopper's New York Movie."

"Inscrutable gringos don't impress me." There was a click on the line. "Hold on." Diamond put me on hold and came back in a moment. "I took your lady out to the crime scene yesterday. She took samples and put them in vials. Quite a job she has."

"Yes."

"Now she's calling in with a prelim on the body. I'll call you back."

I was hanging up the phone when Jennifer walked in. She set a book bag on my desk and went straight to the window and hugged Spot. "Street said you can ride him. Is it really true?" Her eyes sparkled.

"He's not quite like Secretariat in the Belmont Stakes, but, yes, it's true."

"How? Will he let me? What do I do?" Jennifer's sudden youthful enthusiasm was like fresh-cut freesias in my stale office.

Spot was sitting. He leaned his head against Jennifer's stomach. His eyes were closed. Bliss.

"Maybe sometime when we're outside I'll show you."

"Deal." Jennifer turned and sat on the corner of my desk.

"You ride your bicycle again?"

"Yes. Sam Sometimes still hasn't returned. Gramma filed a missing persons report. Neither Gramma nor Helga drive anymore, so you can imagine the chaos around our house. Gramma is looking for a new caretaker. She says Sam is fired no matter what his excuse. So, yes, the bike and me are inseparable." Jennifer held up two crossed fingers.

"Anybody following you?"

"Not that I know of."

"I don't like it," I said.

"What can I do? I have to get to school. I have to go on errands."

"I can give you rides. Street, too. Maybe some of that Salazar money could be turned loose on a full-time car and driver until you find another caretaker."

"I don't think so," Jennifer said. "Gramma is really stingy. And even if she did hire a temporary car, she forbade me to see you. So I'd still have to ride my bike to your office."

"My instincts tell me you shouldn't be alone."

"You think I'm in danger?"

I glanced at the woman in the New York Movie painting. "Yes," I said.

Jennifer saw me. "You think the woman in that painting is in danger, too, don't you?"

I turned toward Jennifer and looked at her for a moment. "Yes," I said.

"That's a Hopper, isn't it?"

"Not too many fourteen-year-olds would know that. They teach art history at the Tahoe Academy?"

"Are you kidding?" Jennifer stifled a laugh. "No. But he's only one of the greatest American painters, right? Anybody would know him." She turned to look at another framed print on the adjacent wall. "That must be a Hopper, too. Same style."

"It's called Lighthouse Hill," I said.

"Tell me about the danger," she said.

"I'm not sure. I don't know that much about art."

"Maybe you're not erudite," Jennifer said. "But you know. Tell me. Besides, if I'm going to have to learn about maggots in bodies, I might as well learn about art." Jennifer was still sitting on the corner of my desk, her arm out petting Spot.

I thought a moment. "I suppose that the woman standing by herself in a crowded movie house and the lighthouse on the hill are two ways of showing our isolation, that ultimately we all are alone. The lighthouse is able to weather the solitude. But the woman is in danger of losing her strength. She might give in to decisions that would be bad for her even though they would lessen her loneliness."

"You mean taking up with the wrong man," Jennifer said.

"That would be one of the dangers."

"The woman in the painting is young," Jennifer said. "Not much older than me. How is someone that young going to know who the right man is? It's not how smart you are. I'm pretty smart. But it takes life experience to learn those things, right?"

"There's a difference between intelligence and wisdom," I said. "But you got a measure of both."

The door opened and in walked Street carrying two large coffees in foam cups and a bag of donuts. "Jennie!" She set the coffee and donuts on my desk and hugged Jennifer. "What a nice surprise!" Then she hugged Spot. I was last.

I didn't mind. I was too busy noticing the fit of her jeans.

"Why the smile?" she said to me.

"The, uh, order of your greetings," I lied.

"Best for last?" Street sat in my lap. She pushed at the desk with her feet and sent us spinning around on the chair.

"Whoa," I said, stopping us.

Street twisted in my lap and looked over her shoulder at me. "What'sa matter? Spinning make you dizzy?"

"You make me dizzy."

"Old guys get dizzy easily," Street said to Jennifer.

"Who's saying I'm old?"

Street spun us around again. I reached out a leg to stop us.

"You don't like to spin," she said. "That's practically a definition of old."

"Can't argue with you there," I said.

Street took a chocolate-covered donut out of the bag and held the bag out to Jennifer.

Street's back was against my chest. I leaned my chin on her shoulder. She reached the donut up over her shoulder and fed it to me. Chocolate glaze smeared my lips.

"Don't get that stuff on my new sweatshirt," Street said.

Jennifer was watching us carefully as she pulled a cinnamon twist out of the bag.

The phone rang and I picked it up.

"Got an address on John Smithson," Diamond said. "And something else you'll want to know, too."

"Hold on a sec," I said. I put my hand over the phone. "Jennifer wants to learn to ride Spot," I said to Street. "Maybe you could show her down in the parking lot?"

Street understood that I wanted to be alone and they all made a fast exit.

I took my hand off the phone. "Ready, officer."

"Your boy is an attorney, no longer practicing. Lives on Lakeshore Drive up in Incline Village. Tony spot. Must have some bucks."

"Tony," I said.

"Gringos got some funny words. I'm learning most of them."

"Address?"

He gave it to me. "Now for the something else," Diamond said. "Mr. John Smithson, well-to-do widower of the late Penelope Smithson, has been around the block before. Wanna guess?"

I swiveled in my chair and looked out the window. Jennifer was draped across Spot's back as he trotted around the parking lot. Street was flapping her arms with excitement. "Penelope was the second wife to die on him?"

"Yeah. Get this. His first wife also died an accidental death. Five years before Penelope. Her name was Alexandra."

"How she die?"

"Drowning," Diamond said. "In Lake Tahoe."

"Happens," I said.

"Sure. Trains collide, too, and people die in the wrecks. But consider which kinds of accidental deaths are easiest to fake. Not train collisions."

"True," I said. "Someone goes swimming and you hold them under awhile. Someone goes hiking and you give them a shove at the edge of a drop-off. Guess I better pay a visit to Mr. Smithson."

"Wait, I ain't done," Diamond said. "This John Smithson inherited from both wives. Alexandra had oil money from some Oklahoma wells. And Penelope's family owns a Wall Street investment company."

"Maybe he's a good lay?" I said.

"Good lay. Good killer. Who knows, maybe both."

I thanked Diamond and hung up. Street and Jennifer were still running around down below. I could tell they were near hysterics. The remaining coffee was cold so I left it on the desk. All I needed was Jennifer's book bag and the donuts. I locked the door and went downstairs.

When I pushed out the glass door Spot ran up to me. Street and Jennifer were sitting on the landscape timbers panting and laughing. Spot pawed my pants leg.

"Sorry to interrupt the rodeo," I said. "Investigation calls. You cowgirls want to come along?"

"Where?" Street asked.

"A John Smithson up in Incline."

Jennifer said, "He's the one whose wife fell up on Mount Rose the day after Melissa died. What could you possibly learn from him?"

"Don't know. But she was the second wife of his to make an accidental exit from his life. Thought I should at least ask him some questions. Can't hurt."

"I can't go," Jennifer said, disappointed. "I'd love to see how you do your work." She looked at her watch. "I have to tutor one of the boys in my trigonometry class in less than an hour."

"You won't be missing much," Street said. "Watching detection in action is a little like watching insects molting their old skin. You wait a long time for action. And when something new finally emerges it looks just like what you had before."

"That's where piercing insight comes in," I said, tapping my forefinger on my temple.

Street stood on her tiptoes, pulled my head down and put one eye to my ear. "Pierced all right. I can see right through."

I looked at Jennifer. "No respect," I said.

Jennifer giggled.

I picked up Jennifer's bike and went to put it up on the bike rack on top of the Jeep. "We'll drop you at school."

TWELVE

Street and I dropped Jennifer at the Tahoe Academy in Zephyr Cove and then drove north up the lake. We went through the Cave Rock tunnel, headed up Spooner Summit. Spot dozed in the back seat.

"Diamond said you took samples out at the crime scene yesterday?"

"Yes. The word is finally getting out to law enforcement that entomologists should be brought in before the body is disturbed. So I did my thing while they took pictures of the body and the surrounding territory. I also set up a hygrothermograph so I can record temperatures and humidity over the next week. You want to see the site? They removed the body to the morgue after I was done."

"Sure." I was impressed with Street's sense of cool even though she'd been pulling insects out of a corpse just hours before.

"Just continue over Spooner Summit and I'll tell you when to turn off the highway. Do you think this body is connected to Jennifer's sister in some way?"

"No," I said. "I wondered about the missing caretaker, but he's been gone only eight or nine days. From what Diamond said, it sounded like the body is female and has been dead considerably longer."

"Yes. Large parts of the corpse were desiccated. Just

skin and bones. The skull was completely cleaned. I found specimens in the abdomen where there was still some moist tissue. But most of the maggots had already left and there were numerous hide beetles making fast work of what was left of the body. The results won't be very specific until I get the temperature records for the ravine where the body was found."

"Temperature affecting the bugs, right?" We'd crested the summit and started down toward the Carson Valley three thousand feet below.

"Yes. It's critical to the development of maggots and hence to the decomposition of the body. After I get several days worth of readings from the hygrothermograph, I'll be able to compare them to the temperatures and humidity reported by the Weather Service. The difference in the monitor's recordings and the Weather Service's recordings will allow me to look back over the last few weeks and extrapolate what the temperatures and humidity were at the site where the body was found. Once I know that, I can establish an approximate time of death."

"You found numerous maggots in the body?" I asked, knowing that maggots were the primary target of Street's forensic inquiries.

"There were a fair number of maggots in the third instar stage. But they were already through feeding and were wandering away from the body to find a drier place to prepare for the pupal stage. Many of the maggots had already formed pupas on shrubs nearby."

"How long does that indicate since death?"

"That is what I'll know after I get the temperature data. Oh, the place where we turn off is coming up. See the giant boulder at the edge of the next big curve in the highway? You can pull in behind it. Then we hike from there. It's about half a mile, maybe less."

I pulled off the highway and parked where Street indicated. There were lots of tire tracks, but all the sheriff's vehicles had left. We got out and Street led the way down an old Jeep trail. The pines were less dense than on the Tahoe side of the summit where moisture was more plentiful. It was easy to see through the forest. Unlike many foot trails, this Jeep trail was wide enough that Street and I could walk side by side. Spot bounded ahead.

"If you were to guess about the time since death, what would that be?" I asked.

Street gave me one of those looks that scientists must learn in school. A small tolerance for those who lack mental rigor.

"I understand that it would be the most flagrant speculation," I said. "And I swear never to tell anyone that you violated the sacred scientific principle of only speaking with benefit of facts."

Street's look became withering.

"Cross my heart," I said.

"Two and a half to three weeks," she said. "And that's only because it has been warm recently."

"How warm must it be for maggots to do their thing?"

"The ideal from a maggot's perspective is eighty degrees Fahrenheit. Any cooler than fifty degrees and they stop all activity. Warmer than ninety-five and they lose most of their liveliness, although they don't die until one hundred twenty degrees or so."

"So, when it gets down into the forties or thirties at night in Tahoe, they would stop their activity?"

"If they were outside the body, that would be true. But inside the corpse they are insulated from the nighttime cold. Further, they generate their own heat."

"But insects are cold blooded."

"Yes. But their metabolism creates heat nonetheless. And the heat of a maggot mass is substantial. The night temperatures could drop to below freezing, yet the temperature of a maggot mass could be as much as seventy degrees warmer." Street pointed ahead to a fork in the trail. "We turn left up here."

"What, exactly, does the maggot mass do?" I asked.

"Eat. A maggot is a highly specialized feeding machine. They use enzymes to begin the breakdown of the tissue before they actually consume it. Their combined heat helps speed the process and they are a critically important part of the decomposition of a body."

"A lovely picture," I said. "After the flies lay their eggs, how do the maggots get inside the body?"

"The female blow fly, flesh fly and house fly all have an uncanny ability to find the natural body openings and they lay their eggs at those spots. In the case of this body, the flies would have also laid their eggs near the bullet holes in the head. When the eggs hatch after a day or so, the tiny first instar maggots have an equal talent for burrowing into those openings where they start eating the moist flesh."

"How long does this go on?"

"It only takes a day or so for the maggot to outgrow its skin. They molt, and the second instar begins."

"You can tell these apart."

"There is a size difference between the different instars," Street said. "But to be certain, you have to look at the posterior spiracles. Those are the breathing structures of the maggot."

"Of course," I said.

"Another day, another molting, and the third instar emerges. This guy feeds voraciously for one to four days, then leaves the corpse to find a safe place to begin pupation."

"That's like a cocoon?"

"Yeah. The pupa looks like a little football. And from that, in a week or so, emerges our glorious little fly."

"How long does the whole process take?"

"Ten to twenty-seven days from egg to adult fly."

"Depending on temperature," I said.

"And species and moisture and position of the corpse and the presence of social insects..."

"Wait. What does position of the corpse have to do with it?"

"A corpse that is buried or even wrapped in a blanket slows down the process. It is harder for the flies to gain access to lay eggs among other things. A corpse that is hanging is difficult for beetles to get to. They come after the maggots and do the final cleanup, so to speak."

"You mentioned social insects."

"Right. The necrophagous species like maggots feed directly on the corpse and accelerate decomposition. But there are predators and parasites of those species, especially among the social insects."

"You mean wasps eat maggots?"

"Wasps both predate on flies and parasitize maggots. Some wasps lay their eggs directly on the maggots. When those larva hatch they feed on the maggots even as the maggots are feeding on the corpse. Then, of course, there are the ants, many of which eat maggots. The ants of a large colony can carry off maggots in great numbers, substantially slowing the effects of the maggots on the decomposition of the body." Street stopped hiking and looked around. She walked to the side of a clearing and looked through a stand of trees. "Over here, Owen."

I walked over and looked where she was pointing.

"The corpse was under that tree," she said.

THIRTEEN

Spot was already there, but, oddly, he stood distant from the place Street indicated. He sniffed the air, then turned his head as if saddened by what he smelled. A strip of yellow crime scene tape fluttered from a pine bough near his head.

"Spot, come here," I said.

He turned and looked at me with drooping eyes.

"Spot, come!"

He walked toward me, his movements listless. When he was eight feet away from me, he lay down in the dirt, tucked his nose down between his paws, and gave forth a big sigh.

Can dogs smell death? Spot's reaction certainly suggested as much. I walked over to him, bent down and rubbed his head. "What's wrong, your largeness?"

He ignored me and kept his nose buried in his paws.

"Okay. Give me a minute to look around and we'll leave."

Street came over. "Come on, Spot. Let's get out of here. The detective can find us back at the car." She patted him on the side of his chest and then walked back up the trail. Spot stood and followed her without looking back at me.

"I'll be there in a bit," I called after them.

After they left I looked anew at the forest.

The body had been found in a shallow ravine that ran vertically down the mountain. I hiked up to one of the low ridges that comprised a side of the ravine. From this vantage point I could see another, parallel ravine. They were twins in size and shape and direction except for one thing. The neighboring ravine had a small stream running. I looked up the mountain above me but saw no evidence of snow. On this arid east side of the Carson Range, the only snow was to the south on the tall slopes of Heavenly ski area and Jobs Peak and Jobs Sister. Where we were, on Carson Valley side of Highway 50, the peaks were mostly under 9,000 feet and all the snow had melted weeks ago. Which meant that the water in the ravine next door came from a spring.

I turned back to the ravine where the body had been found. Nothing unusual caught my eye, which made it a good place for a murder. The jeep trail allowed access to anyone with a four-wheel-drive. And the ravine provided complete privacy from the highway a half mile distant. The nondescript quality of the area made it unattractive for hikers and other off-road types. Anyone could have driven out here with the woman whose bracelet said 'Maria-I'll-love-you-forever' and shot her with a pistol. The killer would have had a reasonable expectation that the body wouldn't be found for weeks.

I took another look at the tire tracks and footprints. They could belong to anybody, pre-murder or post-murder. I hiked back after Street and Spot.

They were resting in the shade of a large Jeffrey pine.

"Find anything?" Street asked.

"No. A general topography affording lots of privacy for murder. A spring-fed stream in the next ravine over. Nothing else."

"Then we should take this canine someplace to get his mind off what he smelled back there," Street said.

"Perhaps a visit to the ex-husband of the woman who died hiking on Mount Rose would do the trick."

"Perhaps."

Lakeshore Drive is a row of millionaire's houses on the water. Many of them are being torn down and replaced with billionaire's houses. Some are made of stone and slate, some are cedar and glass, some are white stucco cubes and cylinders. We drove slowly down the manicured street watching house numbers. Three kids were running through a sprinkler. They stopped and stared at Spot as we rolled by.

The house belonging to John Smithson had a glass front that rose maybe forty feet to a pointed roof. Sky and mountains showed through the glass on the other side. Where there weren't windows there were fieldstone walls interrupted by window bays which were clad in green copper sheets. I pulled into the drive which was made of bricks. I parked in front of a three car garage with a multi-gabled roof. Street and I got out and left Spot in the Jeep.

The front entry was a double door, each one over-sized and made of oak with hand-carved filigree. There was a brass knocker in the shape of Atlas holding the Earth. I picked up the little globe and smacked it down onto Atlas's shoulders.

The door opened and a big woman in her late thirties smiled at us. She had long straight hair, blond as corn-cob silk and was wearing a purple Lycra jumpsuit. "Yes?" she said.

"Hi. We're here to see John Smithson, please."

She smiled and looked over at Spot in the Jeep. As she shifted her weight from one foot to the other I realized that she was muscle-bound. Under the Lycra were distinct biceps, triceps, quadriceps, and more.

"Who shall I say is calling?"

"Owen McKenna and Street Casey. It's about Penelope.""

The woman's smile wilted. "Wait here. I'll see." She shut the door in our face.

She was back in a minute. "He'll see you by the pool. This way." She led us through a large glass-walled room with a marble floor and a marble fireplace on one end. Beyond the glass was a kidney-shaped pool with the sparkle and color of blue diamonds. Just past the pool was the lake with the snow-capped peaks of the south shore in the distance. In front of the pool, in a lounge chair with his back to us, was a man reading a thick paperback. He had on white pants and a tight white T-shirt. He stood and turned toward us as we followed the Lycra lady out to the pool. His muscles bulged.

"You!" he said, the word catching in his throat. His heavy arms levitated slightly from his sides.

"Took the word right out of my mouth," I said.

Street looked at me.

"Mr. Smithson and I have met before. In the woods across from my office. He was following Jennifer, but too dumb and belligerent to admit it."

"Listen little lady," the man said to Street. "You better wait out back. Your man has some explaining to do and it might get messy." His shoulders tensed. The definition around his deltoids and trapezius muscles was impressive.

Years ago at the academy the first rule we learned was always call for backup. "Street, would you please get Spot?"

"What," he huffed. "You brought the damn hound with you?"

"Crowd control," I said.

Street started for the side of the house.

"Should I stop her?" the Lycra woman said.

The man nodded.

The woman stepped in front of Street. The woman had a good fifty pounds of solid muscle on Street. Street stopped and looked at me. I shrugged.

"I'm getting tired of you poking your nose into my business," Smithson said. He advanced on me, arms bulging.

I thought about grabbing the charcoal grill nearby and wrapping it around his head, but it would have been unseemly in such a nice neighborhood.

"You tall boys got reach," he said. He was into his stance. "But I got punch."

I didn't doubt it. I kicked him in the groin.

He bent over, arms between his legs.

I stepped next to him, laid my hand on the massive web of muscles across his back and gave him a push. He fell into the pool. "Okay, Street," I said.

The woman looked at me. She stepped sideways. Street ran around the house.

Smithson sounded like he'd inhaled some water. He coughed and gasped and clawed at the edge of the pool.

I jumped in. I grabbed him by his belt and dragged him to the steps. He was a heavy load. I did my best to make carrying him appear effortless as I hauled him by the belt, up and out of the water. I dropped him onto the chaise lounge. The Lycra woman rushed to his side as he sputtered and coughed up water.

Spot came running around the house. He charged up to me, wagging. I gave him a rough rub. Spot turned and looked at the couple near the swimming pool. He walked over to the edge of the pool, lowered his nose to the water and sniffed. Street peeked around the corner of the house. Spot lapped at the water a couple of times. The man suddenly noticed and went rigid. Spot lifted his head and shook it, water flying from his jowls.

"Spot," I said. I pointed at Smithson. "Watch him."

Spot walked over and sat down in a patch of sunlight next to the chaise lounge where Smithson continued to cough. Spot's head was above Smithson and he hung it down over Smithson's body. He looked vaguely like a hungry vulture. The woman backed away, her steps slow and even.

"Show him you mean it, Spot."

Spot lifted his lips in a little growl. Then he started panting from the heat of the sun, his huge tongue dangling out the side of his mouth. He looked longingly at the pool.

"Spot," I said. "Pay attention."

My dog glanced at me, then went back to watching Smithson.

Smithson quivered. "Don't," he said in a small voice.

"Don't what?" I said.

"Don't let him on me. Call him off."

"You answer my questions and Spot goes hungry."

"Hon, call nine-one-one," Smithson said. "Run."

"Good idea," I said. "We can all talk to the police about how you tried to assault me. Oh, and while we're at it, let's ask them if they've gotten any further on their investigation into the deaths of Alexandra and Penelope."

Smithson jerked his eyes from Spot to me. "What are you talking about?" His teeth were clenched. The woman in the purple suit didn't move.

"I understand they've recently been looking into your file. New evidence or something. When you call, ask for Diamond Martinez, Douglas County Sheriff's Deputy. He'll tell you about it."

Smithson's eyes were intensely black. He looked back at Spot. I saw Smithson's muscles tense, but I didn't think he had the guts to try anything. Spot's eyes wavered from Smithson to the pool and back.

"Let me ask you again," I said. "Why did you run off into the woods that day? Who were you following?"

"Screw you."

I realized that Smithson was not going to talk without more pressure than I was willing to apply. I looked at Street. "Forthcoming," I said. "Let's go." I walked over, took her arm and steered her around the house.

"Call off your dog!" Smithson yelled as we left his line of sight. His voice wavered.

I didn't trust Smithson not to pull a gun, so I waited until we were to the Jeep. "Come on, Spot!"

FOURTEEN

"You didn't know Smithson was the man you met in the woods?" Street asked as we drove away.

"I was as surprised as he was." My clothes had dried somewhat, but swimming pool moisture was seeping from my clothes into the car seat. Spot stuck his head over the front seat and sniffed at the mixture of chlorine and wet seat fabric.

"Are you sure he was following Jennifer that day?" she asked.

"Either Jennifer or the other bicyclist who turned into the woods shortly after Jennifer did. At the time I thought maybe he recognized the other bicyclist and was chasing after him. Now I wonder. I start investigating the death of Melissa Salazar and Smithson comes into the picture two different times. Kind of suggests he's involved in some way." I reached the end of Lakeshore Drive and turned south onto the shoreline highway.

"But if there is a connection between Melissa's death and the death of Penelope Smithson," Street said, "it would seem to be a very loose one. Smithson's wife died on the opposite side of the lake."

"I agree. On the other hand, if there is no connection then his double appearance is a big coincidence. Detectives aren't supposed to abide coincidences."

Street tapped her chin with her forefinger. "One

time I was getting some bar soap out of the cabinet in my bathroom and I saw an unusual insect. It was iridescent green. It looked like a six-spotted green tiger beetle except that they don't live in Tahoe. I tried to catch it, but it got away. I remembered it clearly because except for spiders, I hadn't seen any bugs in my condo in a long time. Later I saw the same iridescent beetle in the hall closet. Same puzzle, really. Was it an unlikely coincidence? Or was there a connection between the two places? I eventually found out that I also had soap in the hall closet. It turned out the beetle was digging in the soap."

"If the analogy holds," I said, "then Melissa's death and Penelope Smithson's death are likely to be connected in some unforeseen way. The soap connection."

"Exactly," Street said. "In this case, John-the-body-Smithson is the unusual insect turning up in strange places. We just have to figure out what the connection is."

"John-the-body?" I said. I took my eyes off the road and frowned at her.

Street giggled. "Well, he does have a body."

"I'll give him that. But he's an Ode to the Steroid gods. He genuflects before the barbell. He's got more beef than a Black Angus bull. He's..."

"Easy, boy, easy!" Street slugged my shoulder. "I was kidding. You've got a body, too."

"You noticed."

"I do. Other women notice, too." She reached over and ran her hand over me, exploring.

"Street, I'm trying to drive."

"I'm not stopping you." She untucked my shirt.

"Street, what if other people see?"

"They won't."

I swerved a little. "Spot's watching us," I said.

"He's watched before."

FIFTEEN

The next morning I was up early having laid awake half the night worrying about Smithson and how to ensure Jennifer's safety. I still wasn't sure that Smithson was involved, but he seemed the likeliest suspect.

I lounged in bed trying unsuccessfully to come up with a way to put a bodyguard on Jennifer without Gramma Salazar's permission. If I staked out their driveway or watched the mansion from the woods, I'd eventually be discovered and she'd try to have me arrested. If I knew exactly when, where and how Jennifer was going to be in greatest danger, I could try and squirrel her away to protect her. But that's called kidnapping and people tend to get upset when children are kidnapped. I could not think of a clear way to proceed.

Spot interrupted my thoughts. He came to my doorway with his big empty food bowl in his mouth.

"You just ate yesterday," I said. "You're a carnivore. You're supposed to binge, then fast for days."

He thumped his tail against the door jamb.

"All right," I said, sitting up and stretching.

Spot is too big to about-face in the hallway, so he walked into my bedroom to turn around, then trotted to the kitchen and waited by the closet where I keep the dog food.

"Sit," I said. Spot dropped his bowl. It's made of metal

and is the size of a hubcap. It clattered to the floor and wobbled to rest. Spot sat down, his front legs splaying slightly on the vinyl flooring. He looked at me.

I got out the Science Diet and chunked about five pounds into his over-sized bowl. A string of saliva dropped from Spot's lips. No manners.

I waited a minute to give the command. Spot stared at me. His eyes were brown laser beams in a white sea filled with black polka dots. Now there were two strings of drool.

"Okay!" I said.

While I loaded the coffee maker, Spot set another world record inhaling what looks like compressed sawdust. To each his own.

I had my usual breakfast of black coffee and two aspirin and thought about Smithson. I didn't have a clue how to catch him at anything except being a nuisance. I thought about Sam Sometimes, the missing caretaker.

Was he the climber who found Melissa's body? If so what did it mean?

Spot finished the last of his food and carefully ran his tongue around the bowl, pushing it down the hallway as he wiped it clean. Then he licked his chops. His out-sized tongue made him look like a Saturday morning cartoon dog. Even the sound effects were the same.

I thought of someone who could tell me about the climber from nine years ago. "Your largeness," I said to Spot. "Care for a post-prandial ride?"

Spot's tail banged the dishwasher.

We walked out into the driveway. A tiny yip came from down the road. Treasure came running toward us at full velocity. Her peach-colored hair was tied up in a ponytail with a red ribbon. Spot lowered himself in the crouch of a hunting mountain lion. Treasure bore in. She yipped and jumped into the air. Spot turned his head at the last moment and Treasure bounced off his chest. Then she did her handstand and pranced around on two legs under Spot. He did his own dance of sorts as she nipped at his feet. She jumped around his head, pawing at his face with little red painted toenails. Spot shut his eyes and endured the assault stoically.

"Okay, boys and girls. Time to go."

Spot came and stood by the Jeep. Treasure did a final pirouette and raced back home.

We drove down the mountain and pulled into the local fire station. There were two men in blue fire department coveralls raking the stones in the landscaping out front. I nodded at them and walked inside.

"Terry in?" I asked the young Hispanic man who was polishing one of the engines.

He stopped, nodded and picked up a phone on the wall. "Sir Terrance. Sir Terrance," he said. "Jose calling. You have a visitor." His English was perfect, native-born American. But when he referred to me he pronounced it Vizeetour.

Terry Drier came down a metal stairway. He was wearing a loose baby blue sport shirt tucked into tight jeans. The muscles in his arms were thin and hard and looked like steel cables under his skin.

"No uniforms for Battalion Chiefs?" I said.

"Owen, I thought you were my lunch date." Terry looked at his watch. "She should have been here five minutes ago." He shook my hand and leaned in close. "Wait 'til you see her. I met her in the personals. Can you believe it? She's a volunteer at the Tahoe Historical Society."

Just then a rusted green Dodge Omni pulled up and a pudgy woman with ratty graying hair got out. Her plain face broke into a huge smile when she saw Terry. Her overbite was severe. "Terry!" she called out. She rushed to meet him and they embraced.

"Hon, I want you to meet an old friend, Owen McKenna. Owen, please meet Emily."

She gave me a quick nod and turned back to Terry. "You ready? I brought a picnic lunch that is going to make you swoon!" She pinched his stomach.

Terry beamed at her. They ignored me and hugged like teenagers. Finally, Terry turned to me. "Guess I better be going, Owen. Nice of you to stop by."

"Just a quick question?"

"Oh. Uh, sure." He walked Emily to her car. "Just give me a minute, darling. I'll be right back." He trotted back to me. "Isn't she great?" He smiled back at her, then gave her a little wave with his fingers. "Can we make it quick, Owen? Don't want to keep her waiting."

"Sure. I know you help coordinate search and rescue. I wondered how long you've been doing it?"

"Gosh, I don't know. Ten, twelve years I suppose." He stole a peak at his sweetheart.

"Nine years ago a little girl named Melissa Salazar fell off the rock slide above Emerald Bay. Ellie Ibsen's dog found the body and one of your climbers brought it up. Do you remember who the climber was?"

Terry screwed up his face in thought. He turned toward Emily in her car, then turned back. "Nine years is a long time," he said. "I remember the incident. But the climber? Been a lot of them over the years. Volunteers, you know. Most of them are just taking a year off from college. They come up to Tahoe to have some fun, stay a few months and then split."

"He was in his early twenties," I said. "Had blond hair. Was a devoted rock climber. He possibly went by the name of Samuel Sommers."

Terry was looking back at Emily. His head turned at the name. "Yeah, sure. I remember him. Good climber. Did a daring rescue for us out at Kirkwood earlier that summer. A young woman was climbing the palisades near the Cornice Chair and fell. She hung on her safety rope for most of a day. Sam went up that rock like Spiderman. He made a sling out of webbing and lowered her down. There was a big fuss at the time because they don't allow climbers up there and they wanted to haul the girl in. I don't know how, but Sam talked the ranger out of arresting her. Mostly, though, he was real quiet." Terry looked off in an unfocused way and smiled.

"I've always remembered the girl's name," he continued. "Maria. They did a TV story on the rescue and when the reporter did an interview with Sam and the girl, they played the song as background music. The one from the musical. 'I just met a girl named Maria.' Isn't that weird the way music makes things stick in your mind?"

"Yeah, music does that. How long did Sam stay with your group?"

"Just that summer. Then he disappeared right after he brought the little girl's body up the rock slide. Someone said he got a job care-taking around here. But I never saw him again." Terry leaned close again. "Just between you and me, there was something funny about him. Like the way he was so protective of that young woman at Kirkwood. He kind of attached himself to her. But no one ever said anything bad about him because he seemed to be a good guy. Doing volunteer work. Saving lives. Can't be too picky about that, can we?" Terry looked again in Emily's direction. His eyes twinkled at her. "Look, is that all you needed? I gotta go."

"Sure," I said. "Thanks a lot."

I drove back home, dialing Diamond on my cell phone. "I've got a possible lead on your body," I said. "I connected the name with the missing caretaker."

"You've got my attention," Diamond said.

"You said the bracelet had the name Maria on it."

"Right."

"I just talked to Terry Drier, Douglas County Battalion Chief. Terry's search and rescue group at the time that Melissa Salazar died had a climber named Sam. The description fits that of Samuel Sometimes, the missing Salazar caretaker. Terry told me that Sam was the one who brought Melissa Salazar's body up the rock slide. Sam also rescued a girl who got stuck climbing on the Palisades at Kirkwood. According to Terry, Sam became quite attached to the girl which, I suppose, isn't uncommon when you save someone's life. Terry remembered the girl's name because of a TV report that used a song from West Side Story."

Diamond broke in, "'I just met a girl named Maria.'"

"I didn't know you were a fan of musicals."

"I'm not."

"I'll see what else I can find out about Sam," I said. "You might want to use your official leverage to see if there is a tape of that TV report, maybe get an ID on the girl."

"I already made a note of it," Diamond said, irritated at my suggestion.

I hung up and drove home thinking about Sam the caretaker. He worked for Salazars, and probably was the climber who brought up Melissa's body and saved Maria on the cliffs at Kirkwood. Now Maria was possibly dead, and Sam disappeared about the same time that Jennifer began stirring up the past.

Then there was John Smithson, whose wife Penelope died from a fall a day or two after Melissa died. It was of note because falls were an unusual way to die and because Smithson inherited from Penelope. He also inherited from his first wife Alexandra, who died in a drowning accident.

Smithson was connected to the Salazars in that he'd been following Jennifer the day she first contacted me.

None of this made either of them killers. I needed another connection.

When I got home, I called Street.

"I was just going to call you," she said.

"Hmmm?"

"I think I might have figured out how Smithson did it!" she said. She sounded breathless.

"You mean John-the-body?"

"One and the same."

"Should I get a beer and sit down?" I said.

"Absolutely. You're going to love this."

I fetched a Sierra Nevada from the fridge and carried it out to the deck. I sat on one of the deck chairs and propped my feet up on the railing. Below me stretched 150,000 acres of deep blue water with a backdrop of snow-capped mountains. I took a swig of the beer. Detecting was hard work. "I'm ready," I said.

"Okay, here we go. You might want to take notes. Let's say that John-the-body and his wife Penelope go hiking up Maggie's Peaks. When she gets to the top of the rock slide she pauses to drink some water and enjoy the view. Smithson sees his opportunity. He sneaks up and gives her a push and she falls to her death. Are you with me?"

"Street, my sweet, I've never left you since we met."

"Great. So John-the-body turns around and what does he see? Little Melissa Salazar. He realizes that the girl saw him do the evil deed. Maybe he advances on her. Maybe she runs. Either way, he chases her down, grabs her and throws her off the mountain."

"You're saying Penelope and Melissa both died by his hand on the rock slide. How did they find Penelope up on Mount Rose?"

"Easy. Smithson knows that both of the bodies are out of sight somewhere down the rock slide. He knows they won't find them for a day or so. He hikes down the mountain, drives home and waits until dark. He realizes the sheriff and the search and rescue people would notice any vehicles stopping in the area. So he gets in his boat and goes across the lake and into Emerald Bay at night."

"Wait," I said. "How do you know he has a boat?"

"Didn't you see?" Street said. "When we were up at his house? The canopy over the dock shades one of those cigarette boats. The kind with the huge prow that look stupid and go a hundred miles an hour?"

"I was too busy trying to keep from getting vivisected by that steroidal maniac to notice any boat."

"Well, trust me. He's got a big, fast boat. So he goes across the lake at night and beaches it at the Vikingsholm castle. Then he hikes up the mountain and climbs up the rock slide to retrieve his wife's body. He carries her down and puts her in the boat."

"That's a big, steep climb to go down at night with a dead body on your shoulders," I said.

"Sure. But he's got the muscles for it."

"So you've pointed out," I said. "Let me guess. He pilots his way back across the lake at night, puts the body in his BMW and drives up the Mount Rose highway."

"Exactly. When he gets up to the meadow, he parks, carries her up the mountain and drops her off a cliff, making it look like an accident."

"But the meadow is only at eighty-five hundred feet," I said. "From what I read it sounded like she fell up on the trail to the summit. Are you proposing that he carried her body up two thousand feet? Even if she had been very slim, that's quite a physical accomplishment."

"Who better to do it?" Street said.

"John-the-body." I said.

"You got it. Aren't you pleased? I've practically solved your entire case."

"So why are you studying bugs?"

"How else am I going to meet rich entomologists?"

"Sorry, I forgot that every girl's dream is to fall in love with a wealthy bug collector."

After I hung up I thought about Street's scenario. Would it be possible to carry a body that far? As for the boat connection, it made sense as long as the weather was not too stormy. Even in August, when Melissa and Penelope died, one didn't go across the lake in a big wind. The water was too cold, and a capsized boat would lead to death from hypothermia. But the reports from that distant time said the weather had been calm. A perfect time for taking a body across the lake at night. If Smithson could carry a body down a mountain and load it into his boat, it would be easy to transport it to his car on the opposite end of the lake and drive it up Mount Rose. Although it seemed a bit far-fetched, it was nevertheless a possible explanation for Smithson's involvement in the case. And I'd learned over the years that people did much stranger things while committing their crimes. But could it all be done in the short time of an August night?

It would be easy to test.

SIXTEEN

Spot and I were waiting outside of Jennifer's school at three o'clock. She came out and walked straight to her locked bicycle. I beeped the horn.

Jennifer looked up and came running over to the Jeep. She grabbed Spot's head and hugged him. "What a surprise!" Then she got serious. "Is everything all right?"

"Sure. I just had a couple of questions. Give you a ride?"

"I'd love it," Jennifer said. She unlocked her bike and we put it on the roof rack. Jennifer sat sideways on the front passenger seat so she could reach back and pet Spot as we drove out of the school lot.

"Your caretaker," I said. "Did he ever have a girlfriend or speak of young women?"

Jennifer laughed. "Sam? No. I mean, I think he's heterosexual, but I can't imagine him having a girlfriend. He's too awkward and nervous."

"Did he ever mention someone named Maria?"

"No. Sam was fiercely private. He interacted with us only enough to do his job. Who is Maria?"

"Just a name someone mentioned in connection with Sam."

"The dead body!" Jennifer said. "The body that Street took samples from. That was Maria, wasn't it!"

I didn't see any reason to withhold the answer. "There was a bracelet on the body with the name Maria engraved on it."

"Was there a last name? Maybe I've heard of her."

"No."

"If Maria's name was connected to Sam and now she's dead right when he's disappeared, that makes it look like he killed her! And with Sam being strange around women... God, it all fits, doesn't it!"

"Jennifer, it is best not to jump to conclusions."

"I get it. We should focus on what we know rather than on what we can speculate about."

"I think you might be too smart for your own good," I said.

"I've been told that before. Sorry."

"Nothing to be sorry about."

"Okay. Next question," she said.

"I need a boat," I said. "I need to test something."

"You have a hypothesis about the murder?" Jennifer asked.

"Street does," I said. I thought about whether it made sense to tell her. Often I don't divulge the details of my investigation to my client. It seemed especially inappropriate with a kid who might be frightened by the information. But Jennifer was already frightened and, if she were lying to me, telling her where my investigation was going would be a good way to tempt her into a protest of sorts if she knew I should be looking another direction.

"Street's hypothesis is that John Smithson pushed his wife off the rock slide to inherit her money. Your sister saw him do it, so he pushed her off, too. He realized that two bodies could only look like murder and not an accident, so he climbed up the rock slide that night and retrieved his wife's body. He carried it away by boat and faked her death up on Mount Rose. I'm wondering if such long hikes and the long round-trip boat ride would require more hours than an August night provides. If I rented one of your boats, I could test it."

"Of course!" Jennifer said. "But you won't rent it. You and I will go together. We have two boats. An eighteen foot runabout with an outboard. And a thirty-two foot powerboat. It's got a big inboard engine. It's very fast. You could use either one."

"With Gramma's permission? Or you could get her permission to take one of the boats out and then pick me up down the shore?"

"Oh, to heck with Gramma. I'm tired of living under her control. I give you permission."

"If Gramma called the cops on me, I'm not sure the courts would agree," I said. "They are no doubt technically Gramma's boats. I'd probably need Gramma's technical permission."

"Then I'll buy a boat."

"They are expensive," I said.

"Four hundred million should give me some choices," Jennifer said.

"Good point. But maybe we can borrow Gramma's anyway."

"When?" she said.

"Whenever you think it would cause the least problems. When - dare I suggest it - Gramma might be somewhere else and not even know."

Jennifer excitedly slapped her hand on the car seat. "Tonight! Tonight would be perfect because Gramma goes to play bridge at Auntie Ethel's."

"Auntie?"

"She's not really my aunt. But I've known her all my life and I've always called her Auntie Ethel. She always sends her driver to pick Gramma up on Friday nights. They play bridge and drink tea until around ten. By then we'll be long gone."

"Won't Gramma panic if she comes home to find you gone?"

"She won't know I'm gone. If my door is shut and my light is off, she'll assume I'm asleep. I can even bunch up some clothes under my blanket so it'll look like me in case she opens my door."

"Sounds too risky," I said. "Better to go in broad daylight. Better to have Gramma know in advance."

"It's not risky at all. It will work perfectly."

Jennifer said it with the marvelous conviction of youth.

"Where will Helga be?"

"Helga never leaves Gramma's side."

"Gramma won't check the boathouse when she gets home?" I asked.

"No. I can set the alarm panel so it looks like the boathouse hasn't been touched."

"How will we get the boat back in the boathouse late at night? Older folks don't sleep soundly. Won't the noise wake them up?"

"No. We can turn off the boat motor when we get close. Then we paddle in. I can sneak into the house and you can run down the beach to the park where you'll leave your car. Besides, Gramma always takes a Nembutal before bed. She loves her drugs because they make her sleep like a baby."

I thought about it as I drove. The gated Salazar driveway appeared on the left. I pulled off on the shoulder and parked. "It seems a big risk for you," I said. "A bigger risk for me if I'm caught with a minor. They'd get me for kidnapping and boat theft."

"Remember the affidavit I wrote you," Jennifer said. "If

that doesn't give you protection, I'll hire the best lawyers in the country."

"You've got some of your grandmother's fire in you. She threatened to run me out of town."

"She did?! Why that... You should have told me! That does it! I'll call you at home this evening and tell you when to come. If Smithson is the man stalking me then I won't let Gramma stand in the way of your investigation!" Jennifer was indignant. She got out of the car. Her face was flushed. "Sometimes that old woman drives me nuts!"

I got Jennifer's bicycle off the roof rack. She rolled it through a tiny space next to the wrought iron gate. "I'll call," she called out to me as she climbed on her bicycle and began to ride down the drive.

"You will not!" a loud voice answered from nearby.

Jennifer was so startled that she jerked to a stop and nearly fell off her bike.

We both turned to see Gramma Salazar step out from behind a tree.

SEVENTEEN

Mrs. Salazar walked out of the woods toward me. She wore an olive green blouse tucked into leather shorts that were held up with leather suspenders, a cousin of sorts to lederhosen. Heavy wool socks came most of the way up to her sturdy knees and her feet were encased in out-sized mountaineering boots. In her hand she held a tall walking stick that was fitted with an iron tip honed to a frightening point. As she got closer I could see a severe scowl across the coarse features of her face.

"Fraulein Jennifer!" Gramma Salazar yelled. "I told you earlier that you are forbidden to see this man!" Her voice was ragged with anger.

"Gramma, you don't understand. I only..."

"Jennie, do not talk back to your grandmother! You have disobeyed my orders and that makes me very cross. For that you will be punished."

"Mrs. Salazar," I interrupted. "I am trying to help."

The old woman cut me off by thrusting out her walking stick, the point raised toward me.

"That's right, Gramma," Jennifer said.

"Not one more word, child! Now go home!" She turned to me as Jennifer disappeared down the driveway. "I asked you to stay away from Jennifer once before," she said. "Obviously, I had better make myself more clear!"

"Whatever you wish," I said.

"We'll walk in the woods," she said. Her voice was a hiss. There was a tremor in the hand that held the walking stick, but I could tell it came not from disease or old age, but from anger.

I stepped to her side as she set off at a brisk pace, swinging her walking stick in a large arc and stabbing it into the ground every fourth step. We headed deep into Salazar property at an angle away from the mansion.

"I know what drives you," she said, venom in her voice.

"Excuse me?"

"Back in Deutschland," she said, "I majored in zoology at the university in Frankfurt. My favorite class was on Darwin." She turned and glared at me as we walked. "Darwin makes it clear that I should deal with you severely."

"And how is that?" I asked, astonished at where this conversation was going.

"It is from Darwin that I learned about the power of the drives that are behind your behavior. Behind most men's behavior. Impulses that you have no control over. You are, of course, familiar with Darwin." Her voice was thick with condescension.

"Not in great detail." Nor did I have any idea where her mind was heading.

"His thesis then."

I wondered what could be gained by playing her game. And I was distracted by her iron-tipped walking stick punching holes uncomfortably close to my foot as we walked. I answered as best as I remembered. "Just that he was the first to understand that species evolve, and that life is ruled by competition. The fittest species survive and the others perish."

"True to an extent," Gramma Salazar said. "If you look closely, however, you'll see that in many species the greatest threat comes not from other species, but from within. Especially for the offspring. Young fish are eaten by older fish of the same species. Young wolves are threatened by older wolves. Everywhere you look, the females must protect their young from the adult males." Mrs. Salazar turned to me to make certain I was paying attention. "In mammals particularly, the threat is often with the lone, predatory male. What drives him? Darwin explained that any behavior that increases the likelihood of a male's genes being passed on to the next generation is a behavior the male offspring will also exhibit. Thus, the behavior of the predatory male is reinforced generation after generation. The result is that females are pursued with little regard for their welfare."

Gramma Salazar stopped walking and bore her eyes into me. "The greatest danger to Jennifer is not the mountain lion I saw just yesterday over in that hollow." She pointed to a cleft in the landscape in front of us. "Nor is it lightening or forest fires or the bears that frequent the trails in the woods where she rides her bicycle. The greatest danger comes from her own species. I've seen what predatory males like you do to girls. Males get fixated on the poor things. And after the union is consummated, the males slaughter the girls and leave their bodies in ditches."

"Surely, you're not suggesting..."

"Hush your mouth, Mr. McKenna! I'm talking!"

We crested a rise. The old woman next to me was not slowed by the brisk uphill walk. Her vice grip on the walking stick was undiminished. The Salazar mansion was visible in the distance. Beyond it the blue waters of Tahoe looked like an advertisement for the good life.

"I agree that Jennifer is in danger," I said. "But not from me. I am only trying to protect her. You can believe that."

"No! I don't! I don't believe anything you say! I asked you to stay away from her, yet you have not respected my wishes! Therefore, I am calling my good friend Judge Gelford. I will get a restraining order prohibiting you from having any contact with Jennifer!" Gramma Salazar looked up at me, her old eyes aflame.

I was exasperated with her drama. "Why tell me all of this, Mrs. Salazar? You don't need to lecture me to get your friends in the legal community to do your bidding."

"Mr. McKenna, I have a moral obligation as well as the moral authority to protect my granddaughter's life above all else. I recognize what kind of man you are. The reason I told you about Darwin is so that you'll know that I understand you and those biological drives men have. I am prepared to take action as necessary. I'm telling you all this because I want you to know what will happen if you defy the law and continue to pursue her."

"I'm a captive audience," I said. I was unprepared for what she said next.

Gramma Salazar stabbed the sharp walking stick into the ground next to my feet. "If you disobey the restraining order, I will have your knees broken!"

EIGHTEEN

Jennifer called at six in the evening.

Her voice was a whisper. "Auntie Ethel's driver just pulled up. Gramma and Helga will be leaving in a minute. Come as soon as you can."

"Where shall I leave my car?"

"The park south of us. Walk up the beach. You'll go past several homes before you come to our fence. Which reminds me, you'll have to go into the water to get around our fence, so maybe wear shorts and bring long pants."

"I'll leave now." I said goodbye and hung up, thinking that I was probably making the dumbest decision of my professional life.

I left Spot on the braided rug where he was deep into a nap.

The park and hike up the beach were as Jennifer described. When I got to the fence I worried that I'd be seen because it was still broad daylight. But only one of the nearby mansions had a clear view of me and I did not see anyone around. That left fifty or so windows from which anyone could be watching. The world's a stage.

I splashed into thigh-deep water, went around the fence and back onto dry land. I took off my shorts, pulled on my long pants and continued to the Salazar mansion.

Jennifer was on the pier waving to me as I approached. "Hi," she said, trying to sound casual, but with obvious excitement in her voice. That we were borrowing a boat without approval was one thing. That we were taking it all the way across Lake Tahoe and back at night was another order of magnitude. She'd probably never done anything so rash in her entire life. But she wasn't going to let me know that if she could help it.

She opened the boathouse doors. "Come on in. We'll take the powerboat."

"You know how to run it?"

Jennifer looked at me with disdain.

"Just checking," I said.

Jennifer got in the boat and put the key in the ignition. She turned on the bilge pump, then opened a side locker and started pulling out life jackets. I was pleased that she knew the routine. Inboards can accumulate fumes in the engine compartment and bilge. If the boat is turned on without first exhausting them, they can blow up.

Jennifer handed me a large life jacket. "This should fit you." We each pulled them on. She turned to the gauges. "That's funny. It seems someone else has used this boat recently."

"How do you know?"

"The gas is down almost a quarter tank. Sam always had a rule. Anyone using the boat had to fill it up when they brought it back." Jennifer pointed to the large storage tank at the side of the boathouse. It had a hose and nozzle on it similar to a gas station. "This boathouse was like the auto garage. Sam controlled both and woe to anyone who broke his rules."

"You all obeyed?"

Jennifer grinned. "Like I said, Sam was a good caretaker. We didn't want to irritate him. So, yes, we, I, always filled the tank when we brought the boats back. Now that Sam's gone, the rules are going by the wayside."

"Who could have used the boat?"

"That's just it. Besides me and Gramma and Sam, no one knows the code to unlock the boathouse. I haven't used the boat since last fall. Gramma hasn't been near the boathouse in years as far as I can tell. The water scares her so bad, she doesn't even walk down the beach."

"What about Helga?" I said.

"Oh, I forgot. Helga knows the code. She sometimes cleans down here. But she's never driven the boat. She wouldn't know how."

"So it must have been Sam."

Jennifer frowned. "I suppose he maybe used it before he ran off." Her eyes widened. "Unless he's sneaked back and used it since." She climbed out of the boat and unhooked the hose from the storage tank. "There is Dr. Hauptmann, the one other person who has driven the boat that I know of, but I can't imagine that he would have the alarm code to open the boathouse."

"He's a friend of the family?"

"Yes. A doctor in Las Vegas. Gramma knew him from way back when Grandpa Abe was alive. Dr. Hauptmann has continued to look after Gramma's health. He prescribes her pills. He comes up and stays for the weekend once or twice a year. Sometimes he takes the boats out, fishing and such."

I steadied the boat while Jennifer filled the gas tank. Jennifer got back in and started the motor. It had the deep, throaty gargle of a powerful engine. Jennifer idled it awhile. Exhaust drifted into the air inside the boathouse. She pushed a radio transmitter and the boathouse door rose up.

I unhooked the lines and Jennifer eased the big powerboat out into the lake. She pushed the transmitter again and the boathouse garage door closed behind us.

I felt as if the whole world were watching us from shore

and picking up their phones to report to Gramma Salazar. Too late now.

"What's the plan?" Jennifer asked as we cruised slowly into deep water.

"I want to time how long it would take to make a boat trip from Smithson's house to Emerald Bay and back. Then I'll add in the time for the hikes he would have made while carrying his wife's body. If the total time is less than the length of a single night then that will suggest he could be the killer of both his wife and your sister.

"Of course," I continued, "he could have brought his wife's body across the lake one night, stashed it in his house and then brought it up Mount Rose the next night. But I doubt he'd do that. His house was so neat and clean that I can't picture him having a body around for twenty-four hours." I glanced at Jennifer to see if this talk was bothering her. She seemed fine. I continued. "Smithson has close neighbors, so I don't think he would dare bring a body back to his dock. Instead, he'd go to a deserted beach where he would have previously parked his car. He'd be able to get the body into the trunk unseen. That would suggest he'd have to do it all in one night."

We were about one hundred yards out when Jennifer eased the throttle halfway forward. The engine roared and the big boat surged forward. The prow lifted up at a steep angle as the boat picked up speed. Then the boat leveled off and planed out.

"How fast does this crate go?" I yelled over the roar of engine and wind. We were both standing, our hands gripping the top of the windshield.

"I don't know," Jennifer yelled back. "I've never run it full out. Probably fifty knots." Her long hair flowed out behind her, snapping in the wind like brown streamers. She pointed to the north. "You want to go to Incline Village first?"

I nodded.

Jennifer put the boat into a big sweeping curve and we cruised north up the east shore. Twenty-five minutes later I pointed toward the shore. Jennifer pulled back on the throttle and the boat slowed and settled down into the water.

"Let's not go any closer," I said, "just in case he decides to look out with binoculars. He'd recognize us."

"Speaking of which, there are a pair of binoculars in the compartment under your seat. Which house is it?"

"The pointy glass one with the big cigarette boat in front." Now that I was looking at the boat, I was amazed I hadn't noticed it before. It was huge and menacing, with a shiny blue hull and a red and white cockpit. "Let's turn here. I can estimate the additional time it would take from his house." I lifted up my seat, got out the binoculars and focused them on Smithson's house.

There was movement on the left. Smithson was bouncing lightly on his toes. He lifted his arms up chest-high and pulled his elbows back several times as if stretching his chest muscles. He walked over to a weight bench and lay down on it. The barbell had four 45s on each side. With the bar it was 405 pounds. Smithson pressed it six times. Then he stood up and bounced around on his toes. His enthusiasm was like that of an athlete getting pumped up for a big game.

"See anything?" Jennifer asked.

"Just Smithson exercising." I put down the binoculars.

"Do you want a straight course across to Emerald Bay or one that follows the shoreline?"

"As you've said before, the weather at the time was calm. So I think he would have gone straight across the lake to save as much time as possible."

"That boat of his would be substantially faster than this one," Jennifer said. "Assuming that was the boat he had nine years ago."

"Right," I said. "But if we get this one up near its top end we should at least get a good idea of the time for the trip."

"You want me to open it up all the way?"

"Sure. Let 'er rip."

Jennifer eased the throttle forward. The boat almost jumped out of the water. I had to keep a tight grip on the edge of the windshield. The wind in our faces grew so strong we both sat down in the seats to get out of the wind stream.

"There's your answer," Jennifer yelled, a big grin on her face. She pointed at the speedometer. It showed 56 knots. She held tight to the steering wheel as the boat rocketed across the water, bouncing on the relatively calm surface.

We conferred in shouts now and then about the exact bearing for Emerald Bay. We eventually agreed on the rocky tip of Rubicon Peak as a west-shore landmark to shoot for, knowing that Emerald Bay would be a few miles to the south of it.

The powerboat was obviously made for speed. Its strong hull successfully transmitted every jarring blow from the waves directly into us. After five minutes, Jennifer stood up and drove from a standing position, her legs flexing with the bumps. Apparently, she preferred the stress of the wind when standing to the bounce of the boat that jolted so severely when sitting.

Soon, we were in the center of the lake, five miles from the closest point of land. The sun was setting and the water turned to a black liquid with touches of silver at the crests of the waves. Realizing that the bottom was over 1,600 feet below us was vaguely unsettling. I concentrated on the mountains ahead.

At a mile a minute, it took twenty minutes to get close to the entrance to Emerald Bay. Jennifer brought the boat in fast toward the first warning buoy and then pulled the throttle back. She glanced up at the darkening sky and switched on the boat's running lights. I could tell she'd spent many hours driving the powerful craft.

"The entrance to the bay is a narrow bottleneck," she said as the boat slowed to the speed of a swimmer. "It's a no-wake zone. Although Smithson might have run it at high speed. If he's crazy enough to murder, he'd be crazy enough to chance it."

"Could be," I said. "But he doesn't want to get caught. There aren't many patrol boats out now in early May. But there are in August. He wouldn't have wanted to attract attention. My guess is his time for the run won't be that much different than ours. And even though his boat would go faster, he probably wouldn't go full speed on the return trip for fear of the body bouncing out of his boat."

Jennifer brought the boat into the channel, going slowly, expertly adapting to the lag between inputs at the steering wheel and actual changes in direction. The water grew very shallow, and even in the twilight I could see the bottom which was sandy white but for the interruptions of large boulders that looked like they would rip out our prop.

Jennifer read my mind. "At the shallowest point the big tourist sternwheelers still clear the rocks so we'll be okay. We only run three feet of draft at no wake."

I nodded. It was clear I was in good hands. I'd been on many boats over the years, but probably none were piloted by someone more capable than Jennifer.

Once we were through the channel, Jennifer throttled up slightly to 15 knots. That was below planing speed, so the boat labored at a steep angle, its prow so high we could barely see over it.

The mountains around Emerald Bay were ominous in the gathering dark. We plowed up the bay past Fannette Island until we were nearly on the beach below Eagle Falls. Jennifer slowed the boat and eased it forward. At the last moment she activated the power lift on the prop. The boat drifted forward until the hull ground to a stop on the sandy beach.

"My time-keeping needs to take into account beaching and securing the boat," I said. "What would Smithson likely do?"

"He'd run an anchor and line up the beach and set it in the sand. Or if he had a long line he might go all the way to one of the trees, but that is less likely."

My sneakers were still wet from when I went into the water around the Salazar fence, so I jumped out of the boat into the shallow water. I walked up the sand as if I were setting an anchor. The Vikingsholm castle loomed in the dark forest, its black windows like eyes.

I walked back to the boat. "I can time his climb from land." I pushed against the prow of the boat. It did not want to budge out of the sand.

"Wait," Jennifer said. "Let me move to the back and shift the weight." She walked back. I heaved and the boat slid back into the water. I ran out, jumped up and boosted myself in.

"Our total time from Smithson's house to this point is forty minutes," I said. "Double that and you've got an hour and twenty minutes round trip. So there's no need to head back north toward his house. We can go straight east across the lake to your house. Hiking and driving will tell me the rest."

Jennifer nodded. We'd drifted far enough back for her

to lower the prop. She started the engine and gently pulled the throttle back into reverse. The water slapped the stern as we backed up. Then Jennifer cranked the wheel, moved the throttle forward and we started up in a sharp turn.

Soon, we were back in the tiny channel at the bay's entrance. We cruised out into the black open water. As we cleared the last buoy, Jennifer opened up the throttle and we roared east across the lake.

I looked at my watch. "If Gramma doesn't get back until ten, we've got plenty of time. We'll have the boat back in its bed and you inside the house long before she returns."

Jennifer nodded. "She always returns from bridge between ten and ten-fifteen. Like clockwork. I'll have the house to myself."

As she said it, I detected a sudden tension. This was the first time Gramma had gone to play bridge since Jennifer's scare earlier in the week. "We'll put the boat away and then I'll wait with you inside until the driver brings them home. I can slip out the back before they come in. Then I'll backtrack to my car same as we planned. You won't be left alone."

Jennifer said nothing. She was standing in the breeze as she drove. Her hands were tight on the wheel. I stayed silent as we raced east. The east shore grew larger. I was searching the trees for a glimpse of the Salazar mansion when Jennifer suddenly pulled the throttle back. The boat lurched and coasted to a halt. Jennifer remained standing. Her eyes were fixed on the shoreline. Her body was rigid.

"What's wrong?" I said.

She lifted her arm up and pointed toward the shore. Her finger vibrated. Small sobs emanated from her throat.

"Jennifer, tell me."

"Our house," she said. Her voice was weak. "Gramma and Helga are both gone. No one is supposed to be there."

Her voice choked off.

"Not for another hour or more, like you said." I strained my eyes to try to see whatever she was pointing at.

"Over there," she said, her voice a whimper that reminded me she was a kid. "See that light?"

"Yes," I said. "What about it?"

"No one is supposed to be in the house, but that light is in my bedroom window!"

As she said it, the light turned off.

NINETEEN

"Let's bring the boat in. I'll check the house."

"No!" Jennifer said. "I won't wait outside alone."

"You can come in the house with me."

"No." She shook her head.

"Okay. We'll dock the boat and go down the beach to my Jeep. We can drive to Street's."

"Can we get Spot first? And bring him to Street's?"

"Sure," I said.

She pushed the throttle forward and we cruised at a slow pace toward shore.

The boathouse was hard to see as we approached the black shoreline. Jennifer pushed the transmitter for the door, turned the boat and slowly backed into the boathouse. Jennifer turned off the ignition. I jumped out before we stopped and walked through the French doors out on the pier. The night was quiet and the Salazar mansion was dark. I ran around to the pier on the other side of the boathouse. The dock was bare. I came back in the other door. I didn't turn on the light. Better to work in the dark. Jennifer was running a line from the bow to the pier. I stepped onto the rear seat of the runabout. It rocked precariously under me as I reached for another line from the powerboat and ran it to the other pier.

When we had the boat secure and the door lowered, we

locked the door and left.

"Are you sure you don't want to check the house?" I asked.

"No. Absolutely not. I don't care if I never set foot in that mausoleum again." She pulled on my jacket, leading me down the beach away from the mansion.

"Okay, we'll go to Street's," I said.

"First we get Spot," she reminded me.

When we got to where the fence went into the water Jennifer muttered about her shoes getting wet. I walked into the water first. "It's not too bad," I said. "Your shoes will dry soon enough."

Jennifer gasped at the cold temperature when she walked in, but plunged on without complaining. We got to the Jeep without incident. I turned the heater on high as we drove up the highway and then up the mountain to my cabin. I heard Jennifer's teeth clattering from shivering at one point, but I didn't say anything. When I opened the door to my cabin, Spot ran out.

"Ooh, Spot," Jennifer said. She hugged him furiously. "I love you, Spot. Will you stay with me? Will you stay at Street's tonight?"

Spot nuzzled her neck.

We loaded back into the Jeep and drove down to Street's.

Street didn't answer the doorbell, so I used my key to open the door. This was getting to be a habit. Jennifer kept her hand on Spot's back and followed him as he walked into the living room and sprawled on his favorite throw rug. I dialed Street's lab and then her cell phone and got her voice mail. "Hey, doll, wanted to let you know that Jennifer and Spot are spending the night with you, so don't bring home any strange men. You know how jealous Spot gets."

I told Jennifer that she should consider calling Gramma

and that I didn't know when Street would get home and that I didn't know when I'd be back. Jennifer barely heard me so entranced was she by his largeness. As for Spot, he appeared to be sound asleep under the influence of her pets.

I left and drove fast up to Incline Village. I wanted to see if John-the-body was home.

He was. Lights were on and I could see him through the expansive glass as I slowly cruised down the street. He was carrying a lowball glass with a dark golden drink in it. He stopped and looked at himself in a mirror. He took a sip. Being a man of class he probably drank scotch. Single malt, maybe.

The question was, had he been home exercising all evening? Or did he just come back from the Salazar mansion?

I'd know part of the answer if I could feel the engine of his BMW. Trouble was, it was in the garage. I parked down the street, put on my gloves, grabbed the tire iron and walked back.

His garage was attached to the left side of the house. Smithson was in the opposite side and there were no lights showing in windows near the garage.

I tried each of the garage doors. Locked. There was a human-sized door around the side. It was also locked. I wondered if the garage was wired to an alarm. Probably.

The easiest way to wire a garage was a motion detector up on the garage ceiling. The harder but more effective way was to wire every door and window and still put a motion detector on the ceiling. A guy like Smithson would probably go all the way to protect the Beamer, being that it was a psychological extension of himself, compact, tough, full of muscle.

The side door to the garage was made of fir and had a fir doorjamb. When will people learn about oak or metal?

Rarely do I commit felonies. But I suspected Smithson of murder so I jammed the tire iron in, twisted and popped the door open with less effort than it takes to get hard-frozen ice cream out of the container.

The alarm didn't go off. I pushed the door open a few inches and stuck my head in. The alarm still didn't go off. There was a window at the back of the garage and a yard light just beyond. Visible in the dim light were the silver BMW, a red Lotus race car and a powder blue Shelby Cobra. The guy had taste if not social panache. The Lotus and the Cobra were toys, so that left the BMW for a utility vehicle of the type to haul dead bodies and such. It was the BMW engine I was after. I walked in to feel the engine and got no more than four feet before the alarm went off. WONK, WONK, WONK!

The shriek of the hidden loudspeaker was loud enough to warn London that the Luftwaffe was coming. I trotted to the BMW, pulled off a glove and felt the hood. Warm. The alarm horn hurt my ears. WONK, WONK! I got down on the floor and pulled myself under the bumper. Reaching up, I snaked my hand past the oil pan, and laid my palm on the engine block. It was hot enough to raise welts. I jerked my hand back and rang my elbow on the concrete floor. I grunted, but couldn't hear myself over the alarm. WONK, WONK, WONK! Between the wonks I heard a door slam. I slid out from underneath the bumper.

I stood up and almost jumped over the hood of the Beamer on my way to the door. WONK, WONK, WONK!

"Freeze, asshole!" Smithson yelled over the alarm. The light flipped on.

But I was out the door. The deep crack of a big handgun echoed off nearby houses. I ran the opposite direction from my Jeep, staying in plain view long enough for Smithson to get out the door and see me. Then I went between some houses and doubled back through backyards, vaulting over fences and running around a variety of swimming pools. I was in my Jeep and cruising slowly down Lakeshore Drive when the first of Incline Village's finest flew by, blue lights flashing.

TWENTY

I knew that Smithson would be long occupied with the police while they performed their investigation. I remembered guys like him from my crime scene days in San Francisco. He would insist that the police dust everything in the garage for fingerprints and then inspect the grounds for clues. If the police weren't sufficiently fastidious, Smithson would threaten to call his lawyers, the chief and the mayor. I felt sorry for the officers on the scene. While I was confident that Smithson didn't see my face, he might have guessed at my identity based on my height. If so, he'd fuss about it to the cops and that would use up more time.

I decided it would be a good moment to time the drive up to Mount Rose. I could take up surveillance of Smithson later.

I turned north on the Mount Rose Highway. The road winds up and over the shoulder of Mount Rose, cresting at 9,000 feet before it plunges nearly a mile down to Reno. As I gained altitude I could see lights sprinkling the far shoreline of Tahoe. The gibbous moon was low in the southern sky, hanging over the lake like a big Jack-o'-lantern. It glinted off the snowy mountains and its reflection in the water was a swath of light twenty miles long. The road climbed up into forest and then onto the big snow-covered meadow under Mount Rose. I pulled over where the trailhead starts up to the summit and noted the time. I turned off the headlights and got out into the full glare of the moon on the snow. The air was cold, with a brisk breeze out of the north. Cross-country ski tracks criss-crossed the meadow, looking in the moonlight like strange giant calligraphy.

The summit loomed above, dark and foreboding. I knew roughly where the trail went, but I decided that nighttime on an icy mountain was not a safe time to go up, even though night was when I suspected Smithson had done the climb with his wife's body over his shoulders. But he would have gone in August when the snow was gone.

I now knew how long it would take to make the boat trip and the car trip. Because of the snow I realized it would be easiest to estimate the time it would take for the hikes on both ends. Then I would know if the trip could be done in one night. From my knowledge of the area around Emerald Bay, I figured he could hike from the water up to the rock slide and back in less than two hours. As I thought about it, I realized that I could probably get an accurate idea of the time it would take to make the climb on Mount Rose by studying my topographic maps. I also wanted to get back down to his house and follow him for the next few days.

I pulled back onto the highway and had just run the Jeep up to fifty when flashing lights appeared behind me. I slowed to let them race by, but the lights slowed and stayed behind me. I pulled over, stopped and got out, keeping my hands in clear view.

"Evening, officer," I said to the dark figure getting out of the patrol car. I wondered why the officer had not turned on the spotlight. The officer reached back in the car, turned off the headlights, then shut the door. Something was wrong.

The man spoke. "They're taking your name in vain on the radio," he said. He had a slight Mexican accent.

"Diamond, aren't you out of your jurisdiction? Douglas County line is way south of here." We shook hands in the dark.

"That's why I ain't arresting you. That's why I ain't bringing you in for questioning on a B & E they had down in Incline an hour ago. When I recognized your car I thought I might let you know how easily confused these Incline cops are."

"Wonder why they're looking for me?" I said.

"Apparently a man named Smithson, the one you called me about, had a burglar bust into his garage. Saw the suspect as he ran out. Said the suspect was very tall. Said he thought the suspect was a man named Owen McKenna who has been harassing him." Diamond leaned back against the side of my Jeep and crossed his arms. His skin was dark in the yellow moonlight. "But of course you've been up on this mountain snow-shoeing or something with friends and so you have an alibi." He turned and looked at me. "Am I right?"

"What if I can't remember their names?"

"Then you might be in deep doo-doo."

"The cops got prints or something?"

"No." Diamond shook his head. "The suspect didn't leave any. Probably some pro who's done B & Es before. But the Incline Village boys will want to question you just the same."

"Thanks for the warning." I turned to my Jeep.

"Oh, I almost forgot," Diamond said. "Mrs. Salazar called nine-one-one right about the time of Smithson's burglary. Wanted to report a runaway granddaughter. Said the girl called her and said she wasn't coming home until the man who was stalking her was caught. The old lady thinks the girl said the man's name was John Smithson. Now, you wouldn't know anything about that, would you?"

"Gosh, Diamond. Stumped me there."

"Trouble is," Diamond continued, "if any adult knows where the girl is staying, then that adult could be brought in on a variety of charges. With her money, old lady Salazar could make them stick, too."

"Tell you what," I said. "If I find out anything, you'll be the first to know."

"Good."

"You get the Medical Examiner's report on the body, yet?"

"Just got it an hour ago. I forget some of the details of what he said. Something about the character of the bone around the entry wounds being consistent with the victim being alive at the time. But there are no marks on the inside of the skull from bullets bouncing around, so maybe the soft lead mushroomed on initial impact and didn't carry much inertia. He also found scrapes on bones that happened long after death which suggests the corpse was moved when it was already mostly decomposed. That could also explain the loss of the bullets. They could have fallen out of the skull."

"There weren't even any tiny bullet fragments?" I asked.

"No. The M.E. said the inside of the skull was totally cleaned out by bugs. So I called Street and she said it is possible that hide beetles could have removed the bullet fragments, although she didn't think it was likely."

"Any idea how the body was moved?"

"No. Could be coyotes, dogs maybe," Diamond said.

"Did the Medical Examiner say anything about what the corpse would have weighed when it was moved?"

"He guessed around forty pounds or less. It would have been down to mostly bones and the ligaments holding them together."

"Any word on a TV tape of Maria when she was rescued at Kirkwood?"

"No. Got a deputy on it full time. One of the TV station people said it wasn't likely any tape was saved. But they're looking." Diamond turned back toward the patrol unit. "Let me know when you decide what you're going to do with your little kidnapping problem," Diamond said over his shoulder. "I have to tell the sheriff what I'm doing about the rich girl who ran away. I'll wait two days to hear from you. After that, I'll have to do a little checking around. Being that Jennifer was recently seen with both you and Street, the Sheriff will want to know if I've looked at the McKenna and Casey residences. I gotta tell him something." He got in his car, pulled out around my Jeep and drove away.

TWENTY-ONE

I drove back down the mountain and turned in on Lake Shore Drive. Smithson's house was dark as I cruised by. The garage door was closed and I had no way of knowing if he was home. I could break in again and see if his BMW was there. Or I could tiptoe around the back side of the house and see if I could spy his sleeping face through a window. Instead, I thought that there was no harm in waiting. Never know if he hired an off-duty cop to sit in the living room in the dark and drink scotch with him.

Down the street was a large pine. I parked behind it. I could just see Smithson's house past the tree trunk. But his view of my vehicle was largely blocked. I was in front of a big brick house. Who would wake up first? Smithson? Assuming he was home. Or the occupants of the brick house who in this neighborhood would call the cops to report a strange man loitering in his Jeep?

The clock on the car radio said 2:00 a.m. in soft green numbers. Having nothing to read I put the radio on scan and let it search out stations. Reception in the mountains is weak at best. I got a hard rock station in Reno, followed by a country music station, followed by one devoted to golden oldies. The radio searched the rest of the FM band before picking up a pop music station that broadcast from up at the lake. I switched over to AM and the scan feature gave me many more choices, bouncing in from all over the west. The minutes crawled by while I watched Smithson's house and listened to talk shows. In Phoenix they were arguing about assault weapons. In L.A. they were discussing liposuction. In Boise, Idaho they were trying to decide whether they should secede from the union. In San Francisco they were talking about how to fund the opera.

For a time I snoozed in the car seat. I woke stiff and cold. When I started the engine the car sounded in the quiet night like a 747 revving up for takeoff. But no lights went on in the nearby houses. Smithson's house was unchanged. The clock said 4:30 a.m. I turned the heater on high and went back to my continuing education.

The Mormons in Salt Lake City were celebrating the jobs and international commerce that resulted from teaching kids foreign languages and then sending them abroad to study. In Seattle they were wondering how to be more than just a labor pool for Boeing and Microsoft. Portland wanted to pass a law that would prevent gays and Californians from buying property in Oregon.

A light went on in Smithson's house. It was 5:00 a.m. I turned off the radio so I could concentrate. Another light turned on. There was movement in one of the big living room windows. Then nothing for a long time. Thirty minutes later the garage door opened and the BMW backed out.

It is hard following a car without being noticed when there are no other cars in the street. But the sky was lightening and I thought I could chance it without head-lights. My Jeep would be harder for Smithson to spot, but it was still dark enough that a cop would pull me over. I waited until the BMW was almost out of sight before I pulled out. The BMW went around the north end of the lake. At one point I got close but couldn't see if it was Smithson or the Lycra lady driving because of the smoked windows. I was counting on Smithson.

The car turned north on 267 and climbed up Brockway summit. I followed at a good distance. We crested the pass and cruised down past North Star Ski Resort. There was a bank of fog that covered the meadow near the Truckee airport. I wanted to slow, but the BMW flew into it as if it were not there. When I emerged from the fog the BMW was nowhere in sight.

I sped into Truckee and raced to the intersection of Interstate 80. The BMW was just disappearing out of sight where the west-bound ramp joins the freeway.

Interstate 80 is busy 24 hours a day so I thought it would be easy to mix in with the trucks and stay unseen behind the BMW. But Smithson liked to go twenty miles over the speed limit. I used the trucks like slalom course gates as I tried to keep up, hoping Smithson wouldn't see my frantic driving in his mirror.

We raced over Donner Summit and down the west slope of the Sierra Nevada. I was watching my gas gauge, figuring my range as we cruised by the gas stations of Auburn. Then we were out of the foothills and onto the Central Valley. Sacramento approached and was quickly behind us. I had maybe enough gas to make it to San Francisco if that was where he was headed. Then again maybe I'd run out. Only one way to find out.

On the other side of the Central Valley we sailed up the low rise through the coastal range. To the north the mountains of Napa were a gorgeous green and lavender patchwork. To the south was Mount Diablo in the distance. The BMW set speed records going through Berkeley. I was amazed there were no troopers out. My gas gauge was on empty as we went around the big turn and cruised up to the toll booths for the Bay Bridge. There were several trucks between us. I was afraid I'd lose him. So I swerved three lanes over to an empty booth, paid my dollar and floored it up onto the bridge.

I caught up with the BMW halfway across the Bay. The City was magnificent, free of smog and framed like a picture by the cables of the Bay Bridge. The Transamerica pyramid sparkled in the sunlight. Over on Russian Hill and Pacific Heights the opulently painted Victorians were an artist's palette of color.

The BMW exited the freeway and went up Larkin. It turned right on Post and drove up and down the hills. Then it went around the block and came back on Sutter. I was half a block behind him when my Jeep ran out of gas.

I coasted to the curb, jumped out of the car and looked for a cab. There were none in sight. I took what I thought was a last look at the BMW when it turned into a parking garage three blocks down. I sprinted down the opposite side of the street and was across from the garage when Smithson walked out and turned down the sidewalk. He entered a hotel down the block.

It was a nice enough place with turn-of-the-century charm, although I would have thought a slick guy like Smithson was more the Marriot type. I waited awhile, then walked up to the lobby door and casually looked in toward the check-in desk. Smithson was not there. I stepped inside and picked up a morning paper off the lobby table. Holding it to my face I perused the hallway and adjacent restaurant. He was gone. I walked over and pressed the elevator button. The light went on but no doors opened. They were on upper floors. Had Smithson taken one of the elevators up? Did he know someone who had a room? Or did he have a room? Being rich, did he keep a permanent room in The City?

I walked up to the counter. A young man with Polynesian features looked up from a desk, stood and walked to the counter. I flashed him the badge I bought at a flea market for a dollar. "DEA," I said. I put the badge back in my pocket. "The man who just walked in. Does he have a room here?"

"I'm sorry, sir, I do not know who you mean."

"Bodybuilder. Six feet. Two hundred forty pounds. Muscles you could sell at a beef auction in Kansas City. Usually goes by the name John Smithson."

"Sir, I'm not authorized to..."

I leaned over the counter and spoke in a hushed, low voice. Intimate. Caring. Uncle Owen is handing out free advice. "What if the city inspectors bring their clipboards," I said, "and apply the rules in the fine print? New wiring. New sprinkling system. New kitchen. New elevators. Complete earthquake retro-fit. Hell, might as well bulldoze the place and start over." I stood up as tall as my six-six allowed and looked down on him. "You wouldn't want your bosses to think you weren't forthcoming to an officer of the law, would you?"

The young man slowly turned, swallowed and punched a few buttons on the computer. "We have a Mr. John Smithson staying through Sunday."

I grinned at him. "Thank you. His room number?"

The man's face paled. "I could get in so much trouble."

His fear was palpable. Even though I knew that I would do nothing that could get him in trouble, I felt bad. But I didn't let it show. "The room number?" I said again.

The young man slowly turned to the computer. "Four twenty-six."

"There a back door to this place?"

"Only a service entrance downstairs. The customers must use the front door."

I nodded, told him thanks and walked out of the hotel.

TWENTY-TWO

Across the street was a tiny twenty-four hour grocery that devoted half its space to liquor, a quarter of its space to girlie magazines and the rest to an astonishing range of foods from caviar to cantaloupes. Though broad in selection, the inventory was shallow to the point of only one sample for each of hundreds of different items stacked floor-to-ceiling. Some were cooked and kept warm in a glass cabinet. I pulled out a plastic bowl that contained an artichoke. I also grabbed a box of crackers while I kept my eye on the front door of the hotel. I knew my plan had a flaw which was how long could I pretend to look at an artichoke while John-the-body was possibly taking a long hot shower to be followed by a four hour nap.

"Yes, please, can I help you, sir?" said a Korean man behind the counter.

I put the artichoke and crackers on the counter and was paying for them, thinking I could sit on the curb and make them last several hours, when Smithson walked out of the hotel.

The shopkeeper sensed my sudden concern and, fearing he might lose a sale if he weren't quick, counted my change in record time, slipping into his native tongue. I grabbed the bag and ran.

Smithson was down the sidewalk, sauntering in the spring sunshine. He'd changed into a white leisure suit. The suit coat swung in the breeze.

I munched crackers while I followed Smithson down three blocks, over one, and down three more. He turned into a small cafe. I approached slowly, aware that my height made me a bad tail. Smithson quickly came back out. I stopped, turned and studied a doorway that had been boarded up with plywood. It had the grading letters CDX 1/2" stamped in several places. Gradually, I turned around and saw Smithson watching the sidewalks.

He was waiting for someone.

If he was, then I was.

We waited, he studying the flow of humanity, me studying the plywood. It was obvious when his date appeared. He straightened up, pulled his shoulders back in his best weight-lifter's pose and stepped his feet apart. She was an equivalent physical standout coming down the sidewalk. Red knit dress. Hem just below her crotch. Charcoal nylons and black spiked heels. She wasn't as graceful as Street, but she looked good. Probably had the brain of a brook trout, but Smithson didn't care.

John-the-body embraced her with feeling. His left hand went to her butt. They forced themselves apart and the two of them went into the cafe.

For the next hour I waited outside. Twice I managed a walk-by. Twice I saw them swooning at each other over a table covered with omelets and hashbrowns and coffee.

When they finally emerged, arms around each other's waists, they were so focused on each other that I could have tailed them in a backhoe.

They had a penchant for up. Whenever an intersection presented a steeper street, they took it. Having forfeited a night's sleep, I was tired by the time they reached the top of Nob Hill.

I followed them across the front of the Fairmont

Hotel and over two more blocks to an exquisitely restored Victorian painted in cream, lilac and periwinkle. John-the-body paused with his concubine at the front door while she fumbled for a key. They entered the sugar-plum palace and moments later the curtains were drawn across the downstairs windows. In a minute the mini-blinds were lowered over the upstairs windows. Obviously, Smithson and the woman in the red dress would not be seen again until their hormones had found a new equilibrium.

This time it was clear I had a long wait, so I moseyed toward the financial district and dialed Street on my cell phone.

"Hi, sweetie," I said when she answered. "Hope I didn't wake you."

"Not me. But Jennifer is prostrate on the couch with her arm draped over his largeness and they have opened one eye each at the sound of the phone."

"Tell them they can go back to sleep after Jennifer talks to me. But first, I need to ask a favor. I want Jennifer to contact her grandmother. Otherwise, you and I are going to be arrested on a kidnapping charge. I'm wondering if you could stay with Jennifer until I get back."

"Sure, no problem."

"Never let her out of your sight?"

"Owen, I said I would. I understand."

"Sorry. I guess my lack of sleep is stressing me. I'll talk to Jennifer now."

There was a pause and then a sleepy, high-pitched hello.

"Hi, Jennifer," I said. "I'm calling from San Francisco. Smithson is here and he won't be back in Tahoe for some time. We still don't know where Samuel Sometimes is, so I want you to have Street with you at all times. But it would be good if you went back home and comforted your grandmother. Take Street along and she'll make certain you are safe. As long as you aren't left alone, you'll be safe."

"No," she replied matter-of-factly.

"Jennifer, if you are, in fact, in danger, that danger will only be present if you are alone. I'm convinced of that."

"It doesn't sound like you are convinced that I'm in danger at all." She sounded wounded.

"I didn't mean it that way. I was referring to danger right now because Smithson is in San Francisco and I'm watching him. My guess is that Smithson is who we need to be concerned about. Whether Sam is dangerous or not, he has disappeared and has probably run away to a different part of the country."

"I don't care. I'm not going home," she said.

I ignored the comment. "What I'll do is call you when Smithson does leave. That way you'll at least know of his whereabouts. Maybe Street can stay with you at your house. Your grandmother never prohibited her from seeing you."

"No," she said.

"Look, Jennifer. I'm worried about your grandmother. Not about her feelings, but about what she will do. If she gets rough with the police then they will be forced to get rough with me and Street for harboring a fugitive."

"I wasn't here. I don't even know where Street lives," Jennifer said. "I think you know about my resolve," she continued. "No matter how they interrogate me I won't betray Street's confidence and help."

I didn't know what to say. The kid had her mind made up. "They won't interrogate you. But they will figure out where you are. They'll find you and come to pick you up. It's only because they are concerned about your safety."

"Then they should leave me alone. I'll stay here with Street and Spot. Street said I could. As long as I want."

I must have breathed heavily.

"Please don't sigh, Owen. I know I'm safe here. I know I'm not safe at home. I think we've seen enough evidence of that." She sounded testy.

"Then you might at least call your grandmother. Tell her you're all right."

"Maybe," Jennifer said.

"May I talk to Street again, please?"

I heard the phone being handed over.

"When are you coming back?"

"Don't know. Probably when Smithson does. I'll keep following him. If he makes any kind of move toward Jennifer then that might be enough to get the D.A. to move on him. I'll lay odds he killed his wives. It would be a nice coincidence to nail him on those murders while catching him making an attempt on Jennifer."

"Well, good luck. Speaking of coincidences, remember the green beetle I couldn't identify that was digging in my soap in the bathroom and the same soap in the hall closet?"

"I'm trying to remember."

"Well, I caught it in the bathroom and put it in a jar. The next day I saw one in the closet. Turned out it was two different bugs after all. Rare insects. But the same kind. Same activity. Just goes to show that coincidences do happen now and then. Thought you'd be interested."

"You keep watching those bugs. Never know what you will learn. What about the maggots you got off of the body? Figure out a time of death, yet?"

"No. I need more readings on the hygrothermograph. Another day at the minimum."

We exchanged I-love-yous and said goodbye.

I walked back to Nob Hill, vaguely hoping that I would find a bookstore that might distract me from the gumshoe task at hand.

I found a newsstand, but it specialized in scandal rags. I wasn't interested in Burt Reynolds' toupee or topless photos of the movie star of the week or the one-legged Florida woman who gave birth to identical twins whose father was an alien from Mars. So I hiked back up Nob hill.

Nothing had changed at the lilac and periwinkle Victorian. The main-floor curtains and the second and third-floor blinds were still drawn. I wandered around the nearby grassy boulevards and found a tiny park with a statue and a memorial plaque that told of the great contributions a Nineteenth Century silk importer had made to San Francisco society. Above the plaque stood a bronze statue of the man. He wore flowing robes. One hand touched his chest and one arm reached out as if he were declaiming his own virtues. I sat down on a concrete park bench underneath his outstretched arm and noted that by craning my neck to the left I could spy on the front door of the woman with the red dress.

Was she rich? Was she Smithson's next victim? Or was he truly finding happiness this time? Maybe she had been the goal of his plan all along. Marry a wealthy woman and then kill her for the money with which to entice and seduce the young nymph in red. Maybe there wasn't enough money? No problem. Find another rich woman and do it again. Eventually, there would be sufficient dollars to buy the nymph her own Victorian with a view of the Bay. But if that was the plan, why stay in Tahoe? Was the Lycra Lady in Incline Village his mountain girl? Did it take two nubile young women to keep him satisfied?

I wasn't sure if any of it made sense. My mind wandered to Street and then to Glennie and from there to the woman in Hopper's painting, New York Movie. Hopper was exploring loneliness. Looking at the painting, it was clear how powerful loneliness is. The young woman's future was going to be shaped by her isolation or her efforts to prevent it.

But is the desire for companionship enough to drive a person to murder?

On first thought, it appeared that Smithson killed his wives out of lust for money. But no one murders because it'll be easier to pay the electric bill. Instead, isn't murderous money lust often part of a dream of finding true happiness with a perfect companion, possibly someone in a red knit dress whose attentions come at a high price? In other words, the ultimate escape from loneliness?

Or maybe Smithson killed because his affairs were found out. Rather than risk divorce and the elimination of his allowance which he used to support his habit, he murdered to maintain his access to those women with tight clothes and periwinkle houses. Women who kept him from feeling the crush of being alone physically if not spiritually.

Of course, some people murder out of jealousy. His wives may have devoted their attentions elsewhere. But what is jealousy other than the fear of losing the companionship that we all desperately desire? Again, fear of loneliness seemed a principle motivator in our actions.

What about anger? Many of the murders I'd investigated in my past career were borne of anger, often the quick anger of a barroom brawl. But just as often the anger was fomented by the onset of loneliness. Boy meets girl. Boy loses girl to another boy. Boy might not even like the girl enough to be jealous. But boy is angry enough, lonely enough, to murder.

Hopper was asking me to focus on loneliness. I munched more crackers and ate the last of my artichoke, flicking the leafy detritus into a nearby trash bin as I thought about Smithson and loneliness. Something wasn't right. Smithson and loneliness weren't natural companions. Instead, if I asked myself the question, where is the most loneliness in the Salazar mix, the answer would be the caretaker, Sam Sometimes. This confused me. Hopper pointed to loneliness and that pointed away from Smithson.

Then I remembered what Street had said about the bug eating the soap that turned out to be two bugs after all. She said they were the same rare species, pursuing the same rare activity.

I sat up straight.

Were two murderers working at the same time? Could both John Smithson and Sam Sometimes be closing in on Jennifer? Was there some other connection to the Salazar family that I'd missed?

I'd limited myself to thinking that there was only one killer in any given situation. If John Smithson killed both his wives, then he was a premeditating killer. I'd seen him follow Jennifer on her bike, and he was gone from his house at precisely the same time we'd seen someone turning on lights in the Salazar mansion. Further, the distance from his house to Salazars was enough that the engine of his BMW would have been very hot, just as I'd established. The combination made him my number one suspect. Yet, like Street's bugs, Sam Sometimes could also be killing in close proximity to Jennifer. First Melissa, now Maria, and possibly others in between. Which meant that just because Smithson was in the house down the block from me didn't mean that Jennifer was safe.

And I'd just told her to go home. Maybe it was better for Street and me to take our risks with the police.

I dialed Street on my cell phone, but my battery died just as it started to ring. I sprinted down the block looking for a pay phone. Of course, there were none in sight. I finally found one in the lobby of the Fairmont Hotel.

"Street!" I nearly yelled when she answered. "Is Jennifer

still there?!"

"Yes, Owen, what's the matter?"

I stood there panting. "Good. Thanks. I've changed my mind. I want you both to stay put. Don't go out at all."

"Owen, talk to me."

"I might be wrong." My breath was labored. "What you said about the unusual beetles. Same kind. Same activity. But different bugs."

"Oh, my God," Street said. "You mean there are two murderers after Jennifer?"

I could hear Jennifer exclaiming in the background. "I don't know," I said. "Maybe. Keep Jennifer there. I'll call you back before you leave for work. In the meantime I've an idea about how to find out about the missing caretaker."

TWENTY-THREE

When I left the Fairmont there was only one cab in the drive and it was being loaded with four men wearing turbans. No other cabs were in sight, so I hoofed it down Nob Hill. The Transamerica pyramid was brilliant in the sunshine. The Embarcadaro buildings stood in homogeneous solidarity against the plethora of architectural designs that surrounded them. Sailboats dotted the Bay, their sails like confetti against the blue water.

I turned right at an intersection and saw where I was heading. To the south, toward the Marriot, just four or five blocks from the San Francisco Museum of Modern Art, was a tall building made of pink granite trapezoids mixed in with long strips of blue, mirrored glass. Up on the pediment, in pink neon regalia, were the words Salazar West.

I wondered about Sam Sometimes as I hurried toward the building. No one seemed to know anything about him. He didn't even have a real name. According to Jennifer, he paid prostitutes for companionship. Could he have murdered Melissa in a twisted attempt to find a family? He was, after all, the first climber to get to the body. That would have been easy if he knew where it was all along.

I ran across Market against a Don't Walk sign. SOMA, the neighborhood South of Market, was under construction, being transformed from a rough, ugly mix of vacant lots and drag queen bars into an upscale combination of restaurants,

shops, art galleries and dotcom startups. The renewal was
spearheaded by the building of the SFMoMA and, to a
lesser degree, the Salazar West tower.

The lobby of the clothing company was a study in
contrasting stone. Black granite made up the floor. The
walls were white marble and tinted glass. Across the top of
the atrium stretched pink neon tubes that shimmered like
tracer bullets in front of the black ceiling.

I walked up to the central reception desk where a
heavy young man sat. Under the wrap-around counter one
would find a bank of TV monitors. But instead of a guard's
uniform he wore a black shirt with a cleric's collar and black
pants. The shirt had a small pink Salazar West logo.

"Yes, sir," he said.

"I'm a writer on assignment from the Salazar family,"
I drawled. I put a lot of space between the words. Never
mind my scruffy unshaven, no-sleep look. We writers are
nothing to worry about. "Specifically, Jennifer Salazar. She
has directed me here to talk to your P.R. manager. Just a few
questions is all. Won't take but a minute." I leaned on the
counter expectantly.

"Your name, please?"

"Owen McKenna."

The man regarded me for a moment, then picked up
his phone. He punched some buttons and waited. "Zack
Hanover at the front desk. I have a gentleman here who
would like to speak with Ms. Ramirez. No, I don't believe
he has an appointment. Says he is working for a Jennifer
Salazar."

Zack waited a minute. "Thank you," he said and then
hung up the phone. He looked up at me. "Someone will be
down in a minute. Please have a seat." He gestured toward
an arrangement of leather couches that were overhung by
potted Ficus trees. Their leaves glistened as though they

were waxed each morning. I sat.

Five minutes later a young Asian woman with long black hair, black dress and sensible-looking black pumps approached me. "Mr. McKenna? I'm Share Woo. I'll take you to Ms. Ramirez's office."

We rode a black marble elevator with recessed pink lighting and got out on the fourteenth floor. The view of the Bay was the first thing I saw through floor-to-ceiling windows. "Nice place you people got here," I said.

The woman looked up at me and smiled politely. "Ms. Ramirez is very busy. But she has a few minutes available before her eleven o'clock appointment. If you'll wait here."

I sat on another leather couch. My watch said 10:50 a.m. I studied the art on the wall adjacent to the big windows. Two large canvases by famous artists. One had two bold areas of color, one red, one cream, separated by a thin line. The other canvas was a mix of black and white stripes super-imposed over a swirl of lines. I could retire in style by selling just one of them.

"Mr. McKenna? Ms. Ramirez will see you now."

I was ushered into a large office. A tiny woman wearing a tan business suit stood up from behind a big teak desk and reached over and up to shake my hand. Her silver earrings caught the sunlight pouring in the tinted windows. Her lipstick was the color of garnets.

I introduced myself and told her I was writing a biography of the Salazar family.

"Please have a seat," Ms. Ramirez said.

This time it was an arm chair, but leather just like the couches. She sat in her leather, swivel desk chair and leaned back slightly. Above her was another canvas, with frantic, gestural lines on a multi-colored background. I pointed at the painting. "You've got some serious art," I said. I spaced the words out slowly.

She raised an eyebrow. "Oh?" she smiled. "You're fond of abstract expressionism?"

"No, not really. I like art where you can tell what it's about."

Ms. Ramirez's smile took on the edge of a sneer. "If you don't understand modern art, you shouldn't judge it. The world is overrun with Philistines."

I shifted in my chair, making myself more comfortable. "Oh, I know I'm naive," I said. "I understand some of the intentions of the New York School." I gestured over my shoulder toward the reception room. "And the impact of the Motherwell out there is undeniable. But when Barnett Newman starts talking about the dichotomy of subject and object with his bifurcated paintings, I admit, I'm just not up to it." I pointed at the painting behind her. "Now that deKooning. There's something a guy like me can sink his teeth into. The painter goes wild with gesture in a splash of abstract lines and colors, yet the nude woman that emerges is unmistakable." I grinned at her.

Ms. Ramirez's smile was gone. She regarded me silently for a moment. "What is it I can do for you, Mr. McKenna?" Her voice was wooden.

"Jennifer Salazar said I should call on the Public Relations manager to get information on the Salazar family, you know, business history, all the thrill-a-minute stuff that makes a family like the Salazars so exciting."

"Jennifer is a little girl," Ms. Ramirez said, her suspicions obvious.

"Was," I said. "They sure do grow up fast, don't they?" I chuckled. "Actually, Gramma Salazar - that's what we call Mrs. Salazar - she said I should just talk to the chairman of the board. She was going to call him. But I liked Jennifer's idea better. I'd hate to bother the chairman. Anyway, Jennifer said that as P.R. manager, you'd probably know better than the chairman who in the company could best fill me in on all those exciting moments where family matters intersect with the business. It's just one side to the book, of course, but an important side nonetheless."

"I'm sorry, Mr. McKenna, but I need to see some authorization from the family before I can proceed."

"Well now, Ms. Ramirez. I'm not like an IRS agent or something. I'm just a writer. We don't carry authorization papers." I reached for my wallet. "If you want my drivers license, see who I am and all that, help yourself."

She gave me a dismissive wave before I had my wallet open. "You must see it from my perspective."

"Of course, you're right." I pointed toward her phone. "Why don't you call up the Salazars. Ask Helga if Gramma is around. She'll tell you."

"Helga?"

"Their housekeeper. She's sort of the gatekeeper for the telephone. Normally, you can't get past her if you're not a family friend. But mention my name, she'll let you through."

Ms. Ramirez hesitated.

"Here," I said, smiling. "I know the number." I stood up and picked up her phone. "You dial nine on this thing?"

"Uh, yes, but..."

"Great," I said, ignoring her protest. "I punched 9, then dialed Street's number.

"Hello?" Street said in my ear.

"Good afternoon, Helga. Owen McKenna calling. How are you this fine day?"

"Owen, what are you doing?" Street said.

"Is the weather still nice, or are you having another one of those spring snow storms?"

"You're talking for someone else's benefit, is that it?" Street said.

"Hot sun, blue skies? Great. Anyway, sorry to bother you, but on this biography thing? I'm here at Salazar West and they need authorization before talking to me. Is Gramma around? No? Okay, how about Jennifer?" I heard Street talking to Jennifer in the background. Then Jennifer picked up the phone.

"Hello, Owen? What's going on?"

"Hi, Jennifer. Owen McKenna here. I'm down in San Francisco at Salazar West, like you and Gramma told me?"

"I get it," Jennifer said. "I'm supposed to play along."

"Right," I said. "So I did like you said and looked up Ms. Ramirez. She's been most helpful. But before she gives me any of the background information that will help me on our little project, she feels she should have authorization from the family. Of course, I hate to bother you, but I'm very glad that they are so protective of your privacy and all. Anyway, Helga said Gramma was out, but maybe you could explain to Ms. Ramirez about the biography of the family and that it is all right to talk to me."

"This is fun!" Jennifer said. "I've never played tricks like these before. Just to make sure I do it right, I should establish my identity, drop a few bits of insider information and then ask her to tell you whatever you want, is that it?"

"Great," I said. "I'll put her on." I handed the phone to Ms. Ramirez.

"Hello. This is Ms. Ramirez. Is this Jennifer Salazar?"

I walked away from the desk and admired a Robert Brady sculpture that stood on a pedestal. It was carved of wood sticks and depicted a woman with wings. Behind me I heard Ms. Ramirez asking some questions that few besides a Salazar would know the answers to. After a minute she hung up.

"It seems, Mr. McKenna, that you are legitimate. I'm sure you understand that I must be careful."

"Of course."

"Now how is it that I can help you?"

"Gramma and Jennifer have told me nearly everything I need about the last eight or ten years. But prior to Melissa's death, I know little. Gramma is still too upset about that horrible event to talk about it. And Jennifer was too young. So what I really need is someone who knew the business and the family well. A family friend who Gramma and Jennifer have forgotten to mention. Or a company officer who's been around for many years, especially if they are familiar with the lake house. Then I'd like you to call that individual and ask them to talk to me."

Ms. Ramirez put her fingertips together. "There is one gentleman who comes to mind. He goes back way before the plane crash that killed Abraham Salazar and his son Joseph." She paused. "But he and Abraham didn't get along well. And he is feeble. He might not be willing to talk to you."

"Will you ask him?"

"Yes." She picked up the phone and started dialing. "He was an early investor in the company. Had a lot of stock. But there was a series of disagreements and he left the company."

"What is his name?"

"Immanuel Salazar. Abraham's older brother."

TWENTY-FOUR

M s. Ramirez placed the call and explained about my request to visit Mr. Salazar. She waited for some time while someone on the other end relayed the information. After a minute she said thank you and hung up.

"Immanuel has agreed to see you. But he's leaving soon for his house in Acapulco. If you want to talk to him you'll have to travel to Acapulco or else see him shortly."

"Where does he live?" I asked.

"On an island off Santa Barbara."

"Is there ferry service?"

"No. It is his private island. You'd have to find a private launch." Ms. Ramirez looked at her watch. "Even if you could, there is not enough time to catch a flight to Santa Barbara and then catch a boat ride."

"You're saying I should plan to see him in Acapulco."

"Either that or charter a plane and fly directly to the island."

"There is an airstrip on the island?"

"From what I've heard, Mr. Salazar's island has everything."

"I don't suppose," I said, "that Salazar West has a corporate jet that is about to make an errand run toward Santa Barbara."

"Actually, we have two jets. But one is somewhere

near Moscow with our V.P. of Marketing. And the other is in Singapore. You've heard of the Pacific Rim Trade Summit?"

"Of course," I lied.

After I left the Salazar West building I spent twenty minutes at a pay phone talking to air charter companies. I finally found one that had a plane available. A turbo-charged Cessna 402, the woman said, that would get me wherever I wanted to go faster than anything else available. She politely explained that I would need to put a deposit on file, a figure that would max out one of my platinum cards. She then told me the fee which would max out another one.

I remembered Jennifer's millions and decided I'd get paid back eventually, so I gave the woman the go-ahead. She said the plane would be waiting by the time I got to the airport.

I found a cab and we raced down 101 to San Francisco International.

An hour later I was the lone passenger in a seven-seat, twin-engine plane with two pilots, one female, one male, both in their middle twenties. The young woman was in the left seat. I heard them file a flight plan as we taxied to the runway.

"We're cleared for takeoff, sir," the woman captain said. "Is your belt fastened?" She looked back at me.

I nodded.

They talked into their headset mikes, pushed the throttles forward and we accelerated down the runway. The plane rose at a steep angle.

"This ship seems fast for a prop," I said to the pilots. "What speed do you rotate?"

"Takeoff around one hundred," the copilot said.

"Cruise at two-thirty. You a flyer?"

"Did some years ago. Sunday stuff. VFR hops around the Bay Area. You shooting for the majors?"

"Like everyone else," the captain said, cynicism in her voice. "But even if we get there, it's not like the old days. Job security went out the window and the pay is nowhere as good as it used to be. An older friend of mine flies left seat on the seven-forty-seven for United. He had the Hawaii route for years. Now they cut him back to domestic flights. Next thing you know, they'll ask him to fill in right seat on the seven-thirty-seven."

We made a sweeping turn over the San Francisco peninsula. In a minute the great blue sheet of the Pacific appeared. We arced out over the ocean and turned toward the noon day sun.

The coast was visible to our left as we shot south at an altitude much lower than the airlines fly. I watched intently as we passed Monterey Bay and then the rugged coast of Big Sur. The Hearst Castle at San Simeon stood regally on the green hills, a monument to another era. Soon, I recognized the big rock that sits in Morro Bay. After that the coast veered out and we did a big turn to stay over the water.

"Vandenburg Air Force Base down to the left," the captain called out to me. "Missile test center, the works."

I saw runways and military facilities on coastal land so gorgeous the federal government could sell it and buy another planet with the proceeds.

"We're coming in toward the Channel Islands," the pilot announced a few minutes later as the plane lost altitude. "Most of them are a national park. The one you want is a bit southwest. Farther out to sea. I'm eager to see it."

We made another turn. I saw out the starboard window a narrow, green isle maybe three miles long and half a mile wide. Near one end were two rugged peaks. The island's perimeter was made of rocky cliffs, caressed with the white foam crescents of crashing waves. On both ends of the island were buildings. A winding road connected them. Near the center of the island I could see the landing strip perched on a high plateau. The plane dropped out of the sky and settled down on a wide, serious runway. We braked quickly and taxied toward an angular building with many tall windows. It looked like a yuppie ski lodge in Wyoming. The pilot braked to a stop next to a Lear Jet. A gentleman in a blue uniform with gold stripes down the pant legs emerged and waved at our plane. He was in his seventies and had a trim white moustache.

"I understand this is a round trip, correct?" the pilot said to me.

"Yes. Only I don't know how long I'll be here. Probably an hour or more."

"No problem," she said. "I'm sure they explained per hour ground costs."

"They did indeed," I said.

We stepped out into warm sunshine and cool ocean breeze.

"Good day, sir," the older man in the blue suit said to me, quickly divining that I was the featured passenger. "My name is Jaspar Lawrence." As he spoke he was looking at the woman pilot, checking the patches on her sleeve. He didn't seem pleased.

"Owen McKenna." I shook his hand. "Ms. Ramirez from Salazar West talked to somebody here and explained that I'd be calling on Immanuel Salazar. By request of his grand niece, Jennifer Salazar."

"So I've been informed. I'm to take you to the house." He turned to the pilots. "You'll find everything you need in the flight building." He pointed toward the lodge. "To the left as you go in the door are the lounge and kitchen.

Help yourself to whatever food you like. And you might like to check out the room to the right. You'll be amused at our electronics. We are," he said with emphasis, "a fully equipped international airport."

"You have a customs station?" the captain asked.

Jaspar grinned. It appeared that if he had to confront women pilots, at least he could impress them. "Mr. Salazar has a special arrangement with those boys." He pointed to the Lear jet. "If you'd like to check out my plane, it's unlocked. But please don't take it for a spin." He gave them a dapper grin. "Mr. Salazar doesn't allow anyone but me to fly it." He turned to me. "Come along now, Mr. McKenna."

"You've got them green with envy," I said.

"Fun, isn't it," he said. "They always dismiss old guys."

"Until," I said, "they find out you own the earth."

I followed him to a gleaming silver Audi Quattro. "How many roads are there on this island?" I asked as we got in.

"Just the one from the house on the south end to the observatory on the north end." He shifted into first gear and pulled away.

"Observatory?"

"Mr. Salazar is an amateur astronomer of some repute. He has discovered and named three comets. Immanuel Eins, Zwei, and Drei."

We drove along the black-topped road that followed the ridgeline toward the south. Jaspar never shifted above third gear. The twisting road was high and often bare of roadside trees, making the ocean visible on both sides of the island.

After a mile, Jaspar slowed. We rounded a bend and came upon a drive lined with Cypress trees misshapen by the buffeting of high winds. Jaspar turned in. After a quarter mile the column of Cypress opened and the drive turned around in a big circle.

Jaspar pulled to a stop and got out.

"Please come with me, sir," he said.

There was an elaborate fountain in front of the house. The artist who designed it had done for flowing water what Escher did to architectural principles. The water tumbled over marble pedestals and landed in pools. The pools were connected at odd angles by marble channels that were cleverly shaped so that it appeared as if the water flowed in an endless perpetual circle, sometimes falling down, sometimes flowing uphill against gravity.

Around the fountains were gardens overflowing with cala lilies. Lounging in one bed of flowers was an amorphous bronze sculpture by Henry Moore. Knowing what most artists are up to, I wasn't fooled. I knew it was another female figure.

Immanuel Salazar's residence was a second cousin to the Sydney Opera House. It sat on a bluff above the sea. It had a bright white roof that curved and swooped up to points that jutted out over the edge of the cliffs.

We walked past the fountain down a path of crushed white stone and entered the house through a glass door that was nearly indistinguishable from the glass wall in which it hung.

Inside was an entry room that looked like a lobby to a modern art museum. On one tall, white wall was a huge Diebenkorn painting from his Ocean Park series. In the center of the flagstone floor grazed a Debra Butterfield horse. The animal was a version of F. Scott Fitzgerald's test. Was I sharp enough to entertain at the same time the two mutually-exclusive concepts in front of me, that the sculpture was as beautiful and graceful as a real horse, and that it was made of ugly rough scraps of junk metal?

Jaspar was part way down a hall when he turned to see

what was taking me.

"Coming," I said.

In the corridor I was introduced to a young Vietnamese housekeeper.

We went past a living room with a wall of glass that overlooked the blue Pacific. The other walls were painted a buttery yellow and were adorned with paintings. In one corner stood a black grand piano.

At the end of the corridor was a bedroom with another wall of glass and another grand view. In front of the glass, propped up on an articulated hospital bed, lay Immanuel Salazar.

Jaspar announced our entrance. "Good afternoon, sir. Your guest Mr. McKenna has arrived."

A thin hand, yellow white, reached out from under the covers and waved us over.

We walked to the front of the bed. Jaspar introduced me and then withdrew from the room.

The man before me looked like a ghost. He was well into his nineties. His skin was so translucent I thought one might hold him up to the light and see the silhouette of his bones. Only his neck and head and left hand emerged from the covers. He was hairless, whether from age or from drug treatments I could not tell. But despite his shriveled body, he had eyes that were bluer than the Pacific. I imagined that little escaped their attention.

"The woman at Salazar West told me your first name, Mr. McKenna." Salazar said in a withered voice. "But I forget."

"Owen," I said.

"Owen," he said, nodding. "A good name. Welsh antecedents, I suppose." Salazar struggled to clear his throat. "I recall that the term Owenism was used to describe the socialistic philosophy of Robert Owen, a Welsh social reformer in the early Nineteenth Century. There was Wilfred Owen, too. The English poet. And of course you know the exploits of Sir Richard Owen."

I grinned at him. "Mr. Salazar, you greatly over-estimate me."

"So they started using Owen as a first name, huh? Now, take Immanuel." The old man coughed several times, then paused to catch his breath. "Imagine being saddled with such a Biblical extravagance. It's a wonder I didn't grow up to be a monk." He gazed off into the Pacific. "Although the work wouldn't have been bad. And I do like illuminated manuscripts."

"Mr. Salazar," I said after a long moment of wondering how much he could be trusted. "I'm a private detective working for Jennifer Salazar. I believe she is in danger and I wonder if I might ask you a few questions about your family. Specifically, the events around the time of Melissa's death."

"Yes, yes. Of course. I thought that bit about writing a biography sounded like a ruse. Sent by the little Jennifer, are you? Haven't seen her for years. I always liked that little fireball." Immanuel Salazar dissolved into a fit of coughing. I was about to run out of the room and call for Jaspar when the old man picked up an inhaler by his bedside and took several breaths. The coughing subsided. He set the inhaler down and groped for an oxygen mask that was connected to a clear plastic tube. He sucked on it before he spoke. "I know her grandmother wondered if Jennifer pushed her sister off the cliff. Don't blame her if she did. Melissa was a twerp, if you don't mind my vernacular. A regular preening princess. Too smart for her own good. If I were Jennifer, I would have pushed her first chance I got. Jennifer might not have been the genius of her sister, but she was smart enough at six to know she could never be punished for murder, never mind that she couldn't be caught. Masterful plan, that cliff stuff. Always looks like an accident."

"So you still think Jennifer pushed her?"

"Probably not. I think it was an accident. But how can you tell?"

"I have reason to believe that the climber who found Melissa's body on the cliff eventually ended up working as their caretaker. His name was Samuel Sommers. Do you know anything about that?"

Immanuel Salazar started laughing. At first it was a high, weak giggle. Then it grew into a hearty laugh from deep within his frail chest. The laugh transformed into another coughing fit and this time he was slower to grab for the oxygen mask. His body shook with great, wracking, phlegm-choked coughs, and I was about to force the inhaler on him when he finally picked it up and sucked on it between his coughs. Eventually, he calmed and he let it drop to the bed sheets. I saw a distinct smirk on his face.

"What's so funny?" I asked.

He slowly raised up his arm and pointed over to a dresser.

"Excuse me, sir. Something about the dresser?"

He continued to point. He mouthed some words but the air to vocalize them wouldn't come.

I walked over to the dresser. It was ordinary, with several drawers and a top covered with mementos. Perhaps he was pointing at the view beyond, something out on the Pacific.

"The picture, damn it!" he suddenly said.

In a gold photo frame was a faded group shot of several people. I picked it up and waved it toward Immanuel Salazar. "This?" I said.

He nodded vigorously.

I took a closer look at the photo. Women with beehive hairdos and men in plaid suits stood precariously in a boat with the shore of Lake Tahoe as the backdrop. The photographer must have been in another boat.

"Bring it here," the old man wheezed.

I sat on the edge of his bed and held it out.

Immanuel Salazar pointed at the various people. "This is my brother Abraham, and this is his son Joseph. They both died in a plane crash, but you probably know that. This is Abraham's wife. You probably know of her as Gramma. And this distinguished-looking man," he said with emphasis, "is me."

"Of course," I said. I was looking at another woman next to Abraham. She was quite young, with a spectacular smile and large, wide-set eyes. Her hair was tied up behind her head. A few curls trickled down her neck which was so thin and graceful it begged nibbling. She had a tiny waist, a big bosom and shapely hips. Hers was the kind of beauty that rivets the attention of all who see her. I pointed to her. "Who's this?" I asked.

Immanuel didn't respond immediately.

I looked at him.

"You asked about the caretaker, a Mr. Samuel Sommers? That, my good man, is his mother." He waited, pleased for the effect his announcement had on me.

"And her name?"

He gave me a grin wide enough to reveal the too-white coloring of ill-chosen false teeth. "Helga."

TWENTY-FIVE

It took me a minute to absorb the implications. I watched Immanuel closely. "And Samuel Sommer's father?" I asked.

Immanuel Salazar was enjoying the moment. "My dear younger brother Abraham had but few weaknesses. Helga's beauty was matched by a cunning guile. Abraham, I'm sorry to say, succumbed to the combination." He shook his head. "Damn women."

I sat on the edge of the bed holding the photo.

Immanuel continued. "The son Samuel, my nephew, Joseph's half-brother, was dispatched to foster care, aided by occasional anonymous checks. At some point, no one will say how, he learned of his true identity. A deal was brokered after Melissa's death. He was given the job of caretaker. They paid him well and he was given a trust fund. He jumped at the offer. But the terms of the trust are that he can never reveal his biological parents. Some clever lawyer arranged it so that even if someone else reveals Samuel's lineage, the checks to Samuel stop. I don't believe that would stand up in court. But nevertheless, my nephew has a large motivation to be sure that no one discovers his connection to the family."

"Could he have murdered Melissa?"

"Absolutely," Immanuel Salazar said. "Young Samuel has always been fixated on our family from the moment he learned that we are his blood relatives. Imagine his jealousy of those kids who are acknowledged as family members and given everything. A young niece of his, especially someone as obnoxious as Melissa, might be the focus of considerable rage. Remember, Samuel gets a monthly check until he dies. But niece Jennifer gets hundreds of millions." Immanuel stared off into the Pacific. A white cruise ship was the only interruption on the blue plane. "If I were you," he continued, "I'd be concerned for Jennifer's safety."

"May I use your phone?" I asked.

"Certainly." He pointed to his end table.

I dialed Street's number. Jennifer answered it on the second ring. "Hi, Jennifer," I said. "I'm glad you're still there."

"I'm not going anywhere. Not until Smithson is caught. Have you found sufficient evidence against him?"

"I'm getting there. Is Street in?"

After a moment Street came on. "Owen, sweetie," she said. "The peripatetic detective."

"Hi, Street. The reason I called is that Diamond said he was under pressure and that he'd be checking both our houses to see if we might be harboring Jennifer. But now I've new information about Samuel and I don't want Jennifer to go back to the Salazar home."

"Okay. What do you want me to do?"

"I think you and Jennifer should stay at your place, but keep the lights low, keep the blinds shut, don't make any noise and do not, under any circumstances, answer the door. Can you get that across to her?"

"Yeah, sure. Can you say what you found out about Samuel?"

"Let me do some more checking, then I'll get back to you as soon as I can."

Street told me good luck and we hung up. I put the

phone down and turned to Immanuel.

"You are, I gather, charged with Jennifer's safety?" he said.

"Yes. There have been some threatening situations. By way of protecting Jennifer, I'm trying to find out who, if anyone, killed Melissa."

Immanuel got a dazed look again. Then he shook himself. "In addition to Samuel, I would take a closer look at Helga."

"What?"

"You shouldn't be surprised. Mothers look after their brood. If Samuel would kill someone in the way of his line to the throne, surely his mother might do the same for him."

"You believe that?" I said incredulously.

"I don't know what I believe," Immanuel said slowly. "But consider this. If Jennifer were dead, then Samuel would possibly be the sole heir to something approaching a billion dollars. There is the stock already earmarked for Jennifer. And Abraham's widow has hundreds of millions of her own. Of course, she has arranged for the disposition of her money and I'd be surprised if Samuel could successfully contest her will. But he doesn't know that. Neither does Helga. I have already given much of my fortune to various art museums. Again, Samuel has no clue. All he and Helga know is that they are related to a family with money and they've been cut out of most of it. Lot's of motivation there, it seems to me."

"You knew Helga when she was younger," I said. "Did she strike you as the kind of person who could push a child off a cliff?"

Immanuel smiled. "Young Helga was as tempestuous as she was beautiful. And she had a temper. Oh yes." He nodded at some memory. "One time she was bitten on the wrist by a dog. A good sized dog, if memory serves. So she wrung its neck. Picked the poor thing up with those strong German arms and twisted its head until it breathed no more. Yes, Mr. McKenna, I can envision Helga pushing a child off a cliff."

Immanuel picked up a remote and pushed some buttons. In seconds the Vietnamese man appeared with a glass of water and some pills on a tray. Next to the water was a shot glass filled with whiskey. "You won't begrudge an old man his medicine, will you?" Immanuel swallowed the pills with water, then picked up the shot glass and downed it.

"I'm an old man," Immanuel repeated. "I'm cynical, bitter and something of a misanthrope. So you should take everything I say with a grain of salt. There is one person, moreover, who understands far better than I the dynamics of Abraham's family."

"Tell me," I said. "The police are coming for Jennifer. They will put her back in her house where she is an easy target. I don't have much time."

Immanuel started coughing, sucked on his inhaler, breathed oxygen, then calmed. "This person is in isolation. Joseph's widow, Alicia Salazar. Jennifer's mother."

"I thought she was institutionalized. Schizophrenic."

"That's what they say," Immanuel said.

"What do you mean?"

"Just what I said. That's what they say."

"You don't believe it?"

"Put it this way," the old man said wearily. He leaned his head back and rested it against the pillow. "There is something wrong with the woman. She is disturbed. No doubt about it. But a paranoid schizophrenic needing to be locked up? I doubt it."

I was beginning to lose my center. Where once I had a simple murder case with John Smithson as my suspect, I now had a complex family where everyone seemed to have a motive for killing Melissa. Even the old man in front of me had admitted to disliking Melissa.

"Where is Alicia?" I asked "Can I talk to her?"

"She is in a secure facility that operates under the name of Saint Mary's Sanitarium of Nevada. It would more properly be called Saint Mary's Prison. It is in the desert north of Las Vegas. And no, I don't think they'll let you talk to her."

I stood up. "Mr. Salazar, I'm indebted to you."

"Owen," Immanuel said. His voice was low and ragged. "If someone really did murder Melissa, I hope you catch him. Or her. I didn't like Melissa, but she certainly didn't deserve to die. Neither does Jennifer. And now I must get ready. I have a villa above the bay in Acapulco. Because my lung ailment is acting up I'm going there this afternoon. It was good to talk to you, Mr. McKenna."

I was spooked as I left the room. The possibility that Jennifer was in imminent danger suddenly seemed much more real to me. I trusted that she would stay quiet and out of sight at Street's condo.

Jaspar Lawrence met me in the hall. "Would you like a drive back to the airstrip, sir?"

"Please."

When I returned to the flight building, the pilots were sipping sodas and watching a football game on TV.

"Ready to return to San Francisco?" the captain said.

"No. I need to fly to Las Vegas. Can we do that?"

The woman thought a moment. "Without refueling? Possibly. Let me run the numbers. Bob? Can you get on the radio and see what they've got for our schedule?"

I said goodbye to Jaspar. Fifteen minutes later we accelerated down the runway, and the turboprop screamed into the sky toward Las Vegas.

TWENTY-SIX

That evening the captain brought our plane into Las Vegas on a low glide path. The lights of the hotels on the Strip sparkled in the twilight as we touched down. The distant mountain silhouettes stood out as rugged black shapes against the navy blue sky.

After we came to a stop, I signed some forms and departed, knowing that I could catch a scheduled flight to Reno/Tahoe International when I was through on the desert.

Inside the airport I headed to the rental car counters, each of which had long lines. I picked one and forty minutes later had the keys to a forest green Ford Taurus. It was dark as I left the airport and pulled onto the freeway, merging with the rush of traffic in America's fastest-growing city.

I'd gotten an address for Saint Mary's Sanitarium out of the phone book. It was north of Las Vegas in a town called Hollybrook. I followed the freeway and then a state highway until I saw the sign for Hollybrook.

The town of Hollybrook was centered around a town square that had a band shell in one corner. I drove down main street past the square and watched the signs. I went several blocks before I found Lincoln Avenue, the street listed in the phone book. I made a guess at the numbering system and turned right.

Lincoln Avenue went up a hill, through a neighborhood of old clapboard homes and then out of town. In the distance I saw a grouping of lights in the night. The lights looked like those of a small refinery in the desert.

I turned in between two stone pillars. A back-lit sign said Saint Mary's in flowing green script. I followed a drive which snaked over and around small desert hills as it gradually climbed up to the collection of lights. Eventually, I arrived at a gate made of chain-link fencing. Flood lights lit the fence and showed six strands of barbed wire across the top. To the left was a gate house. Above it a sign said Saint Mary's Sanitarium. This sign was painted on rough wood and was nothing like the friendly sign out on Lincoln Avenue. A large, solid woman walked out and approached my car as I stopped. She was wearing a maroon uniform with brass buttons and a wide, shiny black belt. She had a .38 revolver in a holster, a radio strapped to her chest, and a sap hanging from a loop on her belt. She was smaller than my six-six, but not by much. I hit the button to roll down my window.

"Visiting hours are ten to noon in the morning and five to eight in the evening," she said.

"Right," I said. "I just flew out from Florida and wanted to see where mom lives. I'll be back tomorrow. Thanks." I rolled up the window, backed up and turned the car around. I didn't like her style and I didn't like the gun on her hip.

I drove back out to Lincoln Avenue and looked for another route into the desert hills toward the hospital. I found only one. It was a street with scattered warehouses. The road went a few blocks and stopped. I turned around and went back. There were few opportunities to leave Lincoln Avenue and none of them went very far toward Saint Mary's. The hospital appeared isolated.

I pulled over and parked behind a junkyard with

a mountain of used tires. I got out and locked the door. Inside the trunk I found the tire iron. Universal tool of bad intentions.

Las Vegas sits on a low desert and gets hot enough to fry eggs during the day. But the night air was cold and, of course, I didn't have a jacket, just a flimsy windbreaker.

I headed into the hills, moving at a brisk pace to stay warm. My footfalls landed on dark sand and rocks. Running on uneven ground at night is a good way to sprain an ankle. I tried to keep my leg and foot muscles tense, preparing for every step to be on a rolling rock.

The air was deceptive, over-flowing with sage and other herbal scents as if I were in a verdant oasis. At the tops of hills I could see the sparkling lights of Saint Mary's floating against the black landscape. In the valleys I plunged into darkness with only the stars to tell me where the rise of earth met the sky. At each hilltop I seemed to get no closer to the hospital. I kept on, up and down, and suddenly found myself at a chain-link fence.

It was the same as the fence at the guarded gate. It stood seven feet tall from ground to the base of the barbed strands. The barbed wires angled in and up another two feet. As I contemplated how to break in I realized that the fortifications were designed to keep people from getting out. Saint Mary's was looking less like a psychiatric hospital and more like the prison Immanuel Salazar alluded to.

Unfortunately, I had no flashlight and the ambient light was too dim to easily see if the fence had an alarm. One aspect of the fence was apparent. There was no visible insulation where it touched the ground. Which meant that it wasn't wired for electric shock. That didn't rule out motion detectors, stress sensors, sound monitors and infrared beams.

I could climb the fence, throw my windbreaker over

the barbed strands and jump to the ground, but that left the problem of escape. Much better to make an opening through which I could exit as well as enter.

The fencing appeared to be imbedded in the ground. One stab in the dirt with the tire iron proved otherwise. I waited for alarm bells and floodlights, but none appeared. So I started at one post and worked toward the next, levering the tire iron under the fence chain and lifting upward. After my second pass between the posts, I'd warped the fencing such that it lifted six inches or more above the sandy desert.

When the chain link seemed to give no more I started in on the dirt. The tire iron made a lousy shovel, but it was effective at dislodging stones and rocks. I dug at the dirt, sweeping it to the side. In ten minutes I'd made an opening that was a foot and a half between the bottom of the fence and the dirt.

I got down and slid on my back, snaking underneath. From the other side I pushed down the warped fencing to make my opening less obvious. If floodlights came on it would not be immediately apparent where I came in. Then again, it would not be easy for me to see where I could get out. So I walked backward toward the hospital and sighted to find a reference point that would lead to the opening. There seemed to be none. I moved sideways and tried again with no luck. Turning, I considered the hospital and all of its lights. Eventually I found a line. If I stood so that the two lights directly in front of the main entrance were lined up, and then I turned around and looked at a flashing red light out near Hollybrook, the opening in the fence was directly before me. To test it, I moved fifty yards away.

I ran across the landscape with my eyes on the streetlights above the hospital entrance. When they lined up I turned to face toward the distant town. Then I ran toward the flashing red light. When I got to the fence my opening was only eight feet to my right. Perfect.

The best way into the hospital was not clear as I looked at its various levels and windows and doors. The main entrance was well-lit, a disadvantage, but it might be unlocked even after visiting hours. The other doors were darker, but would likely be locked and alarmed.

I decided on the main entrance. If only I had a clipboard and a white coat. I hiked through the darkness. When I was fifty yards from the entrance, floodlights lit the grounds and a siren cut through the calm night air.

TWENTY-SEVEN

If I ran away, I'd likely escape without difficulty. But then they'd be suspicious of all strangers. In the morning I might be denied a visit to Alicia Salazar. If instead I sprinted toward the hospital, something they wouldn't expect, I could hide near the building and maybe find my way in.

I was halfway there when the main door opened and two guards spilled out into the flood-lit night, guns in their hands. Sprinting, I dove for a group of bushes near a service door. I was scrambling under the scratchy foliage when the adjacent door opened and another guard ran out. He too had a gun. He swept a large flashlight beam across the landscape and talked on his radio. "This is Clint at the laundry door. I don't see anything. I'm going around to the west side." His light grazed my hiding place. Then he moved off. I thought about their guns. They were out of place even in a hospital that locks up crazy people.

I squeezed out from under the bushes and ran up to the laundry door. It was locked. If I jimmied it with my tire iron, they would know someone was in the building as soon as the guard came back. I wanted them to think it was a false alarm, so I retreated to the bushes and waited.

The guard came back, put a key in the door and went in. This time I was ready. I left my tire iron in the bushes and ran up to the door. Just as it was closing, I slipped my business card into the door jamb. The door shut with a solid sound. No one would know that the latch wasn't engaged.

I stood in the dark for three long minutes and then pulled open the door and stepped inside. The door closed behind me.

I was in a bright room permeated with the smell of hot cotton towels. There were large stainless steel washers and dryers. On a counter were stacks of folded sheets. A door at the other end of the room was closed. I crept across the linoleum tile, ready to grab and subdue anyone who appeared.

When I got to the other door I put my ear to the metal and listened. Nothing. I turned the knob, pulled the door toward me and peeked out.

There was a long corridor that looked like every hospital corridor I'd ever been in. White tile floor, acoustic tile ceiling, pastel green walls. The doors in the hallway had windowpanes in them and the hallway lights were dimmed, no doubt out of concern for the people sleeping in the rooms. Down near the other end of the hall were the bright lights of a nurse's station. A female nurse in a white uniform moved in and out of my sight. I froze against the wall. A male nurse appeared. The two nurses talked. A guard ran up from an adjoining hall, shouted something, then ran away. The nurses moved out of sight.

I stayed against one wall as I moved down the hall-way.

I pulled my flea-market badge out of my wallet and clipped it on my windbreaker. Nerves made my breathless demeanor real as I rushed up to the nurse's station. "Did Graham come by here?" I said.

The female nurse jerked her head up from her computer screen. "Oh! You scared me!"

"Sergeant Graham? Short, wide guy with a moustache?" I held my hands out to approximate his size.

Her eyes went to my badge.

"Sergeant Graham!" I barked. "You see him?"

She shook her head. "No, I..."

The male nurse behind her looked up from the
wastebasket where he was clipping his nails. "Naw, man.
We heard the siren, but nobody been here but our own
guards."

"Damn!" I said under my breath. "Frost and Baum-
garten are on the main entrance, I'm covering the west
entrance and Graham is supposed to be in the center corridor!" I stomped around for effect. "I better run up to her
room myself. The doc will be there, but what if Graham
isn't with him?! Where is it?" I demanded. "Which floor?"

"Excuse me, officer, I don't know what you mean."

"Of course you do! They said you were all alerted!
Christ, I can't remember. The woman the perp's after!"
I paced the floor in front of them. "Alice something." I
clicked my fingers as I paced. "With a Z. No, it was S.
Alice... Her doctor told me himself. Salazar, that's it! What
floor? Her doctor is with her."

"Sir, Dr. Hauptmann is in Baltimore at a medical
conference."

"No, he isn't! Two minutes ago he was driven here
from the airport by Captain Meyer, blue lights flashing,
and three other cops besides me watched him get out of
the squad and run into this hospital! Now what floor is
she on?"

"I'm sorry, sir. Alicia Salazar is in maximum security. Unless I have Dr. Hauptmann's permission, I'm not
allowed to..."

I leaned over the counter and poked my forefinger into
the soft flesh at the hollow of her throat. "If Alice Salazar is

being butchered into pieces while you're sitting on your fat ass quoting me the rule book, I'll personally escort you to Judge Rivera." I scrambled around the counter and lifted her up by her sleeve. "Take me to Dr. Hauptmann and Alice Salazar!"

The woman whimpered, grabbed her keys off the desk and led me away. I turned back to the man who had been clipping his nails. "You see Graham, you tell him to watch this corridor!"

The woman led me toward the elevator.

"We don't have time," I said. "Where's the stairs?"

She turned, whimpering, and walked over to a metal door. I jerked it open and we trotted up two floors. The nurse put a key in the door and let us into a darkened hallway like the one on the main floor.

"Which room?" I said in her ear. She didn't answer me. "Which room!" I yelled.

She jumped at the volume. "Three-fourteen." She was frightened. "I don't see Dr. Hauptmann," she cried.

"He's obviously in Alice's room trying to protect her. Hurry!"

When we got to room 314, the nurse quickly put her face to the window. "He's not there! Dr. Hauptmann isn't there!" She was hysterical.

I held onto her sleeve and grabbed the key she was holding. I put it in the lock and turned the knob.

The nurse resisted me as I dragged her into the dark room and ran my hand across the inside wall feeling for a light switch. There was none. Then I remembered seeing a switch on the wall in the hallway. I reached back outside the door, found it and flipped it on, suddenly enraged at the loss of liberty for the residents of the rooms.

I turned and pushed the struggling nurse into the room. I was vaguely aware of a figure cowering on the bed, sheets pulled tight to her neck, when I was struck on the side of my head.

I went down.

As my consciousness flickered, my rage exploded. I raked my arm out as I hit the floor. My hand struck fabric over hard bone. I clenched my eyes shut, concentrating on awareness, and took hold of the fabric. I jerked on the cloth and rolled to give an extra pull. A heavy man fell to the floor next to me.

He grabbed me and pummeled me with his fists. I held him in a bear hug. My fury about the mis-located light switch was clearing my head. I jerked up and jammed the hulking figure into the wall. He clambered to his feet. But I was already up.

The guard before me was nearly my height and had 30 pounds on me. He had the posture and steps that indicated some experience fighting. He was mad. But I was enraged. I didn't wait for his move. I put two solid punches in his gut. A jab to his chin moved his head back. My hook was inelegant, but it bounced his head against the wall and he slid quietly to the floor.

I slipped the guard's handcuffs off his belt, grabbed the nurse and attached her wrist to his ankle. I found the handcuff key on the guard's key ring and put it in my pocket. I turned to the poor frightened figure on the bed.

She looked like Jennifer, but twenty years older and twenty pounds thinner. Her face was gaunt with dark brown eyes as large as those of a cancer victim. She had coarse, shiny black hair, cut just below her ears. She pulled away in fear as I reached for her.

"You can't!" the nurse said. "She's due for her medicine. She must have it!"

I didn't know about schizophrenia, but I knew that whatever the woman before me was on, it wasn't good for her. And what Immanuel had said had me doubly suspicious. I held my hand out. "Come on," I said to the emaciated woman. "Time to go."

She looked at me, her huge eyes sad and confused and afraid. She didn't move.

"You're going home," I said. "You're daughter is waiting for you."

"Don't listen to him!" the nurse screamed. "He's a kidnapper! Don't listen!"

The woman's mouth moved, but no sound came out.

I stepped closer. "Trust me. I'm here to take you away from this prison. I'm taking you to your daughter. She's fourteen now. She wants to see you."

She mouthed a silent word. Then again. "Jenny," she said on her third effort. "Jenny?" Her eyes were watery.

"My name is Owen, Alicia. Jenny hired me to find you, to take you home. Come." I took her frail, skinny hand in mine. She shifted toward the edge of the bed.

"No!" the nurse screamed. "Dr. Hauptmann will be outraged. She has to have her medicine!"

At the word medicine, Alicia's eyes became alarmed. She looked in fear toward the nurse.

"No more medicine," I said in a calm voice. "I won't let them give you any more medicine." I bent down and spoke quietly to the nurse. "If you say one more word, I'll hit you." The nurse quivered and said nothing more.

The door opened and another guard rushed in.

"What is going on here?" he yelled as the door shut.

I kneed him in the groin. He bent over, gasping. I grabbed his hair and pulled his chin down onto my rising knee. He fell limp to the floor.

I turned back to Alicia. She was sitting on the edge of the bed. The sheets were off. She was wearing a pale blue cotton dress that came to just below her knees. Her feet were bare. I reached for her hands and pulled her to her feet. She was wobbly. I shot a warning glance toward the nurse who kept quiet. Then I quickly led Alicia to the door, stepping over the unconscious guards on the floor. The corridor was empty. Alicia and I did a fast, lurching walk toward the stairwell. I opened the door and heard voices. I let the door shut and pulled Alicia toward the window at the end of the hall.

It had tempered windowpanes with security wires imbedded in the glass. It was also locked. I gently moved Alicia back and aimed my best sidekick at the sill. The entire panel, glass and metal rim exploded outward.

Shouts came from the stairwell. The door burst open. "Come," I said to Alicia. "Jenny is this way. I'll carry you." Before she could respond I picked up all one hundred pounds of her and carried her to the broken window.

There was a ten foot drop to a roof. My choices were limited. Several guards were running toward us. I swung a leg over the shattered sill, leaned forward and got my body and Alicia's through the opening. I whispered in her ear. "Alicia, put your head next to me and hold very tight." In a miracle of faith she tucked her head to my chest and squeezed her arms feebly. I swung both legs over.

My right arm held Alicia. My left hand gripped the window sill. Broken glass ground into my finger tendons. I clutched Alicia's body as I let go.

We hit the roof and crumpled. Alicia spilled from my grasp. She cried out as she rolled across the coarse roof stones. I scrambled to my feet as the guards got to the window. I made a motion with my hand as if I were drawing a gun. They ducked back from the opening. Alicia struggled to her feet. I picked her up and ran across the roof. She held tight and made no sound. Gunfire erupted from behind and above us.

We came to the edge of the roof. It was another twenty feet to the ground. The guards shouted. I scrambled along the edge of the roof until we came to an access ladder.

A door opened. Silhouetted against the light I saw several guards run out onto the roof. There were now six or eight of them running toward us. Alicia bowed her head and clung to me. The guards fired more shots, but didn't hit us.

We struggled down the ladder. Then I ran with her across the flood-lit grounds. When the lights in front of the main entrance lined up, I turned to look for the red light down in Hollybrook.

It wasn't there. I stood motionless, astonished. Then it suddenly flashed. I ran toward it as shouts rose up behind me. I didn't look back until I reached the fence and dumped Alicia in the dirt.

My lungs burned. I sucked air as men with flashlights filled the landscape behind us. My opening in the fence was not there. I ran left and then right. Then I remembered that I'd pushed the fence partway back to the ground. I looked again. It was directly in front of me.

I grabbed the chain-link fencing and jerked up. It rose ten or twelve inches, making a good space above the depression where I'd dug the dirt. "Alicia," I said. "We're going under the fence. Can you crawl? I'll hold it up while you crawl."

Searchlights suddenly fell onto us. I continued to hold the fence. I saw Alicia look at me, her eyes lit by the searchlights. In her eyes was more fear and pain than any human should have to endure. But I was amazed at her resolve despite her drugged state. She dropped to the ground and slid under the fence. I followed and, realizing that her bare feet were not up to rigors of the desert, I picked her up once again and carried her off.

TWENTY-EIGHT

By the time the first guard reached the break in the fence we were down into one of the dark valleys between the hills, away from the searchlights. I set Alicia down and stopped to catch my breath. She stood in the dark, unsure of what to be afraid of or who the enemy was. Although it was too dark to tell, I knew that she was looking to me for the answer.

"Where is Jenny?" she said in a weak voice. Her accent had hints of American Southwest, yet the question had a strange inflection as if English were not her first language. I decided it was probably the drugs they had her on. I had no idea what would happen when the drugs wore off.

"At home in Lake Tahoe," I said between panting breaths. "I'm going to bring you there. My car is about a quarter mile from here. Do you think you can make it?"

I thought I saw her nod. She turned, started to walk away from the hospital and fell in the dirt.

I scooped her up and placed her on her feet. My arms were tired. "Alicia, I'm going to turn and you're going to get on my back. Like kids do. Okay?"

Another nod in the dark.

I turned and backed up to her. I did a deep knee bend. "Climb on my back, Alicia."

She made a weak effort, but she didn't have the strength. Finally, I wrapped her arms around my neck and boosted her up, grabbing her skinny thighs and lifting her into place.

"Are you hanging on tight?" I asked her.

"Yes," came the feeble answer.

"Concentrate on your hands," I said. "I'll hold you up, but you need to concentrate on your hands and keep them clamped around my neck."

She obeyed in concept. But I knew her grip was frangible and I had to bend over at a steep angle to keep her from falling off my back. Nevertheless, it was better than holding her in my arms, and we made good time across the desert.

The rental Ford was where I'd left it. I set Alicia down and leaned her against the hood while I fumbled for my key. I unlocked the doors, set her into the front seat and ran around to the driver's side.

With the headlights off, I pulled out and drove past the mountain of used tires and on toward Lincoln Avenue. A siren sounded in the distance. I stopped well back from the street. In moments the siren and then flashes of lights grew on the road in front of us. The glow of headlights suddenly appeared and a police car flashed by, blue and red lights flickering. A second later the cruiser was followed by an unmarked sedan with a single red beacon stuck on the side of its roof.

I knew they would eventually figure out that I'd parked by the used tire mountain. It would be easy to follow my tire tracks. So I pulled out after them so that my marks in the gravel at the side of the road would show that I had gone that way. When I got to the first intersection where the blacktop widened, I made a slow U-turn and headed back toward downtown Hollybrook.

In front of me, up by the entrance to Saint Mary's, were the lights of more police cars. I took the first turnoff and drove through side streets and quiet neighborhoods.

I knew of only one highway that went through Hollybrook. The police would have the highway covered. And it would not be long before they were searching every street. I could head off into the desert, but the rental car wouldn't get far.

"Where are we going?" Alicia said, her words drawn out slowly.

I didn't want to betray my lack of answers so I said, "Not far." I came to another intersection. There was a trailer park entrance across the street. The sign said Happy Trails Trailer Park and had a picture of Roy Rogers on his horse Trigger. Beyond, in the distance, was the flashing red light I'd sighted on from up at Saint Mary's. Just beyond it was a rotating white light. I realized that the white beacon represented my possible escape.

The local airport.

I drove down the side of the trailer park. A man was walking his dog in the darkness. My headlights were still off. His head turned to watch us cruise by. I immediately turned down the next street, away from the airport, thinking that if he was taking note he'd notice we went away from the airport. I went around several blocks, putting distance between us and the late-night stroller. When I drove back across the road, I looked in the direction of where I'd passed the man and dog. He was out of sight. But farther down the road, coming toward me, was another police car, its lights flashing.

I darted down the block, turned right, raced another block and turned left. Two blocks later I turned right again, keeping my eye out for the airport light. It appeared and then disappeared, although behind what I could not tell.

The town was small and in a minute I was out of the neighborhood and on a barren desert road. The rotating beacon came again. This time I watched it disappear behind a line of trees. Big cottonwood trees. I saw in the starlight a row of them, typical of a stream on the desert. The airport, if it actually was an airport, was on the other side. The road I was on paralleled the stream.

I had to find a bridge. No doubt my road connected with a bridge, but where I did not know. Police lights appeared in my rearview mirror. Then, in the distance in front of me, more flashing lights turned onto my road. I was trapped.

I took my foot off the gas and used the parking brake to slow the car so as not to flash the brake lights and betray my location. The police might not see me in the dark if I got off the road fast enough.

When we slowed, I turned the wheel and we bounced off the shoulder and down onto the desert sand. Dirt flew up from the wheels, making a dust cloud that was certain to be spotted. I drove toward the cottonwoods. The parking brake brought us to an unsure stop in front of the tree trunks.

"Okay, Alicia. Now we have to hurry again." I grabbed the map out of the glove box, jumped out of the car, ran around and pulled her from the passenger seat. "Up on my back like before. Ready? There you go." She was willing but limp.

After I hoisted her up I ran through the trees toward the stream bed that I was certain was there.

The stream was robust, rushing with rapids, and nearly out of its bank with snowmelt from distant mountains. I turned and looked back, wondering if the cops had seen my dust cloud and found the rental car. I saw no lights.

"Alicia, I'm going to carry you across this stream. You're going to feel water on your feet. The water will be cold. Ready?"

I felt her tense.

I waded in. The water was more than cold. It was like ice. I took careful steps, gauging the strength of the current. As long it wasn't too deep, we'd be okay. When the water reached my crotch and Alicia's bare feet we both gasped. I continued on, leaning into the current. The stream got deeper. Soon, it was up to my waist. Alicia started crying as the ice water flowed around her butt. The current pulled hard. I leaned into it. My grip on Alicia was firm, but I felt her arms loosening.

"Hang on, Alicia! Hang on. We're almost there." The water was up to my rib cage. It swept over Alicia's hips. I reached out to take my next step and my foot rolled off a submerged rock. We leaned sideways. I released my grip on Alicia's thigh, shot my arm out and caught an overhanging branch. I was regaining my footing when Alicia let go.

She fell backward into the fast flowing water. Her body turned and her other leg twisted out of my other hand.

I reached for her with my other arm, but she was already gone downstream into the dark, rushing rapids.

TWENTY-NINE

My first impulse was to swim after Alicia. But it was dark. The water was ice cold. If I didn't succumb to hypothermia, I'd likely hit my head on a boulder. It would be better to run.

I pulled on the overhanging branch and jerked myself up onto the far shore. My clothes were leaden with the weight of water as I stumbled down the bank. The cottonwood trees and the bushes at the edge of the water made a maze. I ran through the darkness. Branches scraped my face. There was no point in calling out to Alicia. If she was still alive, she would be too cold to respond.

I ran downstream. When I'd gone far enough that I was certain to be past her, I waded back into the ice water. On my second step I plunged in over my head.

The current pulled me away as I tried to swim toward the bank. My arm hit a submerged log. The blow was numbing, but I hung on. My toes just touched bottom. I lowered myself to gain purchase, then jumped up, vaulting onto the log. From there I leaped to the bank and sprawled in the mud.

I got up and again ran downstream. The stream was wider and shallower where I next waded in. I walked to the middle of the stream with the water up to my thighs and spread my arms wide, hoping to catch Alicia as she floated by.

There was no light except for the rotating beacon at the airport. Its white beam raced across the landscape. I stared upstream, willing my eyes to see in the darkness. The stream was briefly illuminated and then thrown back into darkness.

On the second sweep of the beacon I saw Alicia, mostly submerged, ten yards upstream and coming toward me rapidly. The light was gone as fast as it came and I could only guess where and when Alicia would float by. I judged her to be a bit to my left, so I shuffled sideways.

Something brushed the fingertips of my right hand. I lunged that direction and grabbed Alicia's limp form. There was no tension in her body as I picked her up and carried her out of the rapids.

She was silent when I set her down on the bank. I lay her in the dirt under the cottonwoods and felt her neck for a pulse. There was a slow, weak beat, but she didn't appear to be breathing. I was about to start artificial respiration when she coughed and sputtered and sucked in a breath of air. I pulled her cold, wet hair out of her eyes. She did not seem conscious. She was hypothermic, her core temperature too cold to engage the shivering reflex.

And I had no way to warm her.

I had broken her out of the hospital and now she was going to die if I couldn't get her warm.

I scooped her up, draped her over my shoulder and ran toward the rotating beacon. Two squad cars appeared from the direction of the airport. Their flashers were on. Waving one arm to signal the cops, I rushed toward them across the desert. They didn't see me and drove on toward town.

The white airport beacon suddenly went dark.

It was probably on for an incoming flight of extra law enforcement. Now that they had landed, the beacon was turned off. I continued running. Gradually the airport entrance came into view.

Another vehicle, a dark pickup, cruised out of the airport entrance. It stopped. A man got out, left his door open, and went around and shut the gate behind him. I yelled at him. He couldn't hear me over his blasting radio. I ran faster, hoping to catch his attention. But he got back in his truck and drove off, oblivious to me.

I stopped, near collapse, and lowered Alicia to the dirt. I put her on her side, curled her up in a fetal position and draped myself over her while I gasped for breath, exhaling my hot air under me, into her curled form.

When I regained my strength, I picked her up and we headed for the airport again.

The entrance gate was designed to stop vehicles, not people. I swung my leg over the gate and ran toward the buildings. Alicia was still unmoving and ice-cold. I couldn't tell if she was breathing or not. But I didn't dare stop.

The airport was comprised of two hangars, one work shed with a single dark window and a low building of concrete block. It had windows, a door and a tall utility pole. At its top was the rotating beacon, unmoving and dark.

I carried Alicia to the door and tried the knob.

Locked. Without setting her down, I kicked it open. It swung in and hit a metal garbage can which tipped over and clattered to the floor. There was dim light coming from a Coca-Cola clock on the wall. I found a light switch and turned it on. A row of overhead fluorescent lights filled the room with a greenish, flickering light. I kicked the door shut to keep out the cold breeze and set Alicia down on a faded brown couch. Her skin, in the fluorescent light, was the color of skim milk. There were two doors in one wall. I opened them. One was a utility closet, the other a bathroom. In the bathroom hung a filthy mechanic's shop coat. I grabbed it and brought it to Alicia. "Alicia, we need to get you out of that wet dress. I found a dry coat for you. Help me now."

She was unresponsive. I tried to get the dress up over her hips, but the wet cloth was sticking to her cold skin. I grabbed the fabric at the hem of the dress and ripped it all the way up to the neck line. Then I tore the arm holes apart so that she was freed of the dress without moving. Under the dress she wore wet cotton underpants and no bra. I ripped off the underwear and picked up her clammy nude body. Holding her up I pulled the shop coat over her arms as if I were dressing a manikin. When I had her firmly wrapped up in the coat, I set her down on a dry part of the couch. She was still dangerously hypothermic. I knew the best antidote was slow warming next to another naked human body. But mine, although functional, was wet and very cold.

On the desk was a phone. I picked it up and was about to dial 911 when I saw an old vending machine in the corner behind the door. In addition to coffee, the machine advertised hot cocoa. Just what Alicia needed. I hung up the phone and opened the top desk drawer looking for change. There wasn't any change, but there was the key for the vending machine.

I got the vending door opened, and poured the coins from the collection box out on the desktop. A minute later I had a foam cup of steaming hot chocolate.

Alicia was still lying limp on the couch, her eyes shut, her mouth open. I lifted her into a sitting position, sipped the cocoa to be sure it wasn't too hot and raised the cup to her lips.

"Hot cocoa, Alicia. Drink some cocoa."

Her head lolled. I put the cup to her mouth and slopped some cocoa onto her lips. She moaned as the cocoa dribbled down her chin and onto the shop coat. I'm sure it burned against her frozen skin.

"Come on, Alicia. You need to drink this. Take a little sip." I slopped some more and she cried out.

I set the cup down and patted her on the cheeks firm enough to sting. This time she turned her head. Better. I tried again with the cocoa, and again.

Alicia's eyes stayed shut, but she eventually took a sip. Her right arm came out from her side as if to reach for the cup and then stopped, hovering in mid-air, fingers spread. I got a little chocolate in her and then a little more. She resisted, but I forced it. Eventually, she got down a half of a cup. Not much, but it was heat inside of her.

I could still call 911 for paramedics, but I thought of all those guards and their guns. Something was very wrong at the hospital. Now that it looked like Alicia would make it, I decided to stay with my plan.

We started in on the second cup. I knew it was working when Alicia warmed up enough to start shivering. Her body was wracked by violent spasms, which meant that she was over the worst of the hypothermia.

Alicia opened her eyes. She looked at me and then the room. She appeared frightened but said nothing. Her head vibrated and her teeth chattered. When I raised the cup to feed her more cocoa, she tried to take it from my hand, but her hands shook so much she knocked it to the floor.

By the time Alicia finished the third cup she was much better although still not very cognizant. I was confident enough that she was out of danger that I started searching for keys.

I found them in a masonite cabinet on the wall behind the desk. There were four. Each key hung from a paper fob that was circular and had a thin rim of metal around it. On the fobs were written registration numbers. I took all four keys and turned to Alicia.

"You stay here and drink more cocoa. I'm going outside for a minute. Don't go anywhere. I'll be right back."

Alicia said nothing. She sat on the couch, clutched her foam cup and stared at me. I didn't know what to make of her silence. But her shivering was less violent and her cheeks had turned from blue-white to blotchy red.

I went out into the night and shut the door behind me.

The planes were on the far side of one of the hangars. All four had numbers that matched my keys. One was a Cessna 150 that was missing a prop. Another was a Mooney that was missing the entire engine compartment. Next to the Mooney was an old Piper Cub with canvas wings and only one seat inside. The last plane was a Piper Tomahawk, a trainer built back in the early seventies. It wasn't an ideal plane for cross-country flight, but it looked to be in one piece.

I got up on the wing, opened the door and climbed inside.

I pushed and pulled on the yoke and looked out and behind to see the elevator move down and up. Turning the yoke left and right moved the ailerons on the main wing. The rudder pedals worked, as did the lever that controlled the flaps.

I put the key in the ignition and turned on the navigational gyros. They whirred up a couple of octaves. Both fuel gauges were on full. I turned the fuel selector to the left tank and set the fuel mixture to rich. Then I tried the starter.

The prop rotated one revolution and the engine fired. It ran rough for ten seconds and then smoothed out as the tach climbed to 1500 RPM. The plane buffeted itself with its own propwash. I made sure the brake was on.

Then I throttled back to 700 RPMs and climbed out of the airplane.

Alicia was in the exact same position as I had left her, shivering on the couch. She still had some hot chocolate left in her cup. I got a coffee for me. Then I picked up the phone and dialed Street. It was the middle of the night.

"Hello?" she said, alert and worried.

"Street, it's me. You're awake."

"Owen," Street said. "God, I'm so sorry. They just woke us up."

"Who?" I sipped some coffee.

"The police. Diamond and two other officers. Mrs. Salazar was with them. Owen, they took Jennifer. She struggled against them. She didn't want to go, but they took her! What do you want me to do?"

I saw Alicia looking at me. I didn't know how much she was aware of, but I didn't want to alarm her. "That's unfortunate, but there's nothing to do. I can't talk now. I'm... in a hurry."

"Someone is there," Street said.

"Yes. What I need is a ride. I'm flying in with Jennifer's mother Alicia."

"What?"

"Right. We'll be there in about four hours. Can you be there waiting? Maybe get there early?"

"Sure, Owen. That'll be early morning. I'll have plenty of time to get to Reno. What airline?"

"We're coming into South Lake Tahoe. And we're in a Piper Tomahawk." I drank more coffee.

"Owen, don't tell me you're flying a plane. You haven't flown in years."

"Right. Oh, and Street? Can you bring Spot? We might need him."

"Owen, are you sure you know what you're doing?"

"No. Thanks, sweetheart. I'm looking forward to introducing you to Alicia. She's a real trooper. Oh, one more thing. Did you get an estimated time of...?" I stopped myself, glancing at Alicia.

"Time of death on the body? Yes. It's not what we thought. I took Jennifer to the lab last evening and made some new determinations based on the hygrothermograph readings. I couldn't reconcile the readings with some quirks in the timing of the maggots, the pupas and the succession of insects, especially the arrival of hide beetles. So I asked Diamond if the body could have been moved from a warmer place. He thought a moment and said that the stream in the next ravine over was fed by a hot spring. He didn't think coyotes would drag the body so far up and over the ridge. But if they did, then I could make it work. I figured the heat of the hot spring could raise the temperature where the body was by twenty degrees during the day and forty or more degrees by night. Then my findings made much more sense."

"Which gives us how long since death?"

"Instead of eighteen or twenty days, the body might only be eleven days old."

"Thanks, Street. That is what I needed."

I hung up. Alicia was still watching me. I needed to make one more phone call.

I dialed information for San Francisco and got the number for Smithson's hotel. I dialed the hotel.

"Hello, may I speak to John Smithson, please," I said when the night man answered.

"I'm sorry, sir, but Mr. Smithson checked out this afternoon."

I hung up and guzzled the last of my coffee. Alicia's bare feet caught my eye. They were covered with red scratches and darkening bruises. There was a roll of clear plastic packaging tape in the desk. I tore off pieces of the thread-bare couch fabric, pulled out some stuffing and wrapped the cloth and stuffing around her feet, fashioning makeshift slippers using the tape.

"Time to go," I said to Alicia. I helped her stand up. Her shivering was almost gone. She faltered and I grabbed her. I tried to put her arm over my shoulder, but I was too tall for her. So I told her to hold on to her cocoa and I picked her up again.

I carried Alicia out to the plane. She tucked her head to my chest as we got close to the roaring prop.

"It's okay," I said loudly in her ear. "The plane is safe. I'm going to help you into the seat.

I put a foot up on the right wing and opened the door. Alicia understood my indications and she helped hold herself up as I lifted her into the right seat. After her door was shut, I hustled around the plane and unhooked the line that went from the wings to the tie-down loops in the tarmac. Then I took the blocks out from under the wheels, hoping the brake would hold.

I climbed up into the left seat and shut the door. Alicia was sitting rigidly, alarm on her face.

"It's okay," I said again, strapping the belts across her waist and shoulders. "We're going to see Jennifer," I said, immediately feeling bad for raising her hopes. Now that Jennifer was back home, she was an easy target. Especially when Gramma thought that the only danger came from me.

I made a slow perusal of the cockpit, trying to remember the procedure from years before. The gas, oil and ammeter gauges all looked normal. The altimeter showed 2100 feet above sea level. I didn't know if that was accurate for Hollybrook airport, but I had no choice but to assume it needed no correction. There were King radios, but I didn't want to engage anyone who might figure out what I was up to or where I was going. I decided not to turn on the headlight, running lights or strobes. Better not to attract attention. I found the heat vents and turned them on high.

I leaned-out the fuel mixture, released the parking brake and was easing the throttle forward when I saw the flashing red lights of a police car.

The squad car rushed up to the airport entrance, crashed through the gate and careened out onto the tarmac.

I pushed the throttle forward and, with my lights still off, turned down the taxiway. The police car was driven by a hotdog. He raced out onto the runway and, apparently unaware of our location, turned away from us and shot down the runway.

When we reached the end of the taxiway, I pushed on the rudder pedals and steered the plane around in a big U-turn. I held the throttle partway down and we were going 20 knots when we rolled onto the runway. The moment we straightened out I pushed the throttle all the way forward. I had no idea of the proper position for flaps in a Tomahawk during takeoff. Guessing, I pulled the lever up just one notch hoping the increased lift would shorten our takeoff roll.

The engine roared and we accelerated quickly down the dark asphalt runway. Alicia ducked her head down. Our lights were still off, and I realized the cop couldn't tell if we were on the runway or not when he spun his car 180 degrees and came back toward us.

His headlights bore down on us as we raced at each other from opposite ends of the tarmac. I watched our air-speed indicator. It was crossing over 50 knots. Cop cars accelerate much faster than small airplanes, so he was likely going much faster than we were. Without our lights, he didn't even know that we were there.

When it seemed clear that we were going to crash into him, I switched on the strobes, the running lights and the landing light.

It didn't work. He continued to accelerate toward us. He was only fifty yards away. Our closing velocity was probably over 150 mph. The cop was on a suicide/ murder mission. If we went into the air without enough speed, we might clear the squad car but then crash anyway. But if we stayed on the ground our crash would be much worse.

The cop was almost on us. I jerked back on the yolk and the plane jumped into the air. The police car's antennae scraped our underside as he raced under us.

THIRTY

I looked back as we roared into the night sky and saw the squad car skidding sideways. The driver's door opened. Gunfire flashed. I shut off all the lights on the plane. A bullet tore through the Plexiglass canopy to the left of my head. I turned the yoke to the right and the plane jerked and yawed into a steep right bank. Alicia's gasp was audible over the roar of the engine.

"Don't worry," I said. "We're under control."

I didn't want to present the large target of the aircraft's side to the rogue cop. So I turned back away from him. Over my left shoulder I saw more flashes of gunfire, but now that we'd changed position only a very lucky shot could hit us in the dark. In a few more seconds we were out of range.

I left the throttle all the way forward and gently released the flap lever. The plane sped up noticeably without the drag of the flaps. I put the plane into the steepest climb where the engine could still keep us at 70 knots. As we rose higher, the lights of Las Vegas appeared beyond a ridge in the distance behind us. They were a reassuring landmark. I was flying over an unfamiliar, black desert. Without the lights of Las Vegas I'd be lost.

I pulled the rental car map out of my pocket. It was soggy and hard to open. I turned on the map light and, with occasional glances out into the night, peeled the folded pages apart. Alicia, in her first act of volition, reached out and helped. Her hands were shaking. Looking at her in the dim light it appeared that she was not cold and shivering. Just shaky.

The compass indicated we were flying north, away from Las Vegas. A quick glance at the map showed the area in front of us to be a desolate desert. I put the plane into a slow turn to the west and studied the map.

It wasn't going to be easy. The hazards between us and Lake Tahoe were numerous. There were mountains over 14,000 feet, higher than a small plane like a Tomahawk can fly. Scattered across Nevada and California were multiple military facilities including test sights and firing ranges. But the biggest obstacle was that we had no navigation. I was flying Visual Flight Reference, tricky at times during the day. But very difficult over a dark desert at night. Our only hope was to find and follow highways that were busy enough that they were illuminated by vehicle headlights. In our current location there were none. Our only reference point remained the distant lights of Las Vegas which were now out our left windows.

According to the map we would soon cross High-way 95, a busy artery northwest out of Vegas. But I knew from driving it that farther north it became a winding, sporadically used route as it zig-zagged through uninhabited deserts toward Fallon, Nevada. I was certain that I'd get lost if I tried to follow it.

A much busier highway was 395, the main route from Reno and Carson City down the eastern Sierra to Los Angeles. I was sure that I could follow it to Carson City and then I'd be just minutes from Lake Tahoe. The problem was getting to the highway. We'd have to fly over numerous mountains as well as Death Valley.

After studying the map, it didn't seem we had a choice. My plan was to follow 95 out of Vegas until it turned north. Then I would continue west over the desert. By dead reckoning I hoped to cross Death Valley going straight west toward Lone Pine. The hazards were obvious. If north winds veered us toward the south we'd hit the tall peaks on the southern end of the Panamint Range. And if we made it through those mountains we'd end up over the U.S. Naval Ordnance Test Station at China Lake. I didn't know what would happen if their radar picked us up flying over restricted airspace. But getting shot out of the sky was one possibility. If south winds veered us to the north, we'd crash into the Inyo Mountains or the White mountains. But if I stayed my course we'd make it through.

"Where are we going?" Alicia suddenly said, her voice clearer than before.

I pointed on the map. "We'll follow this road and then fly west over Death Valley. When we get to Lone Pine, we'll turn north and follow 395 to Lake Tahoe.

She was silent for a minute. "How can I help?" she said. Her earnestness touched me.

"Don't let me fall asleep," I said, worried that I might not be able to stay awake two nights in a row.

The road from Las Vegas appeared below and I made a gradual turn to follow it. A light appeared in the sky. It didn't appear to move which meant another plane coming toward us on a collision course. Our lights and strobes were off.

I turned them on and cranked the yoke to the right. The other plane did the same and we arced away from each other.

Alicia had her hands clasped together in front of her. Her eyes were wide in the map light.

"Sorry," I said.

After a moment she spoke in a tremulous voice. "You missed it. That's what counts.

I decided to leave our lights on for the moment as they would probably comfort Alicia. Then I remembered our transponder. It was broadcasting our location to anyone who cared. With half the law enforcement in southern Nevada being alerted to my transgressions I didn't want to advertise our location. I reached over and shut it off.

"What is that?" Alicia said sounding more lucid.

"A transponder. A kind of radio that tells people where we are. I didn't realize it was on until now." I had the airplane pointed northwest in line with the highway. We drifted slowly to the right of the highway. South wind. Maybe 10 knots. Now that I knew, I could make a slight adjustment.

"Will they chase us?" Alicia asked.

I thought of the number of lies she'd probably been told over the years. Living in a psychiatric hospital where you couldn't even work your own light switch was practically a guarantee that you'd deal with medical personnel who obfuscated everything.

"Maybe," I said. "But not in the air unless we fly over a military facility. What they'll do is try to track us and then be ready to grab us when we land."

"What are the police after you for?"

"Kidnapping you." I was aware of her shaking. I turned and looked at her in the dim cockpit lights. Her face was sweaty. "How are you feeling?"

"You did what was right," she said, ignoring my question. "Taking me, that is. I was in there against my will."

I decided that being truthful included asking her the questions I was thinking. "Aren't most of Saint Mary's residents there against their will?" I noticed the highway below turning to the north. Time to depart for points west. I turned the yoke and we banked off toward the blackness

TODD BORG

of Death Valley.

"Yes. But most have severe psychiatric disabilities." She had an edge to her voice. She was coming out of her drugs. Her shakes were intensifying. Sweat was profuse on her forehead and upper lip. "I have my problems," she said, her voice a tight monotone that nevertheless wavered. "But I'm not crazy. I've never been crazy."

She was waiting for my response. No response would be interpreted as disagreement. "You don't seem crazy to me," I said casually.

"Tell me who you are again," she said.

"Owen McKenna."

"How do you know Jenny?" She was more alert now and wary.

"I'm a private detective. Your daughter hired me to look into the death of Melissa."

Alicia didn't say anything for several minutes.

I concentrated on flying. The ground below was completely black. I saw not one light outside of a million stars, something I'd never before experienced while flying. Adjusting for the deviation of Magnetic North and to help adjust for the south wind, I kept the plane crabbing at 5 degrees south of west. A guess.

A small group of tiny lights appeared far to the south. Then they vanished behind a tall mountain. I'd been flying at 9,000 feet. I decided to bring our altitude up to 11,000 feet. It might change the winds and throw me off course. But it would keep me above most of the peaks in the Panamint Range. Any higher than 11,000 and the loss of oxygen might dull my thinking. Besides, I didn't think the little Tomahawk could go much higher. I pulled back on the yoke and we gradually rose toward the stars.

"They didn't let me go to the funeral," Alicia said, breaking my line of thought. "My first-born twin daughter and they kept me locked in the hospital."

"Maybe they thought it would be too hard for you."

"Right," she said with derision. "I was locked in isolation when I protested. Everyone else went to the funeral and had the support of others to help with their grief. But me, Melissa's mother, I was locked away. It was almost nine years ago, and still it hurts like yesterday. I'm glad you're looking into her death. I never thought it was an accident. But what do I know? I'd already been locked up for years when she died." Alicia's fingers were digging through the shop coat into her legs.

"Tell me what happened, Alicia. Tell me why they put you in the hospital."

She took several deep breaths. She relaxed her hands, spread her fingers on her thighs and closed her eyes. She talked slowly, her voice wavering. "Joseph was the first man I ever met who treated me as a whole person. He looked beyond how skinny I was and got to know me. He knew I had an eating disorder, but he worked with me."

"Joseph Salazar."

"Right. My husband. Grandpa Abe's and Gramma's son. We met at an amusement park. I was there with two girlfriends from UC San Francisco. He was there on a Salazar West company picnic. We ended up in the same seat on the LunarTron. Later, we said our match was made in the heavens. The lunar heavens. Anyway, the centrifugal force threw me into him and he held me up while it whirled. After that we went on more rides. He invited me to the company picnic and things went on from there. He was kind and generous.

"We were married three months later. And I had Melissa and Jenny a year after that."

"You were happy then."

"Yes. That was the happiest year of my entire life.

Except for Gramma Salazar. Joseph tried to shield me from her, but she was insufferable."

We'd reached 11,000 feet. I leveled the plane off. Our speed inched back up to 120 knots. "What did she do?"

"She tormented me. Humiliated me for being thin. She said it was a miracle the twins even survived considering I'd starved them during pregnancy. The truth was I ate constantly and never purged myself once the entire time I was pregnant."

"You mean you never vomited on purpose."

"Right. I gained almost the normal amount for twins. I wanted to give everything to those girls."

"What went wrong after that year?"

"Everything. Gramma picked at everything I did. Said I was a bad mother. And then when I had trouble breast feeding two girls at once, she told me I didn't have what it takes to be a real mother. My self-esteem got so bad that I started purging again. Then my breast milk really did dry up. And Gramma told everyone. Joseph tried to intervene and protect me from her, but we would have had to move away from the West Coast. And that was just when he was being readied to take over as CEO. Everyday when he went to work, she started in on me, how I was unfit to be a mother."

"She wanted Joseph to marry a plump German girl?" I said, immediately regretting the weak effort to make a joke.

"Exactly. Instead, he fell for me, a skinny, Irish-Navaho half breed. Gramma never forgave me for stealing her son's heart."

"You and Joseph lived with Abraham and Gramma. Why?"

"Any Salazar would live in their house with them. It simply wasn't questioned. The Victorian in San Francisco has eight bedrooms and nine bathrooms. The mansion at Lake Tahoe is a forty room palace. You'd think it could work."

"How did you end up in the hospital?"

"With Joseph around I could tolerate Gramma. It was hard, but I managed. But after he and Grandpa Abe died in the plane crash, I lost control. I admit, I was an unfit mother during that time. I neglected the girls and I became dangerously thin. On that basis, Gramma and Dr. Hauptmann committed me."

"To a psychiatric hospital?"

"Anorexia nervosa. They said it was a life-threatening mental illness that required a psychiatric hospital. What I didn't know then and only gradually figured out in my drugged state was that that was only the excuse. The proof of that is they've kept me locked up and drugged for more than ten years and have given me no therapy. Just drugs to keep me docile and to keep me from purging. They won't let me out. It's like prison."

"You say *they* won't let you out. Dr. Hauptmann won't?"

"Him and Gramma."

"What does she have to do with it?" I asked.

"She controls him. He works for her."

"What do you mean?"

"He's worked for her from the day she brought him over from Germany. She sends him money, he does what she says."

"Including incarcerating the hated daughter-in-law?"

"Yes," Alicia said matter-of-factly.

A crescent moon had risen behind us. In its dim light I saw black mountains directly in front of us. I checked the altimeter. We'd dropped 500 feet. I brought the little plane back up and we cruised between two jagged peaks draped with snow. The dark rocky saddle between them was uncomfortably close to the belly skin of the aircraft. Alicia put her hand out in front of her and shut her eyes for a minute. In a moment the mountain dropped away and we were 11,000 feet above the desert.

"Do you think Gramma wanted you kept in the hospital so that she could raise her granddaughters without you around?"

"Partly." We were past the tall mountains and Alicia gazed down toward the blackness of Death Valley. "Mostly it was punishment. I had stumbled on her secret and she wanted me put away where I couldn't tell anyone and where my credibility would be weakened if I did tell."

"What secret?"

Alicia continued to stare out the plane's window. I could see her shake in my peripheral vision. "One day," she said, "when the girls were about a year old and we were staying up at Lake Tahoe, I took them out for a day of shopping in Reno. It was my first big excursion alone with them. I had Antonio, our driver at the time, put the double baby stroller and a pile of other supplies in the trunk of the limousine. We left and got as far as Spooner Summit when I realized I hadn't brought extra diapers.

"I didn't want to have to shop for diapers, so I had Antonio turn around and go back to the house. I ran inside and up the stairs and looked in the closet where we kept items like diapers. But they weren't there. I was worried at leaving the babies in the car, so I ran down the hall to ask Helga where she'd put them."

Alicia went silent. The plane droned on above the blackness of Death Valley.

"What happened?" I said.

Alicia answered slowly. "I opened Helga's door without knocking. And there they were."

"Who?"

"Helga and Gramma. Together."

"What do you mean?"

Alicia paused. "They were on Helga's bed. With their clothes off."

"They saw you open the door?"

"Yes. Gramma was even colder to me after that. But not one word was ever spoken about it."

I was considering the implications of what Alicia had said when I saw in the moonlight something very disconcerting. In the distance to the west was a thick bank of clouds.

We could not risk flying into them unable to see the ground. For somewhere in those clouds was the east face of the Sierra Nevada, a wall of granite that included Mount Whitney, the tallest mountain in the 48 states.

THIRTY-ONE

I throttled back, pushed the yoke in and turned to the left. The plane banked into a big downward spiral. We went around several times, caught between the advancing cloud bank and the mountains we'd just flown over. Alicia looked sick, but I had to lose altitude fast. Below us was darkness and I couldn't see the ground. I knew the Lone Pine valley in front of the Sierra was around 4,000 feet of elevation. If the bottom of the clouds was higher than that and we could get underneath without hitting mountains, we could still make it. But if there was fog, we were out of luck.

I had my face to the window trying to see the ground. The altimeter showed us down to 5,000 feet and still dropping. The clouds were now a thick blanket that went up into the night as far as we could see. Our little plane was like a gnat in front of a wall of cotton. I glanced at the altimeter. 4,500 feet. I eased back on the yoke, slowing our descent. Suddenly, a different kind of white lashed the plane.

Snow.

Alicia turned her head sideways as if she were unable to look at the blizzard. I concentrated on seeing through the white, searching for the ground. Our altitude kept dropping, the rotation of the altimeter needle telling me that we were soon to hit the ground whether we saw it first or not.

I eased back farther on the yoke. There was zero visibility out front. Wary of vertigo, that condition where pilots cannot tell if they are flying up or down, I watched the attitude indicator, the airspeed, the altimeter, the compass. We were flying on instruments now without benefit of a radio signal to follow. I didn't dare to continue west or we would hit the mountains. Our only hope was to keep the plane in a circle and gradually reduce our altitude. Dead or alive, we would reach the ground eventually.

Alicia looked around the cockpit as if she were noticing it for the first time. She fingered the fabric of the shop coat. "What is this I'm wearing? Where did I get this?" Her voice had a curious cheeriness, apparently a defensive posture against impending disaster.

In halting sentences, interrupted by my concentration on looking through the snow, I explained what had happened.

"So you saw me."

"I nearly got you killed. I knew I had to get your wet clothes off if you were to live."

"Did you think I..." She stopped and stared ahead.

A hundred feet below us came a light. We flew over it. Then another. I eased back on the throttle. We dropped closer to the ground. More lights appeared. Suddenly, we flew over a road. There were headlights. A big yellow semi went by, fifty feet below us.

Highway 395.

I eased the yoke to the right and we turned to the north. We came back over the road and followed it to the north, barely going faster than the vehicles below us. I kept our lights off. I didn't want to scare any drivers. Without illumination, I was sure we were invisible in the snow squall.

THIRTY-TWO

We flew north in the snow storm. I concentrated on the headlights coming toward us on the highway. If I flew too high, the snow obliterated my vision. But if I flew too low we'd be in constant danger of hitting power lines or even small hills. It was a risk I had no choice but to take. When the road curved I banked the little plane to stay directly over it. If I veered off the highway to the left or right we would likely hit a tree. It was like flying on a roller coaster with death as the penalty for any mistake.

"Tell me about Sam," I said, hoping Alicia's talking would ease my tension.

"You mean Joseph's half-brother. Helga's son."

"Right," I said, glad that Alicia knew his real identity. "He worked as caretaker at the Salazar mansion in Tahoe."

"I don't know him personally," Alicia said. "He didn't show up until after Melissa died. I'd already been in the hospital for several years."

"But you knew of him. How?"

"Joseph told me. Sam was born ten years after Joseph. The family tried to keep Sam's birth a secret from Joseph, but of course you can't hide such things from smart children. Besides, Joseph and Helga were very close. Helga had done most of the work of raising Joseph. Joseph knew that Helga was pregnant and when she went away in the last month of pregnancy it was obvious to him why."

"Did Joseph know who the father was?" The highway made a sudden turn to the left and started climbing up a steep grade. I banked the plane and pulled back on the yoke to follow the road.

"He said he had a good idea. Even to a ten-year-old boy, it was clear how attractive Helga was. And he'd seen his father give her certain looks."

I thought about that as I flew. "Did Joseph ever say how it was handled when Sam was born? How they found a foster family and how they kept it quiet?"

"No. But when Joseph was a teenager he found some papers in Abraham's safe. From them he learned about Sam's whereabouts and how the family was taking care of his finances. Joseph always said that he gained a new understanding of Helga's predicament that day. He said he felt much more sympathetically about her ever since. And when Joseph went off to Harvard he contacted his little brother. They maintained a secret correspondence until Joseph and Grandpa Abe were killed in the plane crash."

Suddenly, the ground disappeared. There was nothing but snow out the window. I pushed in the yoke. We dropped fast, but the road didn't reappear. I was afraid of coming down too fast and hitting the ground. Not knowing the lay of the land made it impossible to tell which course of action would be best. The snow made it impossible to see out the window. I decided to circle back.

I took a reading of the altimeter and the compass, then turned us into a tight circle.

Watching the compass I brought us around in a full circle, and then started back down, roughly returning us near to the point where we lost the road. Alicia sensed my tension and was silent. I strained to see through the snow.

Not to find the highway now meant certain death.

There it was, down to the left.

I brought the Tomahawk back over the road. My chest hurt and my ears pounded from my runaway heartbeat.

When I calmed, I asked Alicia, "Who handled legal matters for Joseph and the family?"

"An old lawyer in Reno."

"Do you remember his name?"

"No, but I can still see him in my head. He was bald, had a pot belly and walked with a limp. I went to a meeting once. The man's son was there, fresh out of law school, getting ready to take over the practice. I remember because the son was the opposite of the old man. Handsome, lots of hair, the picture of fitness. He obviously worked out."

"Think about the name. What was the ethnic flavor? Was it easy or hard to say?

I saw Alicia shake her head in my peripheral vision. "I'd guess it was English," she said. "It might have started with an S. Like Smith, only not so common."

"Smithson?"

"Yes, that's it!" Alicia said.

We flew in silence for several minutes. I thought about the two Smithsons, father and son law firm for the Salazar family. Privy to secrets. Then my mind segued to the woman in the Hopper painting. I thought about her motivations and the motivations of people in general. Loneliness and heartache seemed to rule.

Alicia looked at me across the small dark cockpit. "You are frowning. Is there more trouble with the weather?"

"No, I think we'll be fine. I was thinking about a painting by Edward Hopper."

"I've heard of him. What is it a picture of?"

"A woman in a movie theater," I said. "There are other

people in the theater, but she stands by herself."

"If she is alone amongst people, she feels isolated. Perhaps the painting is about isolation."

I didn't show my surprise. Alicia was as perceptive as her daughter Jennifer. And she hadn't even seen the painting.

"Yes," I said. "Isolation and loneliness. I think Hopper wanted to show that a person who is in a safe place might not be safe at all. If he or she is suffering from loneliness, it could poison their judgement."

"Emotional danger is as real as physical danger," Alicia said. "The stakes are as high and the pain is greater."

I realized that Alicia was talking from personal knowledge.

"It would be hard," Alicia continued, "to make a picture that communicates emotional danger. An artist might have all the visual components, yet the picture could fall flat."

"Exactly," I said. "It's what artists call content. Talent and skill can make for an interesting work of art. But content is an extra quality that's hard to articulate, harder still to achieve."

"It's not just what's in the picture," she said. "Something is required of the viewer. For years people have visited me in the hospital. They all thought I was safe. Physically safe. You were the first to see that I was in emotional danger."

I didn't respond.

"Why were you thinking about the painting?" Alicia asked.

"When Jennifer hired me to investigate Melissa's death, I started to realize that much of what motivates the members of the Salazar family is at first invisible. I was wondering if there were parallels between the Salazars and Hopper's painting."

"You mean what goes on behind the scenes. Content."

"Yes," I said.

"What did you find?"

"A lot of actions that I didn't understand. I thought Hopper could instruct me on the terrors of loneliness and isolation and what it might do to an individual."

"There's a lot of that in my family," Alicia said. She turned away from me and peered off into the darkness.

My mind drifted, no doubt from exhaustion, and the woman in Hopper's New York Movie became Gramma when she had been young. As the painting's viewer, I became Abraham, unfaithful husband, father by Helga of the bastard son Sam. And then out of my mental fog, came an image of the photograph Immanuel Salazar showed me. The happy Salazar family standing in a boat. I realized with a jolt that the photograph pointed to the answer to my questions.

The picture on Immanuel's dresser showed most of the people involved. Gramma and Grandpa Abe when they were young. Next to them the older brother Immanuel and to his side the ravishing Helga who had her arm around young Joseph's shoulders. The only people missing were Smithson and Alicia and those who were not yet born, Sam, Jennifer and Melissa.

I now saw a way to fit the pieces together, and it made a picture as dark and disturbing as it was revealing.

It was a picture of alienation, a picture with deadly consequences for Jennifer. It was finally clear why Jennifer was to be the next victim. If I could get to her fast enough, it might still be possible to save her life. But the killer would strike soon, very soon. Of that I was sure.

At that moment the plane's engine sputtered and died. The cockpit became deathly silent. The only noise was the buffeting of the plane by the storm's wind.

THIRTY-THREE

The little plane dropped its nose and plunged toward the earth. I checked the instruments. Everything seemed normal. I tried the starter. The prop, already doing a feeble rotation from the effect of the airspeed on the blades, didn't change its motion. We were fifty feet above the highway. An eighteen-wheeler was in front of us, heading the same direction as we were. We came down above it, overtaking it. If we landed in front of it, it would smash us into pieces. But it was going too slow for us to land behind it without crashing into it. If I turned off to the side of the highway, we'd hit the trees. Again I tried the starter as I checked the instruments. Then I saw the gas gauges.

Left tank empty. Right tank full. I grabbed the fuel selector and switched to the right tank. Tried the starter. The prop was still turning in a slow circle. We were directly above the truck. The driver had no idea an airplane was about to drop out of the sky in front of him. I kept trying the starter. We were twenty-five feet above the ground. Twelve feet above the semi-trailer. The starter motor made a grinding noise. The plane was buffeted by the airstream thrown up by the truck.

The plane's engine sputtered. We glided over the truck, then came down directly in front of the truck's cab. We settled into the snowy swath of the truck's headlight beams. Light washed over our plane. An air horn blasted.

The plane vibrated under its assault. The truck's head-lights veered away from us and then came back as it swerved behind us. We slammed onto the roadway in front of the truck's bumper. The wheel struts flexed and we bounced. Alicia stifled a scream. The engine fired. I pushed the throttle all the way forward. The prop spun into a blur. I pulled back on the yoke and we roared back into the snowy sky.

Alicia remained silent for a long time. I was aware of her shaking. I wanted to say something that might calm both of us, but no words came. Snow pummeled the windshield and the vents blew a weak stream of warm air.

I stayed close to the road as it crested several passes. Eventually, I recognized the Carson Valley in the distance.

The safest way into the Lake Tahoe basin in a snow storm would be to fly north to Carson City, then go over the broad saddle of Spooner Summit and backtrack south over the lake to the South Lake Tahoe airport. A shorter, more dangerous route was to come in directly from the south. I was convinced that time was everything.

There were few cars as I turned off of 395 and headed up Highway 89 toward Woodfords, but I knew the road well and thought I could fly it in the dark. I flipped on the landing light and stayed close enough to the pavement that the landing light would shine through the snow and show me the way. I didn't think there were any high tension power lines in my path, so I reasoned that we'd be okay if I stayed one hundred feet above the ground, high enough to go over standard utility poles.

Woodfords is a single intersection just up from the desert valley. I flew over it and went like an aerobatic flyer into the canyon that twisted and turned as it climbed up to Hope Valley. When the canyon opened up I banked to the right and powered up over Luther Pass. From there it was a long glide down Christmas Valley to Tahoe and the airport.

My radios were still off and I guessed that other air traffic would be non-existent in the storm. The airport control tower would pick me up on the radar and try to contact me as I came in on my glide path. My intention was to ignore them, land and find Street and Spot as quickly as possible.

The blue runway lights were invisible in the snow storm, no doubt buried. I brought the plane down where I thought the landing strip might be. It was impossible to tell if the runway was covered with two inches or two feet of snow. Wind buffeted the plane. I saw in my peripheral vision Alicia's hand going to the instrument panel. Her legs stiffened. I backed off on our speed. When we were ten feet above the snow, I throttled back to idle. The plane rocked left and right in the wind. Then the wheels plowed into the snow.

The plane slowed. We started to skid. The wheels caught on heavy snow and we flipped over.

My head hit the top of the canopy as the plane slid upside down. The shoulder belts dug into my neck and chest. Alicia made no sound. The plane jerked to a stop. The engine died and the only sound was the wind. I unlocked and pushed open the doors. Then I unlatched my belt and fell in an upside down heap, half in the plane, half outside in the snow. I pulled myself out, ran through deep snow around a broken wing that was dribbling gasoline, unclipped Alicia's seatbelt and dragged her out into the storm. When we were a safe distance from the wreckage I paused and hauled Alicia to her feet. The wind was icy and the snow stung. I held Alicia with my back to the wind and looked across the airport.

There, at the edge of the access road, was Street's little VW bug. Street was near the car, struggling toward us through drifts. Spot was running across the snow-covered tarmac.

He met us halfway, jumped around and sniffed Alicia as I ran with her toward Street.

"Oh, my God!" Street cried when we met. She put her arms around both me and Alicia. "When the plane flipped I thought you..." She stopped. We three hugged, all of us shaking.

Then, calmer, Street said, "You must be Alicia. I'm Street. Good to meet you." It was, perhaps, the strangest meeting two people could have, me carrying the half-dressed Alicia in a snow storm, yet Street handled it as if nothing were out of the ordinary.

When we reached the car, I set Alicia down. She shivered violently.

"God, you poor thing," Street said. "You must be freezing. Here, you and I will get into the back seat." She opened the door and helped Alicia into the tiny car.

Spot got in the front passenger side and I drove off immediately.

"I take it we're in a hurry," Street said.

"Very," I said. I popped her cell phone out of its holder and dialed Diamond's pager. "Diamond, please give a call immediately." I recited Street's number and replaced the phone, noticing that its time feature said 5:00 a.m. I'd been up for nearly 48 hours. I was exhausted but not sleepy, the benefit of adrenaline.

We turned out of the airport and drove toward town on Highway 50. I pushed the VW to its limit in the snow. The car only had two-wheel drive, but it went through the snow well. In the rearview mirror, I saw Street attending to Alicia. "She's a tough one, Street," I said. "Crash a plane and she doesn't make a peep." Street pulled off her coat and wrapped it around the woman. Spot stretched his head back between the front seats, investigating Alicia's shop coat and packing tape slippers.

"Thanks for being here, Street," I said.

Before she could say anything, the phone warbled.

"Yes, Diamond," I said, appreciating his promptness.

"Do you know where Jennifer Salazar is?"

"Actually, I do," Diamond said. "She is at the Salazar mansion. The girl was hysterical so we kept an officer there throughout most of the night. He only left just now."

"Do you know who is with Jennifer?"

"Sure," Diamond said. "Her grandmother. The housekeeper."

"Could there be anyone else?"

"Not that I know of. But I wasn't there. We still have a man at the front gate, though."

"He won't let anyone in?"

"Not without my permission or the grandmother's permission."

"So if the girl leaves the house, no one would see her, correct?" I said. We were almost through town. The early morning streets were bare of traffic. Snow blew horizontally under the streetlights.

"Not unless she went by the front gate. Oh, by the way, Owen," Diamond said. "You might not want to show your face around just yet. There is an arrest warrant out on you. They are considering charges against Street also."

"Thanks, Diamond." I hung up.

"Where are we going?" Street asked as we raced past the casinos and headed north through blowing snow toward the Salazar mansion.

"If my guess is correct, we're going for a very cold boat ride," I said.

THIRTY-FOUR

I turned into the park that is south of the Salazar mansion and stopped in the same place I parked when Jennifer and I went for the boat ride.

The beach, wide, calm and sandy before, was covered in foam from the crashing waves. The huge dark rollers had twelve miles to build their fury as they came across from Emerald Bay. The waves had white caps that vanished when the wind gusts blew them off. When the waves broke on the beach, the wind whipped the icy spray into the air, mixed it with snow and flung it a hundred feet into the woods.

I opened the VW's door and stepped out. Spot jumped out after me. The assault of the spring storm was furious. My windbreaker was immediately soaked with icy snow and spray. I leaned back in the open door. "You should stay with Alicia," I said to Street.

"No way. Wherever you're going, you're going to need help in this storm."

"Spot will come with me."

"So will I."

"Street...

"She's right," Alicia suddenly said. She started taking off Street's coat. "If I can survive thirteen years in an insane asylum, I can manage for awhile in a car. Leave me the keys. I can run the engine for warmth." She handed Street her coat. "Go. Stay with him."

Street pulled on her coat and jumped out of the car. I saw no point in arguing.

"Oh," Street said. She leaned back in the car door and spoke to Alicia. "I have a bunch of candy bars in the glove box. They'll help you stay warm."

"It will help you, too," Alicia said. She opened the glove box. "I'll take two, you take the rest." She thrust them into Street's hands.

Street and I ran down the shore toward where the tall Salazar fence ended in the water. Spot was ahead of us. When we got there I yelled over the roar of the wind. "We have to go into the water to get around this fence. I'll carry you."

Street looked at me with amazement. "This is no time to put on the chivalry act."

"Damnit, Street, this isn't chivalry! The water is dangerously cold! And there's no point in both of us getting wet when only one of us has to. If we get in trouble you'll be a hell of a lot more help to me if you're not suffering from hypothermia!"

Street acquiesced. I picked her up, rushed into the water around the fence and set her back down in the snow.

"I didn't mean to yell," I said as we ran on down the shore.

"You were right," Street said, panting.

When we got to the boathouse I rushed out on the pier and tried the doors. Locked. I ran around the far side to try the other doors. One was shut. The other was blowing in the wind, slamming in staccato bursts against the boathouse wall.

I looked inside the building. It was too dark to see anything. Spot stuck his nose in next to me, sniffed and walked slowly into the dark. I felt around for the light switch, found it and flipped it on just as Street appeared.

"What are we doing?" she asked.

I pointed at the slip where water slapped against the pier. "The powerboat is gone." I went across the walkway at the back of the boathouse to the other pier. "We have to catch it. We'll take the runabout." I started unleashing the lines that held it in place.

"Wait, Owen." Street said, alarm in her voice. "No way is this little boat big enough to take out in this storm. It will swamp in those waves."

I untied the lines.

"Shouldn't we check the house first?" Street said.

"No need to with the powerboat gone."

I looked around for life jackets. They were hanging on a wall. I got out of the boat and fetched several of them.

"Owen, did you look at those waves? Are you blind? I don't want to die."

"Me neither," I said. "But we have no choice. If we hurry, we might save Jennifer. If we don't, she dies for sure."

I threw the life jackets in the runabout and then spied a spare gas tank near a storage locker. I checked the gauge. It was full. I put it in the boat. "You can stay here," I said. "Spot and I will go alone. But it would be better if you came. This boat can use the extra ballast. Riding lower will mean less profile to the wind. With these waves we'll be taking on water and need a baler as well." I grabbed a small bucket that hung on the wall and tossed it in the runabout.

On the side wall hung several rubberized storm coats. I slipped one on, my arms poking eight inches out of the sleeves, and pulled the rest off the wall. I threw all but one of them in the boat. "Are you coming?" I said, holding out the last storm coat.

Street turned and looked out the side door at the howling wind. "Yes," she said. She walked around to my side of the boathouse.

I held the storm coat out so she could put her arms into the sleeves. Then she climbed down into the boat.

"Where do you want me to sit?"

"We'll be most stable if you sit in the bow seat. But pull the hood up and face backward, with your back to the wind. The spray will hit you on your back."

I got down into the boat and sat next to Street for a moment. I kissed her. "Sorry I'm so brusque."

"It's okay," she said.

"I'm afraid for Jennifer," I said.

"Me, too. Here, eat a candy bar, eat two of them."

I grabbed the candy, stuffed one in my mouth, moved to the rear seat and bent over to start the outboard engine, a 40 horsepower relic. It was old, but it would move the runabout along at a decent speed if it worked. I found the priming pump on the gas line coming from the tank and squeezed it several times. Then I pulled on the cord. Over and over. Nothing happened. I twisted the throttle and pulled again. The engine was lifeless. I stopped and looked it over. On the lower left side was a black knob. The choke. I pulled it out and the engine started on the next pull.

"Can you reach the door button?" I said to Street as I unhooked the last line. I pointed to it on the pier next to her. She leaned over and touched it. A motor whined above us and the boathouse door creaked and then rose up into the ceiling.

"Spot," I said. He came running over. "Lie down." I pointed at the space between my seat and Street's. Spot hesitated at the edge of the pier, lowering his head to see just what kind of craziness I was suggesting. Then he reached out one tentative paw and half-stepped, half-leaped into the boat. The runabout leaned precariously in the water as he shifted his bulk and finally lowered himself onto the pile of storm coats on the keel of the boat. I tossed one of the coats over his body. He needed to conserve heat as much as we did. I twisted the throttle grip and eased us out into the worst weather Lake Tahoe had seen in months.

Dark waves smashed across the bow of the runabout as I brought the speed up. The boat plowed up each wave and then plunged down into the troughs between them. I twisted the throttle and the boat surged forward. We almost jumped off the next wave and slammed into the leading edge of the following one. The blow to us and the boat was severe. I backed off on the throttle and found a speed that was jarring but acceptable. Maintaining this speed into the wind, we headed out into the lake.

Street huddled at the front of the boat. Spray soaked her. An occasional wave crashed over the boat and smashed across her back. She jerked with surprise and then braced herself for the next. Spot put his head down as if curling into a circle were the best way to endure such torture. Periodically, he lifted his nose to the storm. I kept us into the wind and kept a lookout for the power boat.

I had no idea where it might be. My only guideline was that the powerboat would head for deep water. But with most of Lake Tahoe over 1,300 feet to the bottom, that left a lot of territory. In the end I thought the powerboat, large as it was, would head directly into the wind to make the ride easier. If we stayed into the wind we'd possibly follow in its tracks.

The snow intensified as we got farther from shore. I could no longer see the land behind us. I was piloting the boat as I did the plane, by dead reckoning.

The snow slowly took on a gray quality. At first I wondered if we were coming near the lights of another boat. Then I realized it was dawn. I couldn't see anything but snow in all directions. Periodically, I veered off my course and the runabout bounced furiously as we cut the waves at an angle. I steered directly back into the howling wind to reduce the violence of the boat's motion. Waves were breaking over us, splashing gallons of water into the runabout. The rear of the boat sat lowest, so the water we were shipping rushed to the stern and was now over my shoes. I grabbed the bucket and bailed as I drove.

As we crested the top of each wave, I looked out into the storm, scanning left and right trying to see the powerboat. There was nothing but snow. We'd gone maybe a mile or more into the lake and, except for the wind direction, we were lost.

Once or twice the outboard coughed and I thought we'd lost any chance of saving Jennifer. Then it came back to life and we continued on, up the crests of the waves, then crashing back down. The boat groaned. I heard wood splintering.

Street said nothing, stoical as statuary at the front of the boat. Spot looked around at me several times, wondering, no doubt, if I'd finally lost it. A wave crashed over him and he put his head down and lifted his paw across his nose. The water was now over my ankles and reached Spot's paws. I thought of asking Street to bale, but I worried that if she let go with either hand she would be swept overboard.

We fought our way into the gray storm for another 30 minutes. The water in the runabout was now over Spot's elbows and eight inches up my calves. I was sure that we'd missed the powerboat. We should have come upon it by now.

We must have been in the middle of the lake, halfway to Emerald Bay, when through the snow storm came a sound that cut the wind and motor noise like a clarion bell.

A woman screamed.

Spot jerked his head up and growled.

"Quiet!" I whispered to him.

I had a vague sense that it came from in front of us. Street turned around, knees on the seat and hands on the gunnels. She pointed to the right. I turned the outboard and we curved off, splitting the waves at an acute angle. The little boat slammed terribly in this new posture. The wind and waves and motor noise were so loud in concert that I heard nothing else. I throttled back just a touch, hoping to reduce the motor noise. We still heard nothing. And at the top of each wave I looked but saw nothing except snow.

Then came another scream.

It was a slow agonizing cry that rose and fell and turned to a wailing before it stopped. The emotion in it was so excruciating that it crumbled a part of my interior. A vision insinuated itself into my mind. Hopper's young woman was being tortured in a darkened theater by a maniac. Then Hopper's woman morphed into Jennifer and the theater faded into a gray blizzard. I tried to see the powerboat, but saw only furious gray flakes. Street gestured ahead to the left.

I twisted the throttle and we shot ahead. The runabout climbed up the waves and slammed down, again and again. Spot was sitting partway up. His front feet were spread wide for stability. Street faced forward, clutching the gunnels of the lurching boat. Suddenly, she pointed.

I looked but saw nothing. I kept the boat heading where she pointed. Spot growled again. Then I saw it.

Off in the blinding blizzard was a dark shape. I could not make it look like anything but a shadow. Gradually, it turned into a boat. I twisted the outboard grip to full throttle. The other boat was broadside to us, rocking violently in the waves. Something moved on the boat. The movement took on distinct form. It was at the stern. Two people struggling. One pushed the other down. A gargled scream rose up to our ears. We raced closer. Spot was standing up high, trying to see. He growled louder. I pointed our boat toward the stern of the powerboat. The person who was down got up. The two people struggled violently. Someone grunted. Then one bent down, grabbed a leg of the other and toppled the person overboard. The person on board bent down, struggled to pick something else up, then threw it overboard. There was a deep chunking sound and then nothing but the wind.

We came up to the stern of the powerboat. The remaining person was moving toward the front of the boat, reaching toward the steering wheel. I throttled back and our boat bumped the powerboat. Street jumped up into the bigger craft.

"Careful, Street!" I yelled. But my attention was distracted by a coiled yellow line that was rapidly running out of the powerboat and into the black water. Spot saw it at the same time. He leaped into the dark water as the end of the line flashed up into the air and then snaked beneath the dark waves.

I heard the distinctive sound of Spot's jaws snapping twice, then nothing. He tried to swim, but his big white, polka-dotted body sunk into the blackness, pulled by the yellow line in his teeth. I took a quick glance at Street and saw her struggling with the other person.

I instinctively gauged where the greatest threat lay, and I leaped into Lake Tahoe.

THIRTY-FIVE

The sudden immersion in ice water was an astonishing shock. But I swam down into the depths looking with open eyes to locate Spot. There, fifteen feet down, was his white hulk. He was trying to swim to the surface, but the line in his teeth was pulling him down into the black abyss.

I kicked furiously and swam down next to him. My right hand closed around the line in his mouth while my left touched his side. Spot seemed to understand. He continued to hold onto the line and the two of us swam upwards, dragging the line.

It felt like it must have an anchor attached. My lungs burned. My body weakened as the pain of no air began to crush my spirit. But I took strength from Spot. If he was willing to go down with the victim below, I would, too. My vision was going as the surface grew near. I saw a dark shape nearby and took it to be a boat. Then my head was above the water and I sucked air as if I'd never breathed before. Spot's head came out next to me, and still gripping the line in his teeth, he snorted and choked through his nose. I reached up and grabbed the water-skier's ledge at the back of the power boat. With my other hand I pulled the line up and wrapped it around a cleat. Still gasping for air I yelled at Spot.

"I've got it, Spot. Get in the boat. Fast!" I reached for him and propelled him toward the boat ledge. He looked at me, the line still in his teeth. "Let go, Spot. I've got it." He hesitated and then let go.

He put his front feet on the ledge, claws scraping fiberglass. Holding onto the ledge, I raised my legs under the water. Spot's rear legs pushed off my thighs and he jumped into the boat. He turned toward me, but I pointed toward the front of the boat. "Help Street. Go help Street." Spot bounded forward. I heard a growl as I rolled up and over onto the ledge.

The end of the line was still in my hand, holding it from snaking out around the cleat. I braced myself against the back of the boat and began hauling the line in, hand over hand.

The line looked like a ski rope which I guessed was 75 feet long. I pumped my arms, about two feet of line with each pull. The weight on the rope seemed to get heavier. I didn't know what was tied to the rope, but I knew it wasn't just a person. Fatigue burned in my biceps. As the pain grew I went into a kind of trance, counting every two feet, trying to get to seventy-five. Faster and faster. A sharp pain grew in the web of muscles across my back. The muscles knotted up, but I kept pulling.

Next thing I knew, other arms were working with me. Street had joined me, meshing her pulls with mine and lessening the work for me. Together we speeded up the pace. My counting got to sixty. Sixty-two, sixty-four, sixty-six.

At sixty-eight something appeared. It was the person tied to the line. Or maybe a body. We tugged and brought it to the surface.

Jennifer. Her long hair swirled lifeless in the black water. We pulled on her but her body was too heavy to easily come aboard. Then we saw the reason.

The line went around her leg in a series of knots and then stretched tight to a concrete block down below.

"Hang on!" Street yelled.

I was too tired to protest. I hung on as told. Street went back behind me and then reappeared. She jumped into the water and swam under Jennifer. I saw a flash of knife and then the line suddenly got much lighter. The concrete block shot down into the depths.

I pulled Jennifer up out of the water and into the blizzard. She tumbled to the floor of the boat. I turned her sideways and squeezed the water out of her chest. She was as cold as her mother had been a few hours earlier. I felt for and found a weak pulse. But unlike her mother, Jennifer wasn't breathing. I filled her lungs with my breaths, in and out. She had a heartbeat and I wasn't going to let her die.

For endless minutes I breathed into her cold body, unwilling to give her up. I was oblivious to what was happening around me, oblivious to the lurching and rocking of the boat in the waves. I didn't feel the snow and I was unaware of the cold. All I knew at that moment was that Jennifer was alive, but not breathing.

She will breathe, I said to myself. She will breathe. I worked those lungs for her, in and out. I got light headed. She will breathe.

The snow came down as if to bury us. Gusts of wind sucked the air from my lungs. With each giant wave the powerboat rocked violently. My body was wracked with cramps. But I willed her to breathe.

And she did.

Jennifer gave a weak choking cry and coughed up water. Then her chest rose and fell as if to never stop, and I bent down and held her while she came to life.

Some minutes later I was aware that the boat had stopped rocking so violently and that a new sound filled the air. I took off my cold wet storm coat and laid it over Jennifer. Then I found another and put it around her. I had no hot drink to warm her. I pulled a seat cushion off and slipped it under Jennifer's head.

Slowly I raised up and looked forward. In the dull light of dawn I saw Street at the wheel, piloting the power-boat downwind through the snow storm. Next to her stood Spot, standing guard over a motionless figure on the floor of the boat. The person was wearing a dark coat and the collar blocked my view of the face. I was reluctant to leave Jennifer, but I went forward.

Even up close, I could not see past the fabric to the face of the murderer. I put my hand on Spot's back as I leaned down. He didn't move. I reached out and pulled the collar away to see two intense eyes staring up at the dog and then at me.

Gramma Salazar.

EPILOGUE

J ennifer was sitting on the floor in front of my wood stove. I'd built a fire in the stove to ward off the cold of the spring snowstorms that were blowing through Lake Tahoe. Spot sprawled next to Jennifer, his head on her lap. She rubbed his head and ears. Spot's eyes were shut. Bliss. Alicia sat in the big leather chair next to Jennifer. I was opposite her on the rocker. Street sat on the floor in front of me, her arms draped over my knees.

"Gramma tried to murder Jennifer," Alicia said, her voice still shaky. "Did she murder my other daughter?" she asked.

"I can't prove it," I said, "but it makes sense that she pushed Melissa off the rock slide."

"Why?" Jennifer asked.

"Unless she tells us, we'll never know. But Gramma had several secrets. My guess is that Melissa learned one of those secrets and threatened to tell. Gramma killed Melissa to keep the secret."

"How could a woman murder her own granddaughter?" Jennifer said.

"She didn't," I said.

"But you just said she did."

"No, I said Gramma murdered Melissa. I didn't use the word granddaughter."

The room went silent.

"Helga had been a quiet and loyal servant," I said. "And she became a quiet and loyal surrogate mother for Abraham and Gramma. She gave birth to both Joseph and Sam the caretaker."

"What?!" Jennifer said. "Helga is my real grandmother?!"

"Yes."

The only sound was the crackle of the fire.

"How did you figure this out?" Alicia asked at last.

"I didn't until you told me that Joseph was very close to Helga and felt even more sympathetic about her when he saw the papers in Abraham's safe.

"Remember the Hopper painting we were talking about when we were in the airplane? I was thinking about the woman in the painting when I had a sudden vision of Gramma when she was quite young, similar in age to the young woman in the painting. I'd thought of Gramma as having everything, money, happy marriage, good son, beautiful houses. Yet from the time I met her, Gramma seemed to be essentially lonely. As lonely as the woman in the painting. How, I asked myself, could a woman with everything feel so alone?

"I thought about the Hopper painting as we flew through the night. Like Gramma, the woman in the painting also appears to have everything. Intelligence, beauty, a place to belong. But that is not enough. Appearances deceive. As an outside viewer, I could only guess that she didn't really have everything which I'd ascribed to her. Something essential to the woman in the painting, something that I cannot see, is missing.

"So I figured the same was true of Gramma. Something that she appeared to have was not really hers. And there was where I found the answer. Joseph belonged to Helga, not Gramma. The papers transferring Joseph from the surrogate mother to Gramma were what Joseph saw in Abraham's safe."

"Was Abraham my real grandfather?" Jennifer asked.

"Yes. I suspect that Gramma couldn't have children, yet wanted them very much. It was a common solution that people have turned to throughout history. What they didn't anticipate was that once Abraham had performed his duty of impregnating the attractive Helga, he kept coming back for more. Helga resisted because she was in love with Gramma."

"What do you mean?" Jennifer asked.

"Physical love?" Street said.

"Yes," I said.

"How do you know?"

"Tell them, Alicia."

Alicia looked down at the floor. She spoke in a nervous voice. "I found them together. It was why Gramma colluded with Dr. Hauptmann and had me committed. So I couldn't spill the secret. Even if I had tried, I would have had no credibility."

Jennifer put her hand on Alicia's leg. "Sorry to say something so harsh, mom, but why didn't Gramma kill you? If she killed Melissa to keep her secrets, why go to the trouble of committing you to get you out of the way?"

"Because," I said, "everyone else was the product of Abraham and Helga. Alicia wasn't a blood relation to Helga. So, in a twisted way, committing Alicia was a kind of mercy from Gramma's perspective."

"Gramma wanted Helga's love for her own," Street said. "Was she crazy enough that she killed everyone else dear to Helga?"

"Yes," I said. "Abraham and Joseph were already dead. Helga's son Sam and Helga's granddaughters were all that were left."

"Did Gramma somehow make the plane crash that killed my father and Grandpa Abe?" Jennifer was incredulous.

"We'll probably never know," I said. "It would be unlikely that she could put a bomb on board herself. But with her money, she could have hired it done. She had the motive what with her husband's affair with her lover and the fact that her son wasn't really her son at all."

"What I don't get," Street said, "is why Helga didn't freak. Didn't she know that Gramma was doing this?"

"No. She thought they were terrible accidents. And because no one knew she was the real matriarch of the brood, she had to grieve in silence."

Jennifer spoke, her voice thick with irony. "Helga had only Gramma to go to for comfort."

Street spoke up. "Did Dr. Hauptmann confirm all of this?"

"Yes. He gave it all to Diamond. They videotaped it. Hauptmann was the doctor who delivered both Joseph and Sam. He gave Gramma her pills, the same pills she used on you, Jennifer, before she hauled you out on the boat. I only guessed that she would use the boat because Diamond said he'd left a man on the front gate. Gramma also paid Hauptmann to keep Alicia confined. According to Diamond, both Hauptmann and Gramma have decided to plead guilty. By doing so Gramma might avoid the death penalty."

Jennifer shifted her position on the floor. Spot moaned. "Did you ever find any evidence that Gramma was Melissa's and Sam's killer?" Jennifer asked. "Anything besides what you got out of Hopper's painting?"

"Well, gosh," I said. "I got pretty suspicious of her after that incident a few nights ago where we pulled you out of the water." I grinned at Jennifer.

"Oh, yeah," she said, embarrassed. "I forgot that little detail." She pet Spot. "Besides that, was there anything else?"

"Yes. Once I realized that Helga was the mother of both Joseph and Sam, I had a motive of sorts for Gramma to murder them all. Then I thought back to my visit with Immanuel Salazar. He had a picture from many years ago on his dresser. It showed the entire family standing in a boat in Lake Tahoe. Among others on the boat was Gramma. I remembered that you said that Gramma was so afraid of the water, she wouldn't even go near the shore.

"So I had the inconsistency I was after. And then there was Sam. Street figured out that the body we'd initially thought was Sam's girlfriend Maria had only been dead eleven days. The timing was perfect for Sam's disappearance.

Jennifer looked startled. "Gramma said she'd gotten a call from him while he was on vacation. She made that up?"

I nodded. "The DNA results suggest a ninety-nine percent likelihood that it is actually Sam's body. Sam was small, hence the bones looked like they were a woman's. And he was wearing the bracelet his girlfriend Maria had returned to him. The holes in the skull weren't bullet holes. They precisely match the iron point on Gramma Salazar's walking stick, which is why we found no bullets in the skull."

Everyone took the news silently.

Jennifer spoke up, "So Samuel Sometimes was my uncle. Why, if both my father Joseph and uncle Sam were Helga and Grandpa Abe's children, weren't they raised as brothers?"

"Because everyone had gotten to know Grandpa Abe and Gramma Salazar when they were already raising Joseph as their son. They couldn't have repeated the illusion when Sam came along because it was clear that Gramma Salazar hadn't been pregnant."

"What about Smithson?" Jennifer said.

"He's the smart one," I said. "According to Diamond, he walks. He knew indirectly about Gramma's evil deeds and she says he took her money to keep silent. He'll be disbarred, but since he retired with the death of his last wife, he won't care. As far as we know he still might have killed both of his wives, probably getting the courage to do so from watching Gramma at work."

"Was he the one breaking into the house at night?" Jennifer asked.

"I don't think so. I called Gramma's friends in Salt Lake City and they said she left for a night during her visit with them. She could have hired a plane to fly back so she could sneak into the mansion and kill you. The same for when she was playing bridge when you and I were out on the boat. Her bridge partners said she had taken ill and their driver took her back home for a time. She told him she was going inside to rest awhile and get her pills. Later he took her back to her bridge partners in order to bring Helga home. Almost for certain, it was Gramma looking for you when we were out on the water and saw the light in your bedroom."

"So Smithson wasn't after me at all?" Jennifer sounded disbelieving.

"Actually, I think he has been keeping tabs on you your entire life. He, with his father, drafted the documents that Dr. Hauptmann used to get Alicia committed. He knew or suspected that Melissa learned secrets that got her killed. And he knew that if you stirred up the whole matter to which he was tangentially connected, it could cause him a great deal of trouble. Especially if - and we'll probably never know - especially if he murdered his wives.

"When he watched you ride into the woods by my office, he probably just wanted to see what you were up to. But now that Gramma and Dr. Hauptmann are in jail, Smithson knows you pose no more threat. Furthermore, the police aren't looking at Smithson anymore. When they wanted to know about his relationship to the family he hid behind attorney-client privilege. Knowing that they might not be able to crack him on either his relationship to Gramma or the deaths of his ex-wives, they probably won't try. Either way, you can stop worrying. He gains nothing from interfering in your life."

Alicia had kept her head low. She was tired, maybe distraught and frightened about her reunion with Jennifer. She raised her face toward me. "We all want to thank you, Owen."

"I just followed the trail. It was your daughter who hired me. It was Jennifer who believed that Melissa was murdered even when everyone else doubted her. My trail was cold until Street figured out that the body could have been in a warmer place and hence her forensics suggested it was only dead from the time that Sam left on vacation."

"What about the plane you stole?" Street asked.

"I can answer that," Jennifer said. "I called up the police in Hollybrook and they got me in touch with the plane's owner. He said it was a used Piper Tomahawk. So I told him to pick out something similar only a new model and I'd pay for it. Diamond fixed things up. He explained to the Hollybrook police what had happened and I paid all their expenses. So the police dropped all charges against Owen."

"I think it's time for a beer," Street said suddenly. "Care to join me?"

"Of course," I said. I stood up and went to the kitchen.

"Make it a whole one," Street said. "We're celebrating."

"A whole one?" I said. "Wow. How about you, Alicia? Would you like a beer?"

Alicia's face showed shock. "Uh, well, I haven't had any beverage besides apple juice, milk and water in thirteen years." Then she grinned for the first time since I broke her out of the hospital. Her smile was huge in her gaunt face, her teeth straight and white. "Yes, Mr. McKenna, I'll have a beer."

"I'm going to pass on Spot because he'd drink us dry. What about you, Jennifer?"

"Well," she said. "I'm almost fifteen." She looked at Alicia. "Is it okay, mom?"

Alicia's eyes immediately filled with tears. But her smile was undiminished. She reached over and hugged her daughter, nodding and crying.

"Owen," Jennifer said over Alicia's shoulder. "We're celebrating. Make it a whole one for me, too."

About The Author

Todd Borg and his wife live in Lake Tahoe where they write and paint. To contact Todd or learn more about the Owen McKenna mysteries, please visit toddborg.com.